Other Novels by Gary L. Ivey

BACKLASH

BACKLASH 2: JUSTICE DENIED

A conspiracy of activists and politicians threatens the livelihoods of hundreds of thousands of people, so Jacqueline James finds herself in the midst of a national controversy. To save her company, her employees and her stockholders, she must launch a daring response called "Operation Backlash."

"It was fabulous!!!! I was so intrigued by the plot... environmental terrorists, murder, politics, moral integrity, a female heroine, hard-core work ethics, and a splash of love made for a great read! (ah...and the evolution/creation thread!)." *L. Z., Facebook post.*

"I found myself cheering Jacqueline on, as she took on Washington and her stockholders throughout the book. The storyline kept me wondering 'what next?' The author meticulously conducted his research, reminding me of a well-developed Grisham-like novel." *D. J., Amazon.com review.*

"Get Ready for a Wild Ride! *Backlash* can be enjoyed on many different levels. As a page-turner, it keeps you on the edge of your seat...but Backlash has a deeper subtext, almost a platonic dialogue being conducted between the lines, that addresses many of the key political concerns of our time." *B. G., Amazon.com review*

www.backlashbook.com

About *Quest for a King*

"In *Quest for a King*, Gary Ivey brings the Bible to life through vivid and intricately-crafted characters with whom the reader can't help but bond. Viewed through the eyes of these engaging characters, the pre-Davidic period of three thousand years ago comes alive like never before. Rich and nuanced subjects that are hard to limn from the terse biblical text become much clearer, such as how the Israelites worshipped their one G-d but at the same time hadn't quite abandoned the Canaanite deities. The Bible records the events of this period, but through the compelling characters of *Quest*, the reader is able to truly live them. As with the best of historical fiction, *Quest* is a deeply immersive experience. I read it cover to cover in one sitting... it is impossible to put down. I wish I had had this growing up. I would have understood biblical history so much better!"

Brett Goldberg,BA, author of A Psalm in Jenin *and entrepreneur.*

"Gary Ivey's wonderful third novel *Quest for a King* is just as riveting as his first two. It's a remarkably ambitious saga exploring the lives of a complex array of Biblical and non-Biblical characters. *Quest for a King* follows several generations of families, some mentioned in the stories of 1st and 2nd Samuel, some not. Deeply researched, the book evokes with remarkable specificity these ordinary and extraordinary people living in ancient Israel, as their lives are swept up and overturned by the move of God and the forces of history."

Terry R. Freeman, BA, MBA, CG, Genealogist, Historian, Author.

"Gary Ivey takes the biblical storyline of Israel's quest for a king and makes it come alive. By adding rich character development and well researched historical details to the Old Testament record, he has created a work of fiction that's both educational and extremely engaging, like an Old Testament *The Chosen.*"

Bill Barley, BS, JD, Pastor, Living Stones Church.

The Quest stories have also been honored at film festivals where Gary L. Ivey has submitted his TV pilot script "Lost Glory" from the proposed "Age of the Kingdom" TV series.

2023 Christian Film Festival: Best Script and Best Movie Poster
2023 Branson International Film Festival: Best Script Nominee
2023 International Christian Film Festival: Best Script Nominee
2023 Golden Draft Awards, Official Finalist
2023 Santa Monica Film Awards, Semi-Finalist

QUEST FOR A KING

Age of the Kingdom Series
Book One

By Gary L. Ivey

Published by
Studio IV Productions, Kailua Kona, HI 96740

ISBN: 987-0-9993968-2-7

www.garyivey.com

Front cover design by SelfPubBookCovers.com and Gary L. Ivey.
Back cover design by Gary L. Ivey using resources from pexels.com, envatoelements.com and wikimediacommons.org.

❧ Acknowledgements ❧

I want to extend my heartfelt thanks to several people who read *Quest for a King* prior to publication while it was still rife with typographical errors, inaccuracies and continuity issues and still gave me encouraging words. Ruth Arthurs and the Living Stones Church Writers Group in Kailua-Kona, Hawaii, listened to my reading of a very early draft when I was calling what would become this volume *Thine is The Kingdom* and gave me notes which I took to heart. Carl Burkhalter, who worships with a Messianic Jewish community, also read and gave feedback on a very early draft. While Sharmaine Magsi, a labor and delivery nurse, didn't read the book, she helped me avoid errors in the several birthing scenes portrayed in the book. My pastor, Bill Barley of Living Stones Church in Kailua-Kona, Hawaii, had given invaluable feedback on one of my other novels and was ideally situated to evaluate *Quest*. Terry Freeman, a good friend and fellow author from my previous home state of Georgia, is also a well-known historian and an authority on the Southern dialect (and barbecue!). As a Christian, he knows these stories well. Especially helpful was longtime friend and business associate Brett Goldberg, who holds dual U.S. and Israeli citizenship and speaks 11 languages fluently, including Hebrew. He has first-hand knowledge of the geography of the Bible lands and knows well the history of the Jewish people from Antiquity to today. His enthusiasm for the book was welcome and he saved me from making a couple of important historical errors. Finally, thanks to my wife and best friend for 50 years, Toni, for suffering through my reading of the book aloud and helping me recognize "bumps" in the flow, continuity lapses and inauthentic character behavior.

❦ Preface ❧

Quest for a King, book one of the "Age of the Kingdom" series, is a work of fiction. It follows several generations of several families against the backdrop of the events found in 1 Samuel in the Bible, which relates the events that birthed the United Monarchy of Israel 3,000 years ago. Other biblical texts shed light on the story, especially 1 Chronicles, but Genesis through Judges also provide background and context. The Psalms of David figure in as well.

Some of the characters who are front and center in *Quest* are entirely fictional. Others are mentioned, but not named, in the Bible. These I have given names and backstories to flesh out the narrative. Still others are the main characters in the biblical narrative, but I have tried to tell their stories from the viewpoints of others.

Quest is in the mode of historical fiction, because I regard the Bible as history, though these accounts of events 1,000 years before Christ, may not have been written with the same philosophy of history which motivates the preservation of history today, the author(s) being more concerned with how God moved within human history.

I relied on a great many books, articles and online sources in the research for the book, in an effort to make it as true to the current understanding of daily life of the time portrayed. Archeology continues to illuminate the past, helping us understand the forces at work socially, culturally and politically.

The conventional wisdom among scholars has been that, as archeology sheds more light on the ancient lands and their cultures, the Bible would become increasingly discredited. However the opposite has proven true. For example, the default position of scholarship was for many years that David was a mythical character, not a real, historical figure. So when the "Tel Dan Stele" was discovered in 1993 containing a reference to "the House of David," the conventional wisdom had to be revised. The engraved stone contained a record of

viii

the victory of a Syrian king over the "House of Israel" and the "House of David," an obvious reference to the northern and southern kingdoms as they existed after the death of Solomon. The southern kingdom, known as "Judah" in the Bible, continued to have kings descended from David for hundreds of years, so the designation "House of David" makes sense and lines up perfectly with the biblical record.

This is NOT a children's book, even though some of the stories are among the most beloved Sunday School lessons, full of adventure and romance. One reason for writing this book was to take an unblinking look at the gritty, difficult lives of biblical characters we think we know.

I was serious about being faithful to the biblical text where it is explicit. Some readers may find events portrayed in this book surprising, so I encourage the reader to revisit the ancient record in 1 Samuel for themselves, which contains some of the most detailed stories in the Bible, yet there is much concerning the inner motivations of the characters which the Bible leaves to our imaginations.

I did not shy away from the supernatural elements of the narrative. While skeptics explain away such things in natural terms, if one is a believer in God, as I am, why would one not believe the God who cares about his children would intervene in earthly affairs?

So, I hope the reader enjoys this novel in the spirit it is offered; as an opportunity to see the events of long ago as contemporaries might have experienced them.

Gary L. Ivey

ANCIENT ISRAEL

(All Locations Are Approximate)
Topographical Map: Wikimedia Commons, EricGaba

❦ 1 ❧

The hot afternoon air stopped dead and all nature fell silent, as if sensing some approaching horror. The birds, which were usually plentiful on these fields, were quiet or had flown away.

Like two malevolent monsters, the opposing armies had trampled forest flora and farmers' fields alike to arrive here. More than 90,000 men faced one another across a field of green, awaiting orders which would soon come.

Eldad stared forward from his position on the front line and squinted through his black forelock, trying to make out faces in the mass of humanity opposing them across the field. The soldiers in the army of the Sea Peoples were nearly obscured by dust and the hazy distance. Through the shimmers rising from the plain, Eldad and the other men of the tribe of Benjamin standing with him could make out teams of horses hitched to iron battle chariots, each with a driver and a bronze-helmeted archer. The sight sent a shiver of fear up his back, in spite of the heat. He licked his lips, but his mouth was dry.

He marched near friends and neighbors from Mizpah, his hometown. Phanuel, Asaph and Zedekiah he knew well. The other man he had never met. Eldad hadn't gotten his name, but he was dressed in the garb of a shepherd.

The shofar, a ram's-horn trumpet, sounded once. Captains barked the order to advance and the men of Israel began walking deliberately forward by ranks over uneven ground. Some carried spears and swords, but many only had tools from their farms and shops; lethal though they could be.

Twenty-seven-year-old Eldad was tall and slender, with muscles made hard by hours of work. His face showed the steel of courage and determination, but his hands trembled with fear. This would be his first experience of war.

Like his fellow Israelite volunteer soldiers, he wore a simple tunic, the hem of which was brought forward and tucked into his belt to free his legs for the battle ahead.

He and his fellow volunteers lacked the heavy armor of the professional soldiers facing them across the field to the west, but he was better equipped than many of his fellow volunteers, thanks to his occupation as a metalsmith in Mizpah in a shop built by his late father, in the heart of the territory claimed by Israel's smallest tribe.

Eldad had fashioned his own sword from bronze with a handle of sycamore wood covered in soft goatskin. It had a curved blade, sharpened on the outside. From its shape it got its name: "sickle sword." Its design originated in Egypt, where it had been known as a "kophesh."

He gripped the handle tighter as he walked. He was unaccustomed to the slap-slap of the leather scabbard against his thigh. In his other hand he carried a shield carved from wood, covered in beaten bronze. His helmet was made of several layers of goatskin, to which his wife, Hadassah, had attached a plume of donkey tail.

The battle lines were arrayed across nearly a mile of ground. Stone fences marking the boundaries of farmers' fields were ignored as the two armies approached each other, their tramping creating its own definition of the land.

The Israelite battle line began moving faster without hearing an order to do so. The men were being driven by bloodlust now. A throaty cry rose from the ranks as their speed approached a run and Eldad heard his own voice join the shouting. Some shouted praise to Yahweh and others cursed their enemy, but eventually their shouting became one loud roar and the men broke into a run. It was downhill and their lines would soon crash into the Philistines.

❧ 2 ❧

ONE WEEK EARLIER

The town of Mizpah of the tribe of Benjamin sat on a prominent hill, which was why it received the name "Mizpah," which meant "Watchtower."

Today the marketplace was abuzz with loud bargaining at the booths of vendors of food, clothing, tools, livestock and more. Eldad, carrying a cloth bag, approached a merchant in a booth.

"Are you from Gibeon?" Eldad asked.

"Yes, does it matter?"

It did matter, because Gibeon, though it was easily visible from Mizpah's lofty elevation, was not an Israelite city. There was bad blood going back centuries to when the residents of Gibeon misrepresented themselves to Joshua, dressing in worn clothing and covering themselves with the dust of the road, saying they were from a far country and wished to form an alliance. When the ruse was discovered – that they only wanted to avoid being attacked – Joshua kept the bargain, but Israel made the residents of Gibeon serve them as laborers.

"It is good you are here," Eldad continued. "I want to expand my trade to Gibeon. My brother and I are smiths. May I show you my samples?"

The merchant motioned his assent wordlessly, accustomed to this process after thousands of transactions.

Eldad opened his bag and began laying bronze items on the table: a sickle, a bowl, a knife, a small bell and a figurine of the fertility god Ba'al in the form of a bull. The merchant looked over the assortment and picked up the knife.

"Hmm. Decent quality."

"We pride ourselves in our workmanship."

Picking up the image, the merchant looked at Eldad and asked, "This is a Ba'al, no?"

"It is."

"So you, a Hebrew, make Canaanite gods? You do not make images of Yahweh?"

"The Torah forbids images of Yahweh."

"So you can't sell those," the merchant laughed, "but you make Ba'als to sell to me?"

"You sell Ba'als, do you not?"

"Not in Mizpah, though maybe I could?" the merchant sat the image down again. "I will take your Ba'als. What would you trade?"

"I need silver."

"Don't we all?" sighed the merchant. "I can give you a half bekah for three of these."

"A half bekah for three! That's 12 for a shekel! I must get a shekel for eight!"

"Your work is not that good. I can find someone else," the merchant waved his hand and turned his attention to arranging his wares.

"Ten then."

"Ten for a shekel?"

Eldad nodded.

The merchant then pointed to the bell. "If I take twenty for two shekels, throw in two bells and you have a deal. When can you deliver?"

"Will you be here next week, fourth day?"

"If it please the gods."

"I will deliver to you then. I require half up front."

The merchant nodded, since this was expected for this type of order. He reached under the table and produced a leather pouch. From it he took two small silver bars and gave them to Eldad.

"Thank you, see you then."

"What is your name, smith?"

"Eldad, son of Elishama."

"See you next fourth day, Eldad."

Eldad moved away, threading his way through the milling crowd.

"Eldad! Eldad son of Elishama!"

Eldad turned to see who called his name. His friend, Phanuel, stalked toward him, carrying a bent sickle.

"What is it, Phanuel?"

"Why do you harm me?"

"I would never harm you, friend."

"You sold me this sickle, but it's junk."

Eldad took the bronze sickle Phanuel held out to him, by its wooden handle. He saw the blade was indeed bent.

"Did you use it to hew stone?" Eldad smirked.

"No! I am not a fool! I was clearing thistles for planting."

Eldad handed the sickle back to Phanuel. "I don't know why that would cause this. Our bronze is of the best quality; tough and strong."

"You will make this right!"

"All right. I can make you a new sickle."

"I don't want another of your sickles. I want my silver back. I will find another smith."

"But your family has purchased tools from my family back to when my father was an apprentice."

"If your father was still alive, he wouldn't have allowed this poor quality! I want my silver back!"

Eldad reluctantly took a silver ingot from his bag and gave it to Phanuel. "Let me take the sickle back to my forge and find out why it failed."

Phanuel gave the damaged tool back to Eldad and disappeared into the crowd.

Eldad puzzled over the way the metal was deformed.

What could cause this kind of integrity failure?

Then light dawned in his eyes.

"Jacob!"

❧ 3 ❧

Eldad, still carrying his cloth bag of bronze samples, hurried along a dusty, rutted street with head-high, mud-brick walls on either side. He stopped at a wooden gate and went through a stone archway into his family compound. The compound consisted of a courtyard and several stone apartments, built side-by-side and a wooden livestock pen in a forward corner. He wasted no time entering an open door to the forge on the main floor of the largest house.

The room was dark except for daylight from the door and a small window, plus the hot fire in the furnace. Eldad could hear the hammer ringing as it struck metal on the anvil.

"Brother! Can you explain this?"

Eldad's brother, Jacob, stopped hammering a bronze shearing knife. Eldad held out the bent sickle. Jacob looked at him, not understanding.

"Phanuel demanded his silver back and vowed to find another smith. Why would this sickle bend this way? Is this not your work?"

Eldad's younger brother took the sickle.

"I suppose it is."

"Of course it is! Why did this happen?"

"Perhaps my experiment didn't work as hoped."

"Experiment? What do you mean?"

"Do you know how much the tin from Anatolia is costing now? And there's precious little of it, so I tried a substitution."

"You changed the alloy?! We have been making bronze the same way for generations. What did you use?"

"Sand. But only a little."

"Sand?! Why would you think that would work? You should have known that would weaken the bronze."

"How do we know, if we don't try it? Actually, when you melt sand, it bonds well..."

"But we can't be selling untried materials to customers! If you want to experiment, do it on your own. Otherwise, stick to what we know works; the formula father taught us!"

Eldad turned and angrily left the forge. It was still light, but the sun would be setting soon. He suddenly realized he was hungry.

The family compound was surrounded by a high wall and included three houses side-by-side with shared walls like apartments. Eldad's house was the largest, because he was the firstborn son. It had been the house of his father and mother and before that, his grandfather. It had been built by Eldad's great grandfather, sometime after Israel conquered Mizpah and it was claimed for the tribe of Benjamin.

Connected to it was a small house for his widowed mother, then Jacob's house. There was room for more, but so far there was no need.

As Eldad walked toward a corner of the courtyard, where a stone oven stood, he shook off his anger. He came up behind his wife, Hadassah, who was absorbed in the baking of a loaf of pita, so she didn't hear him coming. He wrapped his arms around her.

"Oh!" Hadassah exclaimed. At 20 years of age, her slim body was warm and soft in Eldad's embrace and the smell of baking bread brought feelings of hearth and home.

"Oh, what a day I've had!"

"Be careful!" she chided.

"Always. When do we eat?"

"It appears it will be late," came another voice. It was Eldad's mother, Zemirah. Hadassah frowned.

"It will be ready soon enough, if my husband will stop distracting me."

"My son, wash up for supper. You smell of the forge."

"It's the aroma of the work which pays for the bread, mother."

"Still, clean up."

"Yes, of course, I'm starved."

As he went to his house, he saw Jacob's wife, Ophrah, with a tray of food, and their four-year-old daughter, Talia.

"The date cakes are ready," Ophrah said.

"So we only lack the bread," Zemirah looked at Hadassah.

"It's almost done."

"Bring it to the table when it is."

"Yes, mother."

Hadassah remained at the oven alone as the others entered the main house.

The extended family were all seated on cushions on the floor around a low table, which was laden with food. In addition to the pita Hadassah had prepared, there was roasted lamb, greens and leeks, and Ophrah's date cakes. The tableware was baked clay and bronze spoons and knives. Glazed clay cups held wine and water. Eldad said the blessing as they all bowed their heads.

"Blessed are You, Yahweh our God, Ruler of the universe, who brings forth bread from the earth. Amen."

"Amen," Jacob repeated and the family began eating.

Golden light came from a single window, a fireplace and oil lamps mounted on strategically placed stone shelves protruding from the stone walls. The floor was hard-packed earth, but colorful drapes and carpets softened the room. In an alcove on one wall was a small image, a Ba'al, the Canaanite god of harvest.

As everyone reached for food and passed the serving dishes, Zemirah broke the brief silence.

"The forge has been busy?"

"Yes, we have orders for many sickles, scythes and variety of knives." Eldad answered. "Even swords. Today I got an order for the Ba'als."

"Eldad, have you heard the rumors?" Jacob asked.

"About what?"

"That the Philistines are going to march against us?"

"I don't listen to gossip."

"Would they come here?" Hadassah asked softly.

"Not likely," Eldad assured her.

"Would you both have to fight?" asked Ophrah, looking at the two men.

"When the call to arms comes, the men of Israel should answer," Eldad said.

"But both of you shouldn't go. Someone must mind the forge," Zemirah asserted, then looked at her two daughters-in-law. "No one has yet given me grandsons."

"If we had a king, like a real nation, he would have a standing army to protect us," said Jacob.

"This again?" Eldad responded. "Yahweh is Israel's king and His priests and judges tell us His will. That's all we need."

"That's old fashioned, brother. We must look to the future."

"We had no king when Moses freed us from slavery in Egypt! We had no king when Joshua conquered this promised land and we do not need a king now!"

"Nor Deborah, nor Gideon, nor Samson, I get it!"

Ophrah interrupted the feuding brothers.

"If Yahweh is all we need, why do we have the Ba'al watching over us?"

Ophrah pointed to the alcove, with it's bull-shaped statue.

"Appealing to a god of abundant harvest is wise," Zemirah insisted. "Father did. We can honor both."

"Prophets, priests, judges; so add a king, what difference would it make?" Jacob continued.

"To a king, it is weakness to listen to prophets," Eldad argued.

"So, make sure to have a godly king."

"Well little brother, I doubt anyone will ask your opinion."

"Nor yours. Your line won't even survive if Hadassah continues to fail to give you offspring."

"And where is YOUR son?"

"At least Ophrah has proven she is not barren!"

Eldad stood abruptly.

"Sit down, and be quiet," shouted Zemirah. "If I didn't know better, I'd think the two of you were still 10- and 8-years old. Let us continue our meal in peace!"

Eldad sat down again and put a large piece of pita in his mouth. Jacob sulked, but said no more.

Moonlight shone through a gap in the curtains hanging on the window of the upstairs bed chamber. Cool breezes brought brief respites from the summer humidity.

Eldad and Hadassah lay close together, but neither was near sleeping.

"Eldad, will the Philistines come?"

"My beautiful Hadassah, don't worry. There are always rumors."

"But will they come someday?"

"Only if Yahweh wills it."

Hadassah said nothing and Eldad understood she wasn't reassured. He rose on one elbow and passionately kissed her, wrapping her in his muscular arms to love her completely.

❦ 4 ❧

The sun was just coming up, but farmers were already at work many miles to the west of Mizpah. Whereas the highlands of Benjamin around Mizpah were very hilly due to the ridge that ran from north to south through the land of Israel and beyond, this land was mainly flat. It was desirable for growing crops like barley and wheat.

It was virtually no-man's land, where the territory controlled by the Israelite tribe of Judah gave way to Philistia. In fact, Beth-Shemesh, the closest town of any size, was constantly faced with encroachment by the Sea Peoples, who called themselves "Palusata."

It shouldn't have been that way. The land to the west on the way to the Great Sea was to have belonged to the tribe of Dan. They tried to settle there, but the marauders of the Mediterranean rim prevented their occupation of the area.

Called the Sea Peoples because they apparently originated from islands in the Aegean Sea, these warriors invaded, sacked, burned and raped their way around the Sea until they were defeated by Egypt and retired to occupy five great cities and their satellite villages on the coast.

The Danites finally gave up and moved away to the north and occupied land there, just south of Phoenicia. They became the northern-most tribe of the children of Abraham so that it became a saying if you wanted to describe the whole of Israel, one would say "From Dan to Beer-Sheva."

On this day, mischievous boys slipped away from the labor going on at their farms to play. Two nine- or ten-year-old boys, Ammiel and Yoshi, ran laughing and hid behind a rock and a bush beside the road. Their friend, Ali, ran after them.

"Where are you? Ammiel! Yoshi! Where did you go?"

Ammiel and Yoshi stifled giggles, watching Ali through the bush. Suddenly Ali turned to look down the road. The other boys followed his gaze and were surprised to see a Philistine soldier in battle armor over a green tunic, carrying a spear, with a sword strapped to his side.

Ali panicked and began running as the other boys watched from their hiding place. The soldier saw Ali and hurled his spear, impaling him, causing him to fall head over heels and then lie still.

The other boys stifled screams and ran away, but then Ammiel took hold of Yoshi and, putting an upright forefinger across his lips, motioning that they should return to the bush to see what happened next.

Enbol heard a commotion in nearby bushes as he walked over to retrieve his spear from the body of the boy, but didn't see anyone. Using his leather-wrapped foot as leverage, he pulled the spear free and the body settled limp in the dust.

Enbol was big, with massive arms and a broad face covered in black stubble. His hair was relatively short and covered by the distinctive Philistine helmet, with horse hair attached all the way around the crown, pointing skyward.

He turned as a column of Philistine soldiers, in the same uniform as Enbol, rounded a bend in the road. Enbol stood watching them march by, still looking for anyone else who might be around. A few glanced his way to take in the massive soldier and the small dead boy at his feet.

He was about to join the marching soldiers, when the royal chariot approached, with the column of soldiers, flanked by generals on horseback and royal flags. He had a fleeting impulse to hide, which turned to panic, when King Maoch raised his hand, silently ordering the driver to stop.

The driver pulled the reins on the pair of horses pulling the chariot and Clamatos, the king's adjutant, shouted, "Halt!"

Up and down the column, other officers repeated the order and the entire army of Gath jostled to a stop as the king looked down at Enbol and the small boy he had killed.

"What is this?" the king asked. "You have dishonored Gath!"

"Pardon sire, but he could have told that we are coming."

"I could have you killed right here, but I suppose you have a point. Do something with the body or it will cause a bigger uproar than if our approach was revealed!"

Enbol scooped up the body and disrespectfully dropped it into a ditch beside the road, then joined the column as Clamatos gave the order to "Forward, march" and the soldiers began moving again.

There were thousands of them, all marching under the green banners of the city-state of Gath and commanded by the thirty-three-year-old King Maoch. Though this was his first campaign as king, he had been in battle before as a prince and had received the best military training the warlike Palusata could provide.

Maoch was one of five kings of the Philistines and each of the other four were marching with their own armies today, intent on striking a strategic target to the north.

Laboring in a freshly plowed field, Joshua, with a cloth seed bag slung over his shoulder, reached into the bag and with a single motion, pulled a handful of barley seed from it and broadcast it across his field. After each cast he took a step or two and repeated the process.

Ammiel and Yoshi ran up to him just then, both shedding tears and out of breath.

"Father! Father! Come!" Ammiel gasped.

"Slow down. What is it?"

"They killed Ali!"

"What?! Who?"

"The Philistines!"

"Here? Where?"

"Come now!" Ammiel cried and, not waiting for him to agree to follow, the boys turned and ran back the way they came. Joshua dropped his seed bag and ran after them.

Ammiel and Yoshi ran up and looked into the ditch where Ali's body lay. Joshua arrived as well, taking in the scene.

"There were hundreds of them!" Ammiel said through his tears.

"More like thousands!" Yoshi added.

"We must tell his father and mother," Joshua said, not relishing the task that would fall to him. "And then we must warn everyone."

"Will they kill us all?" Ammiel asked, his voice breaking.

"They have passed us by," said Joshua, looking down the empty road. "More likely they are going to Shiloh."

❦ 5 ❦

Shiloh was a city in the central highlands of the territory claimed by the tribe of Ephraim, just a little ways north of Mizpah but just east of the central ridge that formed the backbone of the country. West of the ridge, water ran down toward the Great Sea, whereas east of it, water descended into the rift valley where it joined the Jordan River and ran south from there until it emptied into the Dead Sea.

The wilderness sanctuary constructed during the Israel's 40 years in the wilderness after the Exodus from Egypt had been at Shiloh ever since, on a plateau outside the city. It was an ideal place for it, because it was many miles from the heavily travelled coastal road which ran from Egypt to the north parallel to the Great Sea and connected with the trade routes that went east to the Tigris and Euphrates valleys.

For almost 400 years now, it had been the epicenter of the religion of the one true God, known as Yahweh, which literally meant "Lord," but the word was unique to the Israelites. They might also use "El" to refer to their God, but the Canaanites used that word to refer to one of their gods, so Yahweh was the term to refer to the God who had appeared to Abraham almost a thousand years ago and more recently to Moses.

The "Lord's Tent" was a portable building three times as long as it was wide, with gold-plated wooden walls and a multi-layered covering over top. Inside were two rooms housing ritual furniture which most people had never seen. Only the priests and the Levites who served them were allowed inside the tent, or tabernacle, as it was also called.

The second of the two rooms, the "Most Holy Place" was a perfect cube, its length, width and height being equal. It was entered only by the high priest and only once per year, on Yom Kippur, the Day of Atonement. Yom Kippur was one of three yearly events Israel's men were expected to attend.

A courtyard surrounded the tent, defined by gold-tipped posts with white linen cloth walls. Before the door of the tent was a bronze "laver" or wash basin, and between it and the east-facing gate into the courtyard was a square bronze altar.

Eli, dressed in the white robes and turban of a priest, plus the breastplate of the high priest, carried a censer suspended by three chains, with the smoke of incense wafting away.

His steps were unsteady. At the advanced age of 98, he still tried to be active in service to the Tent, but he could no longer see. Though he was still high priest of Yahweh, others performed most of the day-to-day duties.

"Father Eli! You must sit and rest!"

It was twenty-year-old Samuel who spoke, also dressed in the white robe of a priest, but with long hair tied at the middle of his back, denoting his special status as a Nazarite.

"I will serve Yahweh until my last breath escapes my body," Eli replied, with resolve rather than anger in his weakened voice.

"But others can do this work."

"Other than you, the 'others' remind me of my failure."

Samuel did not answer, because he did not wish to add to Eli's guilt over his wayward sons.

"Yes, you, the miracle child," Eli went on. "Ever since the day your mother dedicated you, you have served me and Yahweh faithfully. You are my sole joy. I only wish I could see your face again."

Eli reached out his hand, searching for Samuel, as his sightless eyes stared straight ahead. Samuel took his hand and guided it to his own shoulder, which Eli patted lovingly. Samuel moved toward the bronze altar near the gate of the compound with Eli's hand on his shoulder.

Samuel had indeed been a miracle child.

For years, his mother, Hannah, had prayed for a son, in vain it seemed, for she had been unable to conceive. "Barren" was the loathsome label applied to women like her, who failed to produce male offspring to carry forward the family line. Her husband loved her tenderly and well, but that didn't stop him from hedging by taking a second, younger wife, who had borne multiple sons and daughters. And Peninnah missed no opportunity to throw it in Hannah's face.

Hannah had been desperate to the point that, when the family went to Shiloh for the feast, she stayed at the gate of the Lord's Tent and prayed, soundlessly mouthing her petition that Yahweh would finally give her a son.

Eli found her there and at first accused her of being drunk in the middle of the day, but after she told him of her prayer, he received a word of knowledge from the Lord and proclaimed her prayer would be answered. Hannah had taken Eli at his word as the answer to her prayer. From that moment on she was certain she would bear a son.

And she did.

And she kept her promise. She had prayed if Yahweh would answer her prayer and give her a son, she would dedicate him to the work of Yahweh's Tent. He was of the tribe of Levi after all, so he would be expected to serve, but she would go the extra step of dedicating him as a Nazirite, which meant he would never drink wine or even eat grapes, never cut his hair and never go near a dead body.

So, from the day he left sucking at her breast, Samuel had become a ward of the high priest. Eli was already an old man – nearly 80 – when Hannah brought her only child to live with the priestly family and be saturated in the worship of Yahweh in Shiloh.

Eli's sons, Hophni and Phineas, were at the bronze altar just inside the gate, receiving the sacrificial animals brought by the penitent worshippers. Assisting them were male and female Levites.

The tribe, which descended from Jacob's son Levi, had been designated during Moses' lifetime to be in direct service to Yahweh. Descendants of Moses' brother Aaron were priests, while other descendants of Levi, including descendants of Moses himself, assisted in the service of the Lord's Tent.

Worshipers were gathered at the gate, each with an animal brought for sacrifice, mostly sheep and goats, but a few with doves in wooden cages, which was permitted for those too poor to afford the larger animals.

A kind of assembly line of slaughter stretched from the gate to the large bronze altar, with Levites assisting the worshipers, providing utensils such as knives and bowls for catching blood, which was an important symbol for the forgiveness of sin.

When a worshiper's turn came to approach the gate into the courtyard, he would lay his hands on the head of the sheep or goat he brought, while confessing his sin.

At the next stage of the assembly line, the worshiper used a sharp knife to slash the throat of the animal. A Levite caught the blood in a bronze bowl and carried it to the altar, where he sprinkled the blood on a side of the altar, symbolizing the cleansing of sin.

Next in the assembly line, the worshiper beheaded the animal, then severed the legs from the torso. He then skinned the torso, slicing it from neck to crotch.

At the next point in the assembly line, the worshiper handed off the dismembered animal to one of the priests and a Levite. The Levite took the head and legs to a pile of discarded parts in a corner of the courtyard. The priest took the parts from the torso, which he placed in a caldron of boiling water. Then, when the meat was softened, the priest used a knife to separate the fat from the organs and muscles.

The fat was placed on the altar to burn by fire that was kept continually burning. The organs would also be placed on the altar to roast. The priests and Levites were allowed to take this roasted meat for their own food. The Torah specified that the blood and the fat were not to be eaten. The fat should be burned as a "sweet savor" to Yahweh.

Hophni, Eli's firstborn son, picked up a three-pronged fork from a nearby table and speared a piece of meat, which he removed from the boiling caldron and started toward the table where meat reserved for the priest's personal use was kept. He had not trimmed off the fat, however, so the worshiper who had brought the animal ran to stop him.

"Wait! Lord, doesn't the Torah tell us to burn the fat; not to eat it?"

"I am the priest. Get out of my way or I'll take it by force!"

The man looked shocked at the callousness of the priest.

Then a messenger ran up to the gate, covered in the sweat and dust.

"Where is the priest?! I have urgent news!"

Hophni, Phineas, Eli and Samuel were all near enough to hear, so they drew near.

"What news?" Phineas asked.

"The Philistine army is on the march on the coastal road! It appears they could be coming here!"

"How far away are they?" asked Samuel.

"They will likely arrive in less than a week!"

The men looked at one another. The worshipers cried out in fear and some began hurrying away, taking their animals with them.

"Have you informed the council of elders?" Hophni asked.

"I will go there next. Can you guide me? Other messengers have been sent to all the tribes of Israel."

❧ 6 ❧

Eldad wiped sweat from his forehead as he pounded a bronze scythe blade. The hammer rang loudly on the anvil as the tool gradually took the shape he envisioned. He stopped and held up the blade to the light to check it's shape and balance.

Then he was startled by the sound of a shofar in the distance. He looked toward the door, alarmed. The rams horn trumpeted morning and evening in the town, every day, but this hour was neither and the sound was more urgent than ordinary. He wiped the sweat from his arms with a rag and put on a shirt, then hurried out the door into the courtyard of the family compound.

Eldad was walking toward the front gate when Jacob entered, obviously winded.

"What is it?" Eldad asked.

"The shofar has sounded. The Philistines are on the march. All men are summoned to Shiloh." Fear showed in Jacob's eyes.

"I'll go. You stay. Mind the forge."

"But, brother..."

Hadassah came out of the main house carrying a bowl of dough.

"I'm the eldest," he added. "As head of this family, it is my duty."

"What?! What is happening?" Hadassah asked.

"The Philistines are marching on Shiloh," Jacob answered. "The shofar has sounded calling us to battle."

"Eldad, don't go!"

"I must go to defend the land. Our village. Our tribe. And my family."

"But I need you here!" Hadassah's eyes grew moist.

"I must go tell mother," Jacob said, turning and hurrying away to Zemirah's apartment.

"Don't leave me here with them!" Hadassah whispered.

"But you are safe here."

"Your mother despises me and I don't like how your brother looks at me."

"I think you are misreading things. They love you as I do."

"Please, don't go."

"Hadassah, I am the man of this house and the eldest. If I do not go, no one will respect me. I have a duty to defend our tribe. I'll be back as soon as the Lord gives us the victory."

From an assortment he kept in the forge, Eldad selected a curved, bronze sickle-sword and leather scabbard, which he tied around his waist. From the wall, he took a wooden shield, covered with beaten bronze. Although he had never carried it into battle, his father had made it for just this type of situation. He also selected a knife, which he tucked into his belt and a goatskin helmet from a shelf, putting it on his head. Finally, he shouldered a bedroll, bound with hemp cords.

Eldad came out of the forge dressed for battle. Hadassah and Zemirah stood waiting somberly. Zemirah kissed him and gave him a leather shoulder bag of supplies. Jacob, Ophrah and little Talia joined them.

"Return safely to us, my son," Zemirah said.

Jacob shook Eldad's hand. "I won't let you down. The work in the forge will continue."

"I'll count on it."

Eldad and Jacob embraced and parted. Eldad and Hadassah walked toward the gate as the others stayed back and watched them.

"I'll be back before you know it," he assured her.

"You can't promise that."

"The God of our fathers is with me."

It appeared to Eldad this did little to comfort her. He pulled her close and kissed her, then from his bedroll he a withdrew a gold ring.

"Here, I made you this. I was waiting for an occasion."

Taking her small hand, he slid the ring on her forefinger.

"I do not often forge gold, but bronze didn't seem adequate for how I love you."

"I'll never take it off."

"Until I return, then."

He kissed her again, then turned and went through the gate. As Hadassah watched him go, she put her hand on her abdomen, tears welling up.

❧ 7 ❧

The open marketplace in the village center was rapidly filling with men equipped for battle. They had no uniforms and little armor, for they were farmers, shepherds and shopkeepers, with improvised weapons, such as sharpened farm implements and kitchen knives. Eldad arrived and joined a group of men he recognized, including Phanuel, Jedediah and Asaph.

"Shalom," Eldad greeted them.

"Welcome, Eldad," Asaph said. "You know Jedediah and Phanuel?"

Phanuel turned away as Eldad greeted the others. The only one standing with the group Eldad didn't know was an older man in the garb of a shepherd. He had broad shoulders and his face was memorable because of deep lines creasing his sun-leathered, perpetually scowling face, heavy, black eyebrows and thick beard. He had no helmet but wore the flowing "keffiyeh" of a shepherd and carried a large, bronze ax with a stout wooden handle.

"Yes, Asaph. When do we leave?"

"Soon, I hope."

"You would not be so eager if you had been in battle before," the shepherd said.

The young men did not argue.

"You," the shepherd said, looking at Eldad. "You are the smith?"

"Yes."

"I knew your father. He was a trustworthy man."

"Thank you. We miss him."

A shofar sounded again, and the men turned their attention to five men who had mounted a raised platform. All the men recognized them as the elders of Mizpah. Kenan, chief elder of the village, stepped forward. He was dressed for battle with weapons at his side like everyone else.

"Your attention! You men have been summoned because the Philistines are moving up the coastal road and we expect them to move inland. It appears they threaten Shiloh, to strike directly at the Lord's Tent. We, along with many others from our tribe of Benjamin will go to Shiloh to assemble with the volunteers from other tribes, then march west to intercept and stop the Philistines. If you have need, purchase provisions from the vendors here in the market, but don't dawdle. We march immediately."

He walked to the stairs with the other elders and descended to where a servant held the reins of a donkey. Kenan mounted it and began riding toward the gate of the village. The others on the platform followed, some walking, some mounting donkeys of their own.

"Do you need anything?" the shepherd asked Eldad.

"No, my wife and mother supplied me well," Eldad answered, patting his leather shoulder bag.

"Then we're off."

They moved along with everyone else, toward the city gate. People lined either side of the street, cheering and waving hands and palm branches. There was a celebratory air, as several hundred men walked toward the city gate, but many women and children had tears in their eyes.

Eldad saw Hadassah in the crowd and waved to her. He saw she had tears streaming down her face. Suddenly she ran toward him and stood facing him. He stopped and was about to tell her again how he must go to defend home and country when she spoke.

"I'm pregnant."

"What?!"

"At least I think I am."

Eldad was suddenly unsure of what to say or do. He turned to watch the other men filing by out the city gate and then looked again at his wife.

"How long have you known?"

"I'm not sure, but my time is late, so I believe I am."

Eldad struggled as he tried to think what he should do. Finally he made his decision.

"I must go fulfill my duty, then I will return. You have Ophrah and mother to be with you."

Her tears had not stopped, but now flowed more freely. He kissed her again and rejoined the men leaving the city.

❧ 8 ❧

The hill-country road wasn't made for this. Hundreds of armed men walked north on the artery barely wide enough for two ox carts to pass one another and the group grew ever larger as men from other towns joined them.

The road rose and fell with the land, alternating between peaks and mountain passes to the right of the men with the high parts dry, but rivulets of water in the low areas. Those rivulets would become rivers as they descended to the west, finally emptying into the Great Sea.

Most of the men knew this road well, having travelled it to Shiloh for feast days many times since being declared a man at the age of 12.

Eldad walked with the shepherd, partly because Phanuel was still not talking to him. Asaph and Jedediah walked with Phanuel nearby.

The elders, who were serving as officers in the volunteer army that would muster at Shiloh, rode donkeys, but there were no horses and no chariots. The terrain was treacherous and not conducive to those modes of transportation.

"Have you fought before?" the shepherd asked Eldad.

"No. You?"

"Yes, but mostly just skirmishes with Canaanites."

"I hear the Philistines are worse."

"It's their training and discipline. They have been warriors for generations in many campaigns."

"But so have we. And we have Yahweh on our side," said a new voice from a young man who overheard.

"Assuming WE are on HIS side," answered the shepherd.

"What is your name?" Eldad asked him.

"I'm Azarel, son of Yohanon. From Anathoth."

"Have you fought before?"

"No."

"Just remember, even when Israel wins, some die," said the shepherd.

This silenced the neophytes for a while.

By the time they arrived in Shiloh, there must have been thousands on the road, both ahead and behind them. Eldad assumed there would be thousands coming from far south in Judah, since it was the largest tribe. Benjamin, where he was from, was the smallest.

There were already many thousands at Shiloh, coming from the North, West and even East from beyond the Jordan river, where two-and-a-half tribes had been given their land by Moses himself before his death and before the land west of the Jordan had been conquered by Joshua.

Eldad and the company from Mizpah didn't enter the city, which was overwhelmed with the arriving men, but joined the throng already there which was moving toward the Lord's Tent. Phanuel, Asaph and Jedediah stood with Eldad and the Shepherd.

"I've never seen so many people," Eldad marveled.

"I just hope it's enough," the Shepherd said.

It wasn't easy to see or hear in the large crowd, but Eldad realized something was happening at the opening in the white cloth wall surrounding the Tent. He could see two priests standing in the gate. One of them said something Eldad couldn't quite hear over the noise of the crowd, but immediately those near the gate fell silent and sat on the ground. Like ripples in a pond, the others followed suit, the men progressively quieted and sat, listening. After the jostling caused by the last being seated, Samuel spoke.

"Your attention, please! Attention! Tomorrow you march toward the Great Sea to meet the Sea People. I am Samuel and I have seen that Yahweh will be with us to prevent them from taking the land God promised us. Each of you has your part to play. Be strong and courageous, for you will be filled with terror, but know that God is with you. The high priest, Eli, will now bless you."

Next to Samuel stood the elderly Eli, holding a smoking censer, hanging by three chains, the smoke of incense rising from it. Behind them, sacrifices roasted on the large altar.

Eli swung the censer forward and back and raised his other feeble hand to speak a blessing.

"May Yahweh Elohim be with you. May Adonai Sabaoth accompany you in your mission. May that which the enemy intends for evil redound to your good, so that the land promised to Abraham, Isaac and Jacob may be increased and the nations will come to the brightness of our rising. May this day mark the beginning of the expansion of God's kingdom on earth, even to the boundaries he has set. Amen."

"Amen," repeated most of the men assembled.

When Eli finished, Samuel stepped forward again.

"Amen. Now make your camp. Tomorrow you march against the Philistines. Go with God."

❦ 9 ❧

Samuel led Eli away from the gate toward the Tent, where they encountered Hophni and Phineas, who had offered sacrifices, appealing to God for victory for the troops.

"You missed an opportunity, Samuel," Hophni said. "With these thousands here today we could have received much gold and silver for blessings of safety on the battlefield."

"My son! I am blind, not deaf," scolded Eli, whose mind was still strong as a lion's jaws. "Will you never stop prostituting the Lord's Tent for you own gain?"

"We just think we should make the most of the situation – for the Lord's Tent," Phineas argued.

"God will bless if we are honest and true," Eli insisted. "The prophets have spoken of your end, my wayward sons."

"Do you mean the babbling of a child who hears voices?" Hophni said, looking at Samuel.

"Do not speak of Samuel's gift that way. God might yet lift the curse," Eli answered.

"And another prophet confirmed the word the Lord gave me," Samuel added.

"There is no shortage of people ready to chime in with the wonder-boy, Samuel," Hophni taunted.

"Do you not fear the Lord's word to this family?!" Eli asked.

"You mean the curse that we will both die the same day?" Hophni snapped. "How would that even happen?"

"Ever since Samuel came to live with us, God has honored him with the gift of prophecy." Eli replied. "What gift has he given you?!"

Hophni and Phineas stormed off and Samuel continued to lead Eli toward the Tent.

There had indeed been a prophecy given to Eli by an old prophet early on, that his two sons would suffer the judgement of Yahweh and die on the same day. Later, after Samuel had been with them for a few years, the Lord began to speak to him, sometimes in a voice he could hear.

The first time Samuel heard the voice in the night, he had assumed it was Eli calling to him, but after the third time, Eli had assured him he had not summoned him, so it must have been the Lord.

The message the Lord had given had been to repeat the curse on Eli's sons, so Eli had to drag it out of Samuel the next morning. When Samuel had related what the Lord said, Eli realized the truth, that Yahweh had chosen to speak to this little miracle child, and when his mother had dedicated him to God, God had chosen him as his instrument.

That was only the first time Samuel would hear God's voice. Gradually it became known in Israel that Yahweh had an oracle in Shiloh.

Hophni and Phineas left the courtyard through the gate, not needing to consult one another about their destination. They were going to their homes.

"Will he never die?" Phineas asked contemptuously on the way to their family compound.

"May I remind you, I'm the firstborn," Hophni said. "Father's death would not mean a promotion for you."

"Maybe not, but it would remove a thorn from my heel."

After entering the gate into their courtyard, Phineas turned toward his house as Hophni also changed direction to go toward his.

A very pregnant Atarah, Phineas' wife, was preparing a meal. When Phineas entered, she was just placing the food on a baked-clay plate.

"Atarah, have you prepared the evening meal? I'm famished."

"I have."

"Then hurry and bring it here."

Phineas sat on a cushion. She brought the plate to the low table and set it in front of him. As she did, she tried to brush his cheek with a kiss, but he turned away from her, immediately taking a bite of pita.

"I heard there is an army marching," Atarah ventured.

"Yes, the Philistines march against us again," answered Phineas with his mouth full. "So the city is crowded with our warriors."

"Philistines? Coming here?!"

"Who knows what they will do, where they will go? Besides, Shiloh is an armed camp. There's no need to worry."

Atarah caressed her bulging belly and left the room.

✤ 10 ✤

The volunteer army was continuing to grow as night fell with men coming from every corner of the territory Israel controlled. As men passed by, Eldad heard accents he hadn't heard before and he realized that the different tribes, especially those located east of the Jordan River, had slightly different speech patterns and pronunciation.

The men had begun making camp after Eli blessed them. They were organized by tribe around the white linen wall surrounding the Lord's Tent, much as they had been in the wilderness 400 years ago.

Eldad, the Shepherd, Azarel, Phanuel, Asaph and Jedediah sat on their bedrolls around a fire, eating the meager rations each of them had brought with them. As far as one could see, thousands of campfires illuminated the thousands of other men sitting around them.

"How many do you think have come?" Phanuel asked.

"It must be tens of thousands," Eldad said. "Every tribe is represented."

"But how many Philistines are marching this way?" Asaph asked, knowing no one knew.

"Remember, Gideon won a great victory with just 300," Jedediah said.

"Yes, but God doesn't do things the same way every time," the shepherd reminded them. "Let us pray Yahweh will fight for us in this case."

The others stared into the fire, each with his own thoughts, until Eldad spoke again.

"When the high priest blessed us, he spoke of expanding the land to promised boundaries. What did he mean?"

"God promised Abraham he would father a great nation," Asaph recalled.

"He meant the prophecy," said the shepherd.

"What prophecy?" Eldad asked.

"When Israel lay dying, God showed him the future of the tribes. It was what was promised to Abraham, all right, but Jacob defined it."

The shepherd didn't have to remind these men that Jacob and Israel were the same person and that Yahweh himself – or at least an angel – had given Jacob the name "Israel" after a night of wrestling, because Israel meant "He who wrestles with God."

"What was the territory?" Jedediah asked. "From Dan to Beer-sheva?"

"Much more than that," answered the shepherd. "North to the Euphrates River and Sidon."

"I never heard of the Euphrates River," Phanuel admitted. "Where is it?"

"It's farther north and east than any of us will likely go in our lives unless we become traders on the spice road," the shepherd answered. "And the promise is to extend to the Great Sea to the west and to the Great Desert to the east."

"For that to happen, the Philistines would have to be driven from the coastal plain," Eldad said.

"And to the South?" Asaph asked. "Beyond Beer-sheva? Into the Negev?"

"And beyond."

The men fell silent as they considered the implications. Then Eldad broke the silence once more.

"When will this happen?"

"That's the thing about prophecy," the shepherd said. "God's timing is unknown, unless He makes it known."

"Would God anoint a leader to do this?" Eldad continued.

"God raises up leaders in every generation. The question is, will we recognize them and follow?"

They stared into the fire, considering the shepherd's words, for a while, until he spoke again.

"Now, I am going to get some sleep before our long march and the terror of battle tomorrow. I advise each of you to do the same."

They all stirred and began to arrange their bedding for the night, as some around other fires had already done. As Eldad wrapped his bedroll around him and drifted off to sleep, he silently sent a prayer to Yahweh for safety and success on the battlefield tomorrow.

The city of Aphek, with its stout walls, stood on the coastal road, a few miles east of the Great Sea. It was one of the cities Israel had failed to conquer, so it was still controlled by Canaanites, the ancient people who lived in the land even before God promised it to Abraham.

Day was just dawning as a long column of professional Philistine soldiers, which seemed to go on forever, marched east past the Canaanite city. They wore uniforms and bronze armor, unlike the ragtag Israelite volunteers. The sentries on the city wall stood watching as each of the military units marched by: infantry, archers, cavalry and chariot troops.

The citizens of Aphek knew they had nothing to fear from the Philistines for, while they were not the same ethnicity, they shared many of the same gods, though in slightly different pantheons. Anyway, they were allies against the Hebrews, their name for Israel, and territory recaptured from Israel would be a boon to both peoples.

"How many were we able to muster?" Maoch, King of Gath, asked his adjutant, Clamatos, riding a horse near the royal chariot.

"Twelve thousand, more or less. There must be 50,000 marching with us from all five city states."

"To the glory of Gath and the Palusata!" Maoch exclaimed.

"To the glory of Gath! To the glory of the gods!"

Israel's ad-hoc army was also marching, going west, downhill. A startled flock of birds flew from a stand of trees and swept in a broad arc above the army.

Azarel ran up to the men from Mizpah.

"I have news! Our scouts confirm the Philistines are marching east from Aphek."

"The way to Shiloh," the shepherd noted.

"How far?"

"We could meet them in an hour. Spread the word. I must tell others," Azarel said, already running down the line of men to relay the news.

"May the Lord of Armies be with us!" the shepherd said.

"Amen!" Eldad agreed.

Soon, Kenan rode by on his donkey.

"Men of Mizpah! Make camp here! The Philistines are ahead. Prepare to meet them yet today."

Eldad and the others stopped and began making camp, something some were more accustomed to than others.

"We will fight after marching so far?" Asaph asked.

"Take what rest you can, but be ready to march again," the shepherd advised.

❧ 11 ❧

By mid-afternoon, they had made camp and the Israelites were ordered to march again. Eldad noticed the terrain was much flatter now. He and the others crested a low rise to see a cloud of dust in the distance.

Only a great many men and horses could create such a cloud of dust, Eldad realized.

"Prepare yourselves now, for we meet them within the hour!" Kenan called out to the men from Mizpah as he rode by on his donkey. "May Yahweh, the God of Abraham, Isaac and Jacob, be with us all."

Eldad squinted into the sun in the western sky. He could just make out individual soldiers through the haze and shimmering heat waves.

He drew his sword and tried the blade's sharpness, though he knew it well, having forged it himself. He put it back in its leather scabbard and took his shield from his back, slipping his left arm into its leather straps.

Eldad looked around at the broad field with trees lining either side.

"What is this place?"

"The Stone of Help," the shepherd said. In the Hebrew tongue it was pronounced "Eben-ezer." Eldad noted the name.

It will be famous after today.

"Then let us gird ourselves for battle," the shepherd said. The men watched what he did and then followed suit, adjusting their clothing and weapons to make running and fighting easier, pulling the hems of their tunics forward through their legs and tucking them into their belts, freeing their legs for running.

Kenan drew his sword and called out: "You men form ranks facing the enemy. Spread out!"

The men attempted to follow the order, but they were inexperienced and the line was haphazard. Kenan rode up and down, directing men to fill in the holes in the line. "You! Here! You and you, beside him. Line up facing the enemy!"

Eldad happened to look at the sky and called, "Look out!"

The men looked toward the approaching Philistines. Some saw the danger in time, others did not. Philistine archers had loosed hundreds of silent arrows which were arcing toward the Israelites.

Eldad raised his shield and an arrow struck it and held. Around him others were struck down because they had no shields or raised them too late.

"Now! Forward!" Kenan called out.

The men started moving toward the army facing them. Kenan, on his donkey, was now out front facing the Philistines with sword raised, leading the charge.

"Forward!" called a captain of the Palusata, echoing a hundred others passing down the ranks of professional infantrymen. The command was a word that came from deep in the past of Mycenaean warfare and had been heard from the Aegean Sea to the Nile. With practiced precision, the soldiers moved as one man toward the Hebrews across the field, their wood- and leather-shod feet pounding a drumbeat that bounced back from distant hills. To add to the ominous rhythm, the bronze-helmeted soldiers beat the flats of their iron swords on the fronts of their shields with each stride.

Under the green banner of Gath, King Maoch stood tall and proud in his gilt-edged iron battle chariot. With him rode his armor bearer and bodyguard, who would defend him to the death if the battle got too hot around him. The driver of the chariot was a warrior himself and could be counted on to defend the king as well.

Flanking the royal chariot was the general staff; commanders of the army of Gath. The generals rode horses; regal animals trained on the plains near the Great Sea; powerful steeds which could overrun wave after wave of infantry and the slow donkeys ridden by the Hebrew officers.

King Maoch looked across the field and saw that he could make out individual Hebrews now.

On the right flank of Maoch's army was the army from Ashkelon, the city by the Sea. Their numbers were not as great as the army of Gath, but they had come the farthest. Their uniforms and equipment varied from those of the army of Gath mainly in the color of the tunics they wore under their breastplates. Gath's was green, but Ashkelon's was purple, thanks to a dye made from a liquid secreted by a shellfish. Their banners were the same purple.

To the left, Maoch could see Gaza's army, with more than 10,000 men. Beyond Gaza, the men of Ekron and Ashdod marched. In all, the army of the Palusata was 50,000 strong.

Maoch could hear the Hebrews shouting as they ran straight at his position.

❦ 12 ❦

Eldad had forgotten his fear as he rode the fury of the speeding battle line and felt his own voice joined to those around him. He felt his people unstoppable as their legs pumped in unison, their feet pounding the ground.

Now they could see the faces of the Philistines, cold and dark. At a shout from their officers and the front line lowered spears. Eldad's fear rushed back but it was too late to stop.

"Careful of the spears!" Eldad cried out.

The two advancing armies crashed together and the throaty shouts broke apart in chokes of pain. All order was shattered as many around Eldad fell on the lowered spears.

Eldad was surprised that he had not fallen, but had gone between two spear points and was still moving forward through the Philistine front line. He slashed to both sides and saw two Philistines fall by his sword. A thrown spear glanced off his shoulder, spinning him around and his outstretched sword caught another Philistine across the throat. But in spinning around, he could see that he was almost alone between the first and second ranks of the enemy.

He ran back a few cubits to where the two armies had crashed together. Suddenly he fell, but he was not wounded. He had tripped over the body of one of his fellow volunteers from the tribe of Benjamin. Then he saw that the ground was covered with bodies; a few Philistine but mostly Israelite.

He had no time to consider it because the Philistines were pushing forward. Eldad leapt to his feet and raised his shield just in time to stop a Philistine sword from splitting his head. He spun around before the Philistine could raise his heavy iron sword again and sliced the bearded man's arm below the shoulder. The man cried out in pain and fell back, but the wound would not be fatal.

From King Maoch's vantage point three ranks back, he could see his soldiers were chewing up the Hebrews. He motioned to the trumpeter, who nodded, then sounded the call to the archers. Immediately in front of Maoch and the generals, the archers raised their bows and bronze-tipped arrows and their officers ordered, "Release!"

Several hundred arrows flew in a silent, graceful arc over the heads of those locked in desperate struggle in the front ranks and sliced through the Hebrew's third and fourth ranks. Maoch could see that it had exactly the desired effect. Those still standing in those ranks panicked, turned and ran, bumping into the ranks behind them. Now his troops could completely eliminate the first two ranks.

Eldad sensed that he was alone among the Philistine soldiers. All those near him had fallen and the ranks of Israel behind him were falling back. Then he heard the shofar sound "Retreat." At that moment he was set upon by three Philistines at once. He had no choice but to leap backward, where he again stumbled over a mound of dead and wounded and rolled back onto his feet.

"Fall back!" Eldad heard the shepherd shout. He turned to face the enemy but was moving away from them as fast as the mass of men to the rear would allow. He continued to face the Philistine line as he retreated, but for some reason they had stopped pursuing them.

The sun was low in the sky as the Israelite army withdrew from the field, badly bloodied.

"Why did they stop?" Eldad asked the shepherd as they limped away from the battle line.

"They follow orders. We meet them again tomorrow."

❦ 13 ❧

Once in camp, Eldad the others of the unit from Mizpah conducted a head count and realized they had lost 23 men out of their original 100. In the deepening darkness Kenan left to report to his superiors while the men bound their wounds and tended to their equipment.

"Where's Asaph?" Jedediah asked, looking around.

"I didn't see him after the volley of arrows," Phanuel said.

"He didn't make it," The shepherd answered.

Eldad gulped, realizing how fortunate he had been.

Inside a tent at the heart of the camp, a circle of dust-covered elders-turned generals gave their reports one by one, their faces illuminated by torches.

"The final tally is 4,000 men killed," one said. "And many more wounded."

"That's almost a tenth of our force!" another exclaimed.

"We must cry out to Yahweh!" one said.

God was their supreme ruler, but He did not speak except through judges, prophets and priests. For an hour they prayed and cried.

"We should send for the Ark of the Covenant to come from Shiloh," one of the men said finally. "That will ensure that Yahweh will be with us and make us victorious!"

The others agreed.

"Perhaps a gift of silver, for Yahweh's Tent?"

"I have no silver," the young woman told the priest nervously, looking about, realizing they were alone in a building near the gate of the courtyard surrounding the Lord's Tent where records of the sanctuary were kept.

"In that case," Phineas licked his lips, "I might accept other 'payment' from you."

His meaning was unmistakable. The young woman was slight, and the priest was both tall and heavy. She was shocked that a priest of Yahweh would suggest such a thing.

"But, you are married!" she protested.

And my wife is as big as a cow and cares nothing for me, Phineas thought bitterly. She would give birth sometime in the next couple of months, but it could not be too soon.

"You do want Yahweh's blessing, do you not?"

"Yes," the girl said. "My mother is very sick."

Suddenly a man covered in sweat and mud burst in upon them. It was Azarel.

"Are you the priest?" he shouted.

"Yes, can't you see I'm counseling?"

"Forgive me, but the battle went badly for Israel. We need you to come and bring the Ark that Yahweh might be with us tomorrow. Otherwise we will be overrun by the Philistines!"

Phineas growled, frustrated that he would need to send the young woman away. "Your blessing will have to come later." Then to the messenger: "Come, let us find my brother."

"What is happening?" the sightless Eli asked Samuel, hearing the commotion as Hophni and Phineas supervised the removal of the Ark from its place in the Most Holy Place of the Tent.

"Hophni and Phineas are taking the Ark to the battle."

Eli did not ask anything further, but the creases in his brow deepened and he lowered his head, his chin resting on his chest.

❧ 14 ☙

The next morning, Eldad munched on a meager breakfast of dried mutton and figs from his bag. The sun was already well above the horizon. He wondered why they had not yet been ordered to array themselves for battle.

Suddenly, he was startled by a cheer and shouting in the camp nearby. He turned and stood to see the reason for the commotion. Other Israelites were running toward something borne on the shoulders of four white-robed Levites, the keepers of the Covenant. It was covered with a royal robe of some kind. Behind them were four more Levites and two important-looking, if bedraggled, priests, riding donkeys. Eldad knew it could only be the Ark of the Covenant.

Israelite soldiers danced around it as it was carried to the center of the camp. "God will be victorious," they chanted. The Levites set down their important burden and the soldiers continued to dance.

How can we fail, now that God's presence is with us?

He knew it was a dangerous game, but it paid well. He had been able to get near enough to the Hebrew camp to see what was happening without getting caught. The advantage he had was that he was neither Israelite nor Philistine, but was obviously Phoenician, being from Sidon. Now he had to report back to the Philistine officer who was paying him, but he had to enter the Philistine camp without getting killed by a sentry.

"Stop! Who goes!" came the expected challenge from a sentry. The Sidonian raised his hands to show he was unarmed and turned to face the sentry.

Gary L. Ivey

"I have information for Clamatos. And King Maoch."
"All right, this way," the sentry said, gesturing with his spear, but keeping it ready as he walked behind him.

"Why are the Hebrews singing and dancing?" demanded Kogn, king of the Philistine city Ekron.
"They bring their god to fight for them," answered the dark Phoenician with bushy black brows.
King Maoch saw alarm in the faces of several of those in the tent. All of them knew the stories of how the Hebrews devastated Egypt and the Canaanites 400 years ago by way of supernatural victories where armies were swept away by the sea and walled cities collapsed.
"How will we prevail if their god is with them?" a timid officer blurted out before he thought.
"Remember who you are!" said Maoch. "You are the Palusata; the fiercest warriors in the world! Acquit yourselves like men!"
"Yes! Dagon be praised!" the men answered.

"Men of Benjamin! Forward in the Lord!"
"For Yahweh!" Azarel joined the voices of his kinsmen in answer to the rallying call of their captain as his cohort moved out to meet the Philistines again. He was fatigued after the battle yesterday and his trek to Shiloh and back to take the elders' request for the Ark to be sent, but he knew he must do his duty.
He was not tall enough to see over the men ahead of him, forward to the enemy across the field, but he knew they were there. Also, because it had taken many hours to bring the Ark from Shiloh, it was now afternoon of the second day of battle and the sun was shining in his face, making it all the more difficult to see their enemy.
Perhaps it's better I can't see them yet, he told himself. Besides his sickle sword, he carried a sling which could give him an advantage to be able to strike a blow from a distance. But for close fighting, he also had a knife in his belt at the

small of his back. He hoped he would not be in hand-to-hand fighting, where the tall, well-equipped Philistines would definitely have the advantage.

Today the armies would meet on a field to the east of yesterday's battle, at a point to which the army of Israel had withdrawn after being beaten back. Azarel's position was near the middle of the battle line and about three ranks back. The rank ahead of his was the slingmen, expert marksmen who would fling their deadly hail of stones over the heads of their fellow Israelites and into the advancing enemy when they were in range.

"Our brothers from Judah strut like peacocks!" The man to Azarel's left said, referring to the corps of the tribe of Judah, which made up the heart of the army. "Just because they are many, they should not think they are better fighters than we are."

"They may strut like peacocks if they wish, Jehoida, if only they will fight like eagles," Azarel replied. The man was his kinsman.

Kenan stopped his donkey at the top of a hill and directed the line to split, companies alternately going to the right and left, arraying themselves on the ridge, looking down at the Philistines in the valley. Eldad, the shepherd, Phanuel and Jedediah stood on the front line looking forward, but having to shield their eyes against the sun.

"This is not ideal," the shepherd remarked.

"But we have the high ground," Eldad said.

"Which will be of little use if we cannot see the enemy because the sun is at their backs."

The others looked forward, shielding their eyes, realizing the shepherd was right.

"Faster!" said King Maoch to his adjutant, loud enough for all to hear. Clamatos loudly called the command for "double-time, march."

A trumpet sounded and then another and another down the line, and the Palusata soldiers slammed their swords against their shields with vigor, as their blood flowed faster to the rhythm. As they began to half-run, they glared from under their bronze helmets, looking forward to the Hebrew lines now only a hundred yards away.

Having bested their enemy the day before, Maoch had no doubt that they would crush them today. The king nodded to one of his generals, who in turn nodded to a trumpeter. When the trumpeter blew his horn once, the infantry paused their advance and the archers raised their bows. Another blast of the trumpet and they released thousands of bronze-tipped arrows in high arcs across the field.

There was a bustling as another rank filed in behind Eldad. Each carried a sling and a heavy shoulder bag. The shepherd turned and looked at them.

"Oh, good. The slingmen. They will return the favor for the volley of arrows we took yesterday. Prepare to kneel when they let fly if you don't want your melon cracked!"

"Front rank! Kneel!" called Kenan.

Eldad, the shepherd, Phanuel and Jedediah, as well as others up and down the front line, obeyed and knelt.

"Slingmen, ready!"

The slingmen loaded five-pound stones into their slings and began swinging them overhead, making a strange humming sound.

"Release!" Kenan shouted.

Maoch watched the arrows descend toward the Hebrew ranks, but before any of the arrows found targets, their enemy answered in kind: the slingmen let loose their stones.

He quickly pulled his small shield from its hanger on the wall of his chariot, slipped the bronze shield's leather strap over his arm and raised it just in time. The infantrymen all around him raised their larger shields and Hebrew stones clattered down upon them. Maoch felt a stone bounce from his shield down his right arm and skip off his leg. He winced in spite of himself, surprised at how heavy it was.

Maoch looked around to be sure no one saw him flinch, but everyone was too busy dodging the stones themselves. Mostly their shields protected them, but a few men cried out and fell in pain. His eyes were wide as he watched one man writhing in pain nearby, blood covering his face.

A spontaneous cheer exploded from the Israelites, but Eldad saw the Philistine ranks stabilize and continue forward, other men replacing those who fell. Eldad and his fellow soldiers rose and instinctively gripped their weapons for the inevitable clash, now just seconds away.

❦ 15 ❧

The volley of arrows had struck down random Israelites whose shields were inadequate or raised too late, but they had been left behind to suffer and die.

"May Yahweh grant us victory!" Eldad shouted, his voice breaking in the middle of the sentence as he marched forward in the battle line, struggling to conceal his fear as he remembered the fierceness of the battle yesterday and anticipated what lay before them.

"Amen," said the shepherd to his right without taking his eyes off the Philistines. He took a long, deep drink from the waterskin slung over his shoulder and wiped his mouth with his hand without putting down his ax.

Eldad could see the individual Philistines in their front line now. They were trotting and would very soon be upon them. Their flowing banners, matching armor and brightly colored tunics were an imposing sight.

Kenan rode up on his donkey in front of them.

"Forward!"

As Kenan turned his mount and pointed his sword forward, the men begin to take steps forward, descending the hill toward the Philistines in the valley.

"Charge!" Kenan shouted.

The men began to run with weapons forward, but then they saw something that gave them pause. At an interval of about every 12 men, the Philistine ranks swung like a gate opening. Through the openings came battle chariots, each containing a driver and an archer.

"Oh no! Save yourselves!" shouted the shepherd.

Unsure what to do, Eldad watched the chariot speeding right toward of him and, at the last second, hurled himself to one side to avoid it. But Jedediah couldn't get out of the way and was trampled under the horses' hooves. Eldad saw that Phanuel somehow avoided being hit.

Those who escaped found themselves the object of the archers in the chariots. More men fell. Israelite discipline, tenuous as it was, was now destroyed and everyone fought for himself.

Eldad saw the shepherd use his ax to shatter a chariot wheel as it went by, causing the chariot to spill over.

Eldad caught the side of another chariot and jumped in. He used his sword to kill the archer, then pushed the driver out. He took the reins and brought the dangerous horses to a stop. He then jumped down to face the oncoming infantry.

A big, black conscript attacked Eldad, who stopped the African's sword with his shield, then hacked at the man's shoulder. He cried out, but swung his sword again. Eldad dodged it, but fell backward over a dead Israelite. The big Philistine raised his sword to strike again, but Eldad was surprised when he was struck down. Eldad looked wide-eyed at the shepherd who now stood facing him, blood dripping from his ax.

"Come on! There're more of them to kill!" the shepherd shouted at Eldad.

As if to cruelly fulfill the shepherd's words, something hit him hard enough to make his whole body fly to the right about six cubits, crashing through struggling Israelites and Philistines before hitting the earth where he lay still.

"No!" Eldad cried out.

He then saw what had killed the shepherd.

Before him Eldad saw a man larger than any he had ever seen; indeed, taller than he thought possible. He towered above the other soldiers, both Israelite and Philistine, in fact, he was nearly twice as tall as any of the Israelites. *He has to weigh many times that of a normal man,* Eldad reasoned in a moment that seemed to stand still. He had heard rumors of giants among the Philistines.

It was the huge man's massive battle ax that had killed the shepherd and he was raising it again, ready to swing it through the Israelite line like a scythe through barley. The men of Israel, terrified at the unexpected threat, turned and collided with their comrades in the ranks behind them.

Eldad scrambled to his knees and tried to move away so he wouldn't be caught by the next swath the frightening giant would cut.

In the midst of the surprise created by the appearance of the giant, Philistine spears rained down, felling fleeing Israelites.

To his side, Eldad saw a Philistine with a raised javelin. Eldad instinctively rolled over to face him, then dodged and was missed by only a finger's breadth as the Philistine drove his spear into the ground. Eldad grasped and held the wooden spear's shaft and, with the other hand, swung his sword at the shaft, splitting it in two.

Deprived of his weapon, the Philistine responded by slamming his shield into Eldad's face. Stunned, Eldad fell back and everything went black.

The Philistine soldier cast away the useless javelin shaft and drew his double-edged sword, drawing back to stab Eldad, but he stopped when a Philistine arrow struck Eldad in the thigh.

He looked up to see a volley of Philistine arrows descending. He was hit twice and fell across Eldad's waist.

From a safe distance, King Maoch, watched the bloody fighting on the front line.

"Why did you wait so long to release The Giant?" Clamatos asked him.

"To complete their confusion. Now we finish them."

His plan had worked as he had thought it would: The Hebrews were panicked by the site of this unexpected behemoth. When they turned in fear, they made easy targets for his soldiers.

"The Giant" was the hero of Gath and the perfect secret weapon. He was part of a clan of giants who had been driven out by the Hebrews when they came out of Egypt. They had taken refuge in Gath.

Maoch again gestured to his trumpeter. When the call for the archers sounded again, they sent arrows raining down on the retreating and vulnerable Hebrews.

His well-trained and disciplined troops were visiting great destruction on this motley army of farmers and merchants. Soon the bloody business would be done.

The first two ranks had been decimated now and Azarel and his kinsman braced for what was coming. The Philistine warriors broke over the pile of bodies like surf breaking on the boulders of Ashkelon with fire in their eyes.

One of them reached Azarel's kinsman first and unceremoniously hacked at his shoulder before he could raise his sword. The Philistine's second blow split Jehoida's helmetless head. He fell to the ground with blood gushing from the fatal wound.

Azarel screamed his rage and hacked at the Philistine with his sickle sword. To Azarel's surprise and relief, he fell with a low choke of pain. But Azarel had no time to rejoice. Suddenly a wave of Philistine chariots hit the Israelite line, laying them low in one violent moment.

Azarel was narrowly missed but was spun around by a horse violently rushing by.

❦ 16 ❦

The westering sun was blood-red through the choking dust as Azarel scrambled to the crest of a ridge. The guttural cries and clatter of combat was behind him now; Azarel had turned away and not even realized that he had run, until now, a few seconds later.

His stomach convulsed with the memory of his kinsman falling at his side. After he limped to the top of the ridge he involuntarily turned to view the larger battlefield and gasped at what he saw. The battle line was moving slowly across the plain eastward like some menacing pestilence, devouring as it went. The Philistines, the dreaded Sea People, were meting out an unmitigated slaughter on his people.

The din of battle assaulted his ears: screams of pain mixed with the clang of iron against bronze, the angry roars of warriors melding with the thuds of lifeless bodies on the sandy soil.

Then his attention was captured by another developing crisis. Between the Benjamites and the larger ranks from Judah marched the golden Ark of God, draped in scarlet, purple and gold, borne on poles like a royal sedan on the shoulders of white-robed Levites and escorted by the sons of the High Priest on donkeys. The enemy was overwhelming the ranks before the Ark now and were getting close.

It made no sense.

Why has God left us just as we invoked His presence?

To the rear, behind the Ark and the two priests, the generals, each representing one of Israel's 12 tribes, watched from their own donkeys, the animals dancing nervously.

Then a Philistine archer loosed a bronze-tipped arrow, which struck a forward-most bearer of the Ark and he fell, his corner of the Ark dipping and its weight shifting. Another bearer stumbled and Azarel watched in helpless horror as the Holy Ark of God tumbled sideways to the ground, pinning one of the Levites under the heavy, gold-plated box and the twin, solid-gold cherubim that stood guard atop it. The scarlet and purple drape fell to the ground, revealing the golden glory that was meant to be always hidden from mortal eyes.

A startling cheer arose from the ranks of the Sea Peoples and they surged forward. As Azarel watched from the height, Yahweh's priests instinctively drove their donkeys forward to get between the Ark and the charging Philistines, but they were unarmed. Only a few Israelite soldiers remained between the enemy and the two acolytes of Yahweh's Tent. The Sea People slashed through the thin remnant of Israelite defenders with terrible fury. Within seconds, the priests were cut down, their white robes slashed with heavy, iron swords and stained with crimson. The Ark was now in the hands of their godless enemy.

Panic seized the Israelites who remained alive and they broke and ran, with the elders leading the retreat. Many took only a couple of steps before being cut down by Philistine arrows and javelins.

Azarel saw that all was lost, so he cast handfuls of earth into the air over his head in grief and despair. Then he turned and ran once again, as fast as his thin, weary and bruised legs could move, down the back side of the ridge toward the brook that cut a path to the sea. He did not know if any of his fellow Israelites were escaping with him, or if the Philistines were pursuing. He reached the brook and splashed through it without looking back, turning now to follow its route to the East, toward the highlands of Ephraim.

After about a mile he paused and turned to see that no one had followed him. He buried his face in the water of the brook, drinking deeply. Until now he had not thought of where he was going, but seeing no other survivors around him made him realize he must go on.

God must have chosen him to be the one to carry the bad news to Shiloh.

It was late and the sun was low in the west when the battle finally ended. The ground was covered with dead and wounded; some Philistine, but mostly Israelite. A few Philistine soldiers remained on the field as the sun went down, but no one thought the Hebrews would counterattack.

Then, Philistine camp followers came onto the bloody field, intent on scavenging anything they thought they could sell and killing any moaning wounded they found. Vultures began circling, hardly visible against the moonless sky.

Threading his way through thick brush, Azarel climbed out of the valley to the main road that traversed the hill country from the sea to Shiloh, and paused to sit on a boulder as twilight descended on the fertile slope. He still had perhaps 20 miles to travel to reach Shiloh where he would have to inform the priests and the prophet that Israel's cause was lost, as was the Ark.

Azarel marveled when he realized he had looked upon the Ark of God and lived. Even more amazing, the Philistines had taken the Ark and they also were not struck dead. He wondered if Israel had offended God so much that His presence was completely gone from the Ark.

Azarel had seen the Tent many times, but of course he had never been inside the mysterious Tent itself; that was only for the priests. There was only one man living who had seen the Ark, which was kept in the innermost room of the Tent with its gold-plated, wooden walls; the high priest entered the Most Holy room of the Tent only on Yom Kippur to obtain atonement. That is, only one man living had seen the Ark until today.

For many miles he moved in the deepening darkness, gradually slowing as weariness overtook him.

❧ 17 ❧

Eldad, nose bloodied, lay unconscious, with the body of the Philistine on top of him. Then he stirred and his eyes opened. He winced from the pain in his head. He tried to get up, but gasped and fell back.

In the darkness, he saw the torches of the camp followers in the distance. He realized if they got to him, they would finish him. He tried to move his legs, but had to cover his mouth to prevent crying out from stabbing pain of the arrow in his leg.

He felt about in the darkness for something to use to push the heavy Philistine off him. He found the broken javelin shaft. With great effort, he used it to roll the heavy Philistine off. Again he nearly cried out because of the arrow through his thigh.

Now free of the weight, he found the Philistine's double-edged sword. He rolled over slightly and felt the bloody point of the arrow coming out the back of his leg, having gone all the way through. With great care, he raised the sword and let it fall on the point of the arrow, which snapped off.

The pain caused by the arrow moving in his leg momentarily blinded him. When he recovered, he pulled with all his might to extract the arrow through the front of his bloody leg. Again he fell back with the pain, holding his hand over his mouth.

He knew he had to get away from there, checking the progress of the camp followers.

"Help me, Lord God," he prayed.

Picturing beautiful Hadassah and the new life she carried within her drove him to try to get up and move.

Gary L. Ivey

He tried to stand, but was too weak, so after falling back, he used the sword to help himself crawl away, over bodies and off the battlefield. It took several minutes, but he was finally able to rest briefly under the trees on the outskirts of the battlefield. Again noting the location of the camp followers, he began slowly crawling again until he was far enough away he wouldn't be found. He lay back against a tree and was soon asleep.

Azarel's stomach complained with hunger. He had eaten a scrap of pita just before the battle began but that was twelve hours ago. The cool water of the brook was a distant memory. His legs screamed for relief and rest. Bruises and scrapes he had sustained in the battle, of which he had barely been aware until now, nearly halted him. The bottoms of his feet were bruised and bleeding. The sand between his feet and sandals tortured his every step. He looked in the dim moonlight for a place of shelter. If he could just rest for a few minutes, he could continue.

He came to a place where a fig tree grew next to an outcropping of rock. He approached it and saw to his delight that it had fruit. Eagerly he tore a few figs from a low branch and quickly ate them, the juice soaking his hands and beard. He sat down against the gnarled trunk to enjoy his feast.

He suddenly realized he had dropped his curved sickle sword on the battlefield and had only his short blade that was better used to cut meat for a meal than for defense. That sword had been his grandfather's in the wars under Barak and Deborah. He was pained to have lost it.

He rose and continued up the never-ending slope. From the position of the moon he judged that it was perhaps three hours until dawn.

<h1 style="text-align:center">❧ 18 ❧</h1>

It was still dark when Azarel arrived in the mountain village of Shiloh with its rows of low stone houses and pens for animals. The village was surrounded by a massive stone wall, high enough so a man couldn't easily climb over it at any point and, at some places, a height of 15 cubits. The gate on the west wall was open and the wall unguarded. The few people out in the marketplace in the morning mist stared at Azarel as he entered the gate. He realized he must look frightful. Some of them followed him curiously.

He made his way through the narrow streets toward the east gate which led to the Tent of Meeting. On the way, he encountered a Levite in a white robe, probably on his way to the morning sacrifice.

"I must speak to the High Priest!" Azarel said, louder than he intended, while gripping the Levite's arm. "I have news of the battle." Others in the street stopped to hear what was being said.

"What is the news?" asked the Levite.

"All is lost. The army of Israel lies on the field. The Ark was taken and the priests, Hophni and Phineas, are dead!"

The Levite's face went white as the mist and the people nearby who overheard gasped and wailed loudly. Several people began running to other parts of the town, apparently to share what they had heard. Azarel could hear more wailing as the word spread.

"Come, then, I am Zedekiah, a Levite," he said with wide eyes. "We must find Eli."

They went out of the eastern gate, where they found him seated on a backless bench outside the entrance to the courtyard of the Sanctuary, its white, linen wall glowing and blowing eerily in the predawn gloom. By now, the whole town was in an uproar and Azarel could hear wailing in the streets as the word of the disastrous battle spread.

"What is the meaning of this outcry?" Eli asked anyone who could hear.

"This man has news of the battle, lord," the Levite said.

The old cleric opened sightless eyes and turned not quite toward Azarel. He thought about how he must look, caked in dust and blood, his clothes torn and hair afright.

How thankful I am that Eli is blind.

"What of the battle my son?" Eli's voice cracked as he asked it. "The news must be bad, for if you returned in victory, I would hear cheers and the blowing of trumpets, not a lone messenger smelling of sweat and blood."

Azarel hesitated, but knew he must tell what he knew.

"Israel fled before the Philistines," he began. "The army suffered heavy losses. Also, your sons, Hophni and Phinehas, are dead and the Ark of God was captured."

Immediately Azarel regretted blurting out so much at once. He looked at the Levite and saw alarm in his eyes. Looking back at the High Priest, Azarel saw immense weariness and sadness in his milky eyes.

Though he was 98 years old and could not see, the old priest's memory was sharp. Twice before, prophets had foretold this day – one of them only a boy– how both of Eli's wayward sons would die on the same day; a judgment of the Lord. But their corruption was as much Eli's fault as it was their own; so the prophets had said. He had never reined them in as a good father should. Their mother's early death had led him to be indulgent of them, but it had spoiled them and brought reproach upon them all.

Guilt and grief descended upon Eli, greater than the anxiety he had felt since the Ark left his care. They had removed the Ark from its place and now it was lost forever.

Eli felt his head getting light and was vaguely aware that he was listing backward, then falling from the backless chair. He sensed both the messenger and Zedekiah reaching to catch him, but it was too late. The full weight of his body came down on his head and all was black.

<h1 style="text-align:center">❦ 19 ❦</h1>

The onlookers cried out in horror and began wailing in grief after seeing the High Priest die before their very eyes. An old woman standing there knew Hophni's and Phinehas' wives and she immediately left to give them the tragic news.

The stone house where the priest Phinehas and his wife lived adjoined the house of Eli just inside the city gate. The woman knocked hard on the wooden door and called to the priest's wife through the wool-cloth-covered window.

"Atarah! Awake, for there is much evil to report!"

Atarah opened the door, moving slowly with the weight of her unborn second child.

"The battle went against Israel," the old woman began, "I'm sorry, but your husband and his brother are both dead and, upon hearing the news, the high priest died as well. Not only that, the Philistines took the Ark of Yahweh!"

Atarah's dark eyes grew wide and pooled with tears. A low sob escaped her lips and she gripped the door frame as the full weight of shock and grief descended upon her. Suddenly she slipped to the floor and began to moan and hold her belly. The woman shrieked and called out to anyone who would hear, "Get the midwife!"

The midwife arrived shortly and immediately set to work. The old woman who had borne the bad news helped her try to get Atarah to squat in the usual birthing position, but she was too weak and unresponsive. Finally, with difficulty, they carried Atarah to the bed in the dark room. Atarah's water had broken and her tunic was drenched, as were the bed clothes now.

"Atarah, you're in labor. You must push the baby out!" the midwife told her.

Atarah moaned and thrashed when the contractions came, but otherwise did not respond.

"Hold her down while I check her," the midwife said to the old woman. "She's only seven months along."

The midwife pushed her wet clothing and the bed clothes out of the way and examined Atarah. "She's not completely open. It will take a while."

Just then, Hophni's wife and Atarah's sister-in-law, Raquel, entered. "What is happening? Is Atarah in labor?"

"Yes," the old woman said.

"I heard mourning in the city."

"The battle went badly for Israel. Your husband and Atarah's were both killed and your father-in-law, the high priest, died when he learned of it. And the Ark of God was taken as well."

Raquel burst into tears and sat down hard on a wooden bench. The old woman came over to her and put her hand on her shoulder.

"There, dear..." the old woman said.

"Come! I need help," the midwife shouted as she struggled to get Atarah to stop thrashing and be still. The old woman returned to the bedside and held Atarah's right hand and shoulder to the bed to keep her relatively still.

"Atarah, you must help to push the baby out," pleaded the midwife. "You must save your baby!"

But Atarah didn't seem to hear. She continued to thrash and moan as the two women tried to hold her until the pain of contractions subsided again.

Then, Raquel was there. She slipped in front of the old woman and took Atarah's hand. "Atarah, it's me, Raquel."

Atarah didn't look at her, but seemed to calm a bit, then stiffened as a contraction rocked her body once again.

❧

Azarel helped Zedekiah and two other men lift the heavy body of the high priest onto an ox cart so that he could be taken away and prepared for burial. That done, he turned and went to find a place he could wash and perhaps get something to eat. He found just one vendor in the marketplace, but Azarel had nothing to trade. Thankfully, the merchant had mercy on him and gave him some raisins. He went to the well and was able to drink from a clay jar attached to a rope which he lowered into the dark depths. He drank some of the precious water and used the rest to wash his hands and face. He then sat down against the wall of a nearby building and was soon asleep.

After many difficult hours, a baby boy was born.

"Don't be sad," said the midwife, as she gently laid the baby on his mother's breast. "You have a son!"

Atarah did not respond, except to say, "The glory has departed from Israel." She kept saying it over and over and wouldn't even look at the baby.

"The glory has departed from Israel."

"The glory has departed from Israel."

"The glory has departed from Israel."

A few minutes later, she died. The three women, exhausted from the difficult labor, wept and embraced.

Raquel was overwhelmed. She was not yet 30 and had been betrothed to the much older Hophni when she was 15, though, because she had not been able to have children, her husband had taken a second wife. She would need to be found and told of their husband's death as well.

The midwife sadly looked at the little newborn boy who would never know his mother and father and declared they would name the baby "Ichabod," which meant, "the glory has departed."

Raquel's tears stopped when she saw a small face peering at them from the door. Immediately she went to the child, her nephew, Ahitub. The 10-year-old had no doubt heard the commotion of the birth and his face was distorted by questioning and fear.

"What's wrong with my mother?" he asked Raquel.

"Come with me," Raquel said, taking his hand and leading him outside, even as he strained to look back at the bed where his mother lay motionless.

"Your mother has given you a baby brother," Raquel said wiping her eyes and trying to appear brave. "His name is Ichabod, but, I'm sorry, your mother has gone to be with our fathers. You can stay with me for a while."

The boy appeared to understand. Perhaps he had already suspected the truth. His eyes brimmed with tears and he looked down, appearing to steel himself.

"Where is my father?"

The question hung in the air while Raquel tried to decide what to tell him.

How can I burden him with the death of both parents and his grandfather at once?

"You know he went to the battle?" Raquel said finally.

"Yes."

"Then we will have to wait."

The old woman came out and said, "Raquel, I will get my sons to help with the burial."

"Thank you."

❦ 20 ❧

A sound like that of an animal caught in a snare, multiplied by a thousand, floated through the damp morning air, across the blood-soaked field. The hoarse voices of the vultures made macabre music as a background to the ghoulish work going forward now.

It was now the second day that the dregs of the Philistine army and a motley assortment of non-military camp followers had been prowling the battlefield, stripping the dead and dying of anything of value, while others buried the dead and mercifully hastened death for those few wounded who still suffered on the field. The Philistine wounded they had put on oxcarts soon after the battle and they had been taken away for crude medical treatment, but their chances of survival were not good.

Overhead and landing occasionally, the vultures did their part in disposal of the bodies. Sometimes shooed away by those working among the dead, sometimes ignored, the vultures competed for the spoils of war.

The Israelite army was either dead, wounded or fled, since there was no such thing as a truce to bury the dead when one fought the Philistines. To have a presence after the battle, one must carry the day.

A scrawny Amorite who had adjoined himself to the Sea People as they came up from Gath stood up after taking a bronze sword from a disemboweled Israelite and squinted at something, or someone, on a stony hill to the East. The bright sun just above the spot made it difficult to tell what, or who, was there.

The horrific spectacle sickened the bearded man as he surveyed it from a safe distance. Dressed in a grey woolen cloak as he was, it was unlikely that the godless Sea People would notice him among the rocks as he leaned upon his walking stick. Even if they did see him, it was unlikely that they would bother coming after him; they were too absorbed in their ghastly work. Nevertheless, he pulled the cloak over his long, tousled, soot-black hair, which cascaded far down his back and was now covered in the grey soil of the ridge on which he stood, after he cast dirt in the air over his head to show his deep sorrow. His grief darkened his face more than the woolen veil, as he wept without shame.

Today Samuel was dressed much older than his time on earth; in a gray cloak with a hood over his long hair, giving him the wild look of a prophet, because that is what he was, as well as a priest and a new judge in Israel besides.

After the army left Shiloh, he had gone to Ramah of Benjamin, his ancestral home, where his elderly mother still lived. He had learned belatedly of Eli's sons' misadventure on the battlefield.

When the Philistine army moved inland and north to Aphek, they needed to be stopped so, with Eli's blessing – and with Yahweh's, the prophet had believed – Israel had met them on this field. More than 50,000 Israelites heeded the call. They were farmers and shop keepers, nobles and their servants. When the emergency was past they were to go back to their crops and their markets, their wives and families.

But those lying here would not be going back.

And now, the Ark was gone. His office as seer had not enabled him to foresee this. It was an unimaginable disaster!

"Samuel! I mean, master!" the servant boy's voice startled him out of his dark reverie.

"Yes, my son?" Samuel answered absent-mindedly.

"Should we not be going? It is dangerous here."

"I suppose. There is nothing to be done here today. This is hallowed ground now, Jabal."

Young Jabal nodded, but was unsure how to reply.

"May God forgive me!" Samuel exclaimed.

"Lord?"

Samuel said no more, but turned and led his young servant to their donkeys.

❧ 21 ❧

Azarel was startled awake by a loud cry, realizing he had slept several hours. He looked around Shiloh's marketplace to find the source of the noise that had wakened him.

"Men are coming!" the shout came again.

Azarel arose and ran in the direction of the cry, bounding up the stone steps onto the city wall near the main gate, as other men gathered in the courtyard below

. There he found the young man who had sounded the alarm. He appeared to be perhaps 13 or 14.

"Where?"

"There," the young man said, pointing to a cloud of dust near the horizon and distant figures barely distinguishable from one another.

Azarel squinted in the hazy distance, wondering if this was the remnant of the Israelite army finally returning. As he looked, however, he saw something that made his heart nearly stop: the unmistakable silhouette of a Philistine officer on a horse.

Trying not to panic, he turned to the young man. "Do you have weapons here?"

"Maybe some, in the storeroom beside the gate."

Azarel looked at the small group of men from Shiloh gathered in the courtyard. They were all either old men or barely more than boys. "Philistines are coming! They will be upon us in less than an hour." he shouted. "We must shut the gate. Can you fight?"

The men looked at Azarel, then at one another, and their faces told Azarel all he needed to know. Their best option was to escape.

"If we can't fight them, we should leave the city to the east," Azarel said to the boy. Then he shouted to all the men, "We need to get out before they get here. Get your families and warn everyone that the Philistines are coming and we must leave immediately!"

The men in the courtyard went to shut and bar the south gate, laying the heavy timber in metal brackets across the double gates, then turned and ran to their houses and began sounding the warning along the way: "Philistines are coming! We must go out the eastern gate, now!"

Azarel turned to the young man, "You must go warn your family, but first, show me where the weapons are."

"Will you fight them?" the young man asked, wide-eyed.

"I don't know. I'm trying to figure out what we can do."

The young man took Azarel to a room under the parapet, inside the casemate wall, beside the gate. There he saw two spears, three sickle-swords and a single bow with about five arrows in its quiver.

"The men took most of the weapons to the battle," the young man explained.

"Yes, I understand," Azarel answered, knowing that most of those men would not be coming back. "Go ahead and warn your family. Get them out of the city."

Zedekiah, upon hearing that the Philistines were approaching, ran back to the Tent of Meeting. He had only recently come to Shiloh to serve his assigned stint at the sanctuary, after which he would return to his home in Benjamin. He ran past the ancient sacrificial altar and the laver, the bronze bowl in which the priests performed their ritual washings and went between the gold-banded pillars, through the purple, blue and scarlet embroidered curtain, into the first room of the Tent. He looked only briefly at the golden wall panels and the golden furniture that had been there for nearly 400 years, knowing that without the Ark in the next room, the holy of holies, it was all meaningless. There was no way to save it, anyway.

However, there was one thing he could do: he could save the ephod: the breastplate through which God spoke and which the high priest wore on feast days and other special occasions. It was beautifully embroidered and had twelve precious stones in golden settings, one for each of the tribes, plus the Urim and Thummim stones, which God used to answer the requests of the nation. That he could do.

It was stored next to the beaten-gold menorah, wrapped in an embroidered, fringed cloth. He scooped it up and left.

Now there was another precious something which must be saved: the heir to the priesthood.

"The Philistines are coming! We must all leave through the east wall!"

Raquel heard it, but she couldn't believe it. She shouted at the man who spoke: "How long until they are here?"

"A matter of minutes! Leave now."

Raquel went and found Ahitub. "We must go. The Philistines are coming."

"But I want to wait for Papa."

"There is no time. We must go now."

Just then Zedekiah ran up, carrying the ephod. "Raquel! You and Atarah and Ahitub must come with me. The Philistines are here!"

"Atarah is dead," Raquel answered, then looked at Ahitub, who was crying. "And she had her baby."

Zedekiah's eyebrows went up, "Then you must get both children and come with me. We must go. Now!"

"Is there no time to gather belongings for the trip?"

"None. We will be lucky to escape with our lives."

❧ 22 ❧

Azarel crouched low on the parapet near the gate, peering over the relatively low wall at the approaching company of Philistines. He estimated they would arrive in about a quarter hour. He had brought the spears, one of the swords and the bow and arrows with him and had laid them in a pile.

His mind raced as he tried to think of what he would do when they arrived. Obviously, he couldn't stand on the wall and fight. He wouldn't last a minute. He tried to imagine what the Philistines would do. Would they try to break down the gate? Would they mount the wall? Gradually he settled on the most likely scenario and formulated a plan.

Then, the young man was at his side again.

"What are you doing here?" Azarel demanded. "You must get out of the city with your family."

"My father went to the battle. He's not coming back, is he?"

"I don't know. Many of our number fell." Azarel watched as the young man processed what he had said.

"I want to fight – for my father."

Zedekiah took Raquel's hand and helped her over a rock as they descended through the woods from the heights of Shiloh. The baby was crying loudly and Raquel was trying to muffle his cries. They had left the city through the gate in the east wall and were descending the gentle slope that, if they went far enough, would take them to the Jordan River. There were hundreds more citizens of Shiloh all around them, mostly women, children and old men. Zedekiah helped up an old man who had fallen.

"Please hurry!" Zedekiah urged Raquel. "They may pursue us."

"I'm moving as fast as I can with the baby," Raquel answered. "Ahitub, are you coming?"

"Where is my papa?" Ahitub demanded, hanging back stubbornly. "Why did we leave my mother behind?"

Raquel turned and took his hand. "Ahitub, the Philistines are coming and they will kill us all if we don't quickly get as far away as possible. They cannot hurt your mother."

"But, where is my papa?"

"I don't have time to explain that to you right now," Raquel said loudly and she began sobbing.

"I think we should go south, to Benjamin. I have kin there," Zedekiah said.

"Yes, all right," Raquel said wearily. "Lead the way."

The Philistines were at the wall now.

"People of Shiloh, surrender now and you will find mercy!" a Philistine voice cried in a Canaanite tongue with a strong accent. It was similar enough to Hebrew that Azarel could understand. He and the young man at his side said nothing in answer. Everyone else had moved to the other side of the city or, Azarel hoped, were already outside and safely crossing the countryside. It was his hope that they could delay the Philistines until the others could get away.

They were crouched on the stairs where they could see the top of the wall near the gate, but could not be seen by the Philistines. Azarel heard the Philistines talking to one another, apparently to decide what to do, since there had been no answer. Azarel guessed there were a couple of hundred soldiers on the other side of the wall.

Azarel now heard shouted orders being repeated and more noise he couldn't identify. A minute or two went by, then he smelled smoke. He looked down and saw smoke coming from the gate.

They are going to burn through the wooden gate!

But before he could take that in, another order was given and arrows flew over the wall in a graceful arc, each one tipped with flaming cloth. Some of them fell harmlessly on the packed earth of the courtyard, but others found wooden roofs and doors or stacks of harvested flax. Soon there were several fires burning. Then another wave of flaming arrows came and more fires started.

"Let's go!" Azarel whispered. "We can't fight against this. If your father is dead, he wouldn't want you to die, too. We should escape with the others."

The young man looked sadly at his home town as it slowly turned into an inferno, then nodded to Azarel.

Azarel and the young man hurried to the east gate as fast as they could, knowing that the Philistines might be moving there as well to surround the city.

Only when they were some distance away did they feel it was safe to turn and view the huge column of black smoke arising from the city.

❦ 23 ❧

In Mizpah, no messenger had come to share news of the battle, even though it had been a week since the men left. In the marketplace, merchants conducted their trading activity as usual, but bargaining often devolved into arguments.

Hadassah drew water from the well in the center of town, as usual, pouring it into a clay jar. When it was full, she put it on top of her head, expertly balancing it there, and began the walk home.

She stopped when she saw some exhausted, dirty and ragged men walk through the city gate. Recognizing one, she excitedly set down her water jar.

"Phanuel! Phanuel! Is that you?"

Phanuel looked at her through tired, glassy eyes.

"Where is everyone?" Hadassah asked. "Where is Eldad?"

"I - I don't know."

"Didn't he return with you?"

"I didn't see him after the Ark was taken. So many fell..."

Hadassah turned to another of the men.

"Do you know my husband, Eldad, the smith? Did you see him?"

He shook his head "no," so she appealed to another.

"Did my husband, Eldad, return with you?"

The men only shook their heads.

Later that night, the word had spread. Very few of those who went to battle would return. In the main room of Eldad's house, the family sat around the table but no one was eating. Zemirah rocked back and forth, moaning. Hadassah wept.

"Oh, my Eldad, my firstborn!" Zemirah moaned.

"We don't know he's dead," Ophrah argued.
"Then why didn't he return with the others?" Jacob said. "They are saying 40,000 men were left on the field."
Hadassah got up and ran upstairs.
"Can you never control your tongue?!" Ophrah snapped.
"Do not speak to me that way!" Jacob retorted.
Ophrah got up and followed Hadassah.

The next morning, the talk was all about the battle. Women everywhere were dressed in black, since pretty much everyone was related to or knew well a man who had not returned.

Hadassah was no exception. Dressed in the black robes of a widow, she again went to the marketplace to find produce to put on the table for the family, but she was numb.

Suddenly there was a commotion near the city gate. Hadassah turned to look and gasped, as did everyone else.

A column of about 20 heavily armed Philistine soldiers marched in. An officer gave the command to "halt" and they stood in ranks in the square. Their commander, rode through the gate on a horse. Many of the townspeople scattered to hastily located hiding places in fear.

"People of Mizpah! Hear me well! I am Clamatos, your Palusata master and new governor of this province. We will enforce Palusata laws. Who is chief of this place?"

Kenan, who did return from the battle, limped forward.

"I am elder of this city," he shouted defiantly.

Clamatos motioned to a soldier who immediately struck Kenan, knocking him to the ground. The people cried out in alarm. The soldier roughly picked Kenan up by the arm.

"Take me to your house." Clamatos demanded. "It will be my headquarters. You and your family can find another."

Kenan stared daggers at Clamatos but there was little he could do but lead the Philistines away to his house as the townspeople cowered.

Hadassah returned home emptyhanded.

❦ 24 ❦

It was dark in the little house until the door opened, revealing the silhouette of a young woman carrying a baby, who was crying. A young boy ran past her and began exploring the room. The young woman entered and went to a window, pulling the curtain aside to let in some light.

It was Raquel, carrying Ichabod. She was exhausted and dirty from the journey, which took a couple of days.

They had stopped midway on the journey and found a wet nurse for the poor, hungry baby and Raquel was even able to bring a little with her, but it was almost gone. Tomorrow she would have to find another wet nurse.

Ahitub looked around, picking up objects curiously in the sparsely furnished room. Zedekiah then appeared at the door, carrying a cloth bag, which he set down by the door.

"I apologize that the house is so small. It was the only thing available."

"I'm very grateful for all you've done for us," Raquel answered, too exhausted to care about the accommodations.

"I will come back soon to check on you. Do you need anything now?"

"You don't need to worry about us for now. You've done enough. I just want to rest. Tomorrow we will know more."

"But you will need food. And milk for the baby... I will return soon... Welcome to Nob of the tribe of Benjamin."

Zedekiah closed the door left and Raquel looked around the room forlornly. Ichabod continued to cry, but Raquel had no experience with babies. She found a place to sit and wearily took advantage of it, trying vainly to soothe the baby.

"Auntie, I want to go home," whined 10-year-old Ahitub.

"I told you, we can't go back. Our home is destroyed."

"How will my Papa find us?"

"Sit down here, son. I suppose I shouldn't wait any longer to tell you the truth."

But before she could tell the boy what happened to his father, she broke down in tears.

❧ 25 ❧

"They approach! Let us go to meet them!" Pietros cried to all who could hear, and many of the people in the square joined him in running through the open city gate. He was the high priest of Dagon in Ashdod and was excited about the privilege his temple had been accorded after the great victory at Aphek.

Among those accompanying Pietros to meet the procession was Methusia, King of Ashdod, dressed in his finest embroidered, ceremonial robe and a tall, purple mitre growing out of a golden crown on his head. Within a minute, they met the mounted men at the head of the column.

"Greetings from Ashdod and the temple of Dagon!" Pietros shouted, then he saw that Methusia was peeved that he had spoken first.

"Indeed welcome, I am King Methusia of Ashdod," the black-bearded king said with a dip of his festooned head. "Our hospitality is at your disposal."

"Thank-you, my lord. I am Captain Kaigon, commander of the mounted troops of Ashkelon," said the red-caped officer seated on a powerful white horse. He was a commanding figure, in scarlet and bronze, though caked in blood and dust. "I have been ordered to meet you here. My men will require food and lodging for tonight. And you, priest."

"Yes," Pietros looked at the Captain expectantly.

"We have an offering for Dagon, may he be praised!" He gestured to a horse-drawn cart well behind him.

"Thank-you," Pietros said without waiting for an explanation. "May Dagon's blessings be on you throughout your long life!" With that, he ran back to the cart.

When he got there he was surprised by what he saw. The Hebrew's god sat upon the cart to be sure, but it was not what Pietro had expected. The gilt box had, not one, but two figures on top of it. Did the Hebrews worship two gods at once? He climbed onto the cart and examined them. The workmanship was not the best. Any smith in Ashdod could have done as well. The two identical figures faced one another and appeared to be bent either in prayer or perhaps in a defensive posture. It was unlike any other god he knew of, but he didn't want to think about that now. He could hardly wait to arrive at the temple and begin the ceremony. But he had no choice but to sit back and let the horses strain to pull their heavy cargo the remaining distance.

Finally the procession passed through the gates of Ashdod and continued through the narrow streets as the citizens cheered and threw flowers at the victorious heroes. Pietros waved at the crowds as they went by, though he had done nothing toward the victory except burn incense and send prayers to Dagon.

The soldiers who had been weary on the road now revived and shouted back at the cheering townspeople, who were beginning to follow them to the center of the city. When the temple was in sight, Pietros jumped from the cart and ran to the front of the column to rejoin Methusia and Captain Kaigon, who were leading the column to the plaza before the temple of the lord of lords – god of fertility and the bounty of the land – Dagon.

When they arrived, the column halted but the cart continued to the platform. When the cart stopped before the temple steps, Pietros motioned for waiting acolytes, tanned boys wearing only loincloths, who rushed forward to carry the golden god up to the place of sacrifice. Bidden by the king, the captain dismounted and climbed the steps to the sacrificial platform with Methusia and Pietros. Already on the platform were members of the temple staff, ready for the ceremony that was about to begin.

Methusia motioned to the cheering throng to be silent and after a few seconds they were.

"People of Ashdod of the Palusata, hear me this day. Our god Dagon has given us a great victory over the Hebrews."

The people once again cheered wildly and Methusia had to motion again for silence so he could continue.

"I am Methusia, lord of Ashdod..."

Again the people cheered and again Methusia motioned for silence.

"Ashdod has been given the privilege of being the first of the Palusata city-states to host the god of the Hebrews!"

This time the cheering from the square continued for a full two minutes and there was nothing that could be done from the temple steps that would stop it. When the noise abated, Methusia continued.

"Captain Kaigon has brought it here and I hope you will extend every courtesy to his valiant men during their stay with us. We will worship our great god who has given us this victory and then we will place the god of the Hebrews before Dagon so the Hebrew god can worship him."

That was Pietros' cue, so he motioned to his temple staff, ranging from elderly priests to young boys. As temple musicians began playing rhythmic music, lively with drums and finger cymbals, they came forward, half dragging six goats and, in teams, slaughtered them expertly as the people looked on, randomly cheering and dancing to the music. The temple celebrants laid the fresh carcasses on the altar and soon the smell of burning flesh was heavy in the air.

The people's dancing became more frenzied as time went on and, as the smoke of the sacrifices billowed over the crowd, Pietros and his ministers brought out wine, which they offered to Methusia and Captain Kaigon, then more wine, as well as beer, was passed among the throng.

Torches were lit as the sun set beyond the sea, which lay just west of the city. The music continued, the wine and beer kept flowing most of the night and the people danced as if entranced in the flickering torchlight.

Finally the music stopped and the weary, slightly crazed people watched as Pietros and the ministers of the temple carried the Hebrew god into the temple of Dagon. Once more they gave a cheer and slowly dispersed.

Once inside, Pietros directed his men to position the Hebrew god before the tall statue of Dagon, not too close, but at a distance befitting a worshipper. This was the ultimate subjugation of the Hebrews: their god worshipping Dagon.

Once Pietros was satisfied, they stood for a moment looking at the magnificent statue of their god. Many times the size of a man, the statue of iron covered in gold towered above the small Hebrew god. Spontaneously the ministers of Dagon knelt before him and gave thanks for his blessings.

❧ 26 ☙

It was too early for vendors to be selling in the booths in the marketplace. The large open space before Ashdod's temple of Dagon was littered with the remains from the great celebration the night before.

Two rats circled a puddle in the muddy street and continued across. Pietro hopped over the puddle and almost skipped to the stairs going up to the entrance to the temple where he was met by an acolyte, rubbing his eyes sleepily.

"Good morning, master."

"Good morning indeed. Yesterday was a triumphant day for Dagon! Have you recovered from the celebration?"

"Yes, master. Mostly."

"How fitting the god of the Hebrews was brought here, to the premier Palusata temple of the god of harvest, when we have just won the fertile land in the north! It is a strange god, though, with two sphinxes atop it, looking inward."

"Yes master. Do you require anything?"

"No, you go and get some sleep. I will worship for a while, before the others arrive."

"Thank you, master."

The acolyte left to go home. Pietro entered the temple.

Once inside he took off his sandals, went to a pillar on which a golden talisman was embedded. He kissed his fingers and touched the talisman, picked up an oil lamp from a stand, then passed into the darkened inner sanctuary.

Pietro used the oil lamp to light two torches in sconces on the wall, then turned to do the same on the opposite wall. He glanced upward and stopped, shocked at what he saw, or rather didn't see.

There was nothing in the space where the image of Dagon should be. He lowered his gaze and saw the image of his god on the floor, lying face down, as if prostrated before the Hebrew god, the box they called the Ark. He rushed to light the other sconces and looked again at the fallen god.

"Why have I been summoned? Does the king of Ashdod do your bidding, priest?" demanded King Methusia, who was accompanied by bodyguards. His head still ached from last night's celebration.

"Forgive me, sire – may you live forever. I would not have sent for you if it was not important that my message not be spoken in earshot of gossiping tongues in the palace. I fear we have a problem with the Hebrew god."

"Is it not still in the sanctuary where you placed it yesterday, with all due pomp and ceremony, I might add?"

"Yes, majesty, but what I'm trying to tell you is, when I arrived this morning, Dagon was on his face before it."

"The image fell?"

"Yes!"

"Well, it has stood there a hundred years. I'm sure it just needs repair. I will send workers to help right it and make sure it is stable and well supported."

"Thank you, sire. I hope that's all it is."

"Of course that's all it is. That's the problem with you priests: always seeing a connection to the spiritual when there isn't one. It will be fine."

"Thank you, your grace," Pietro said, bowing, though the king's apparent lack of spirituality grated on him.

That night, after the workmen had finished restoring the image of Dagon to its place, Pietro entered the inner sanctum and admired the majestic statue. The sconces were lit, but the acolyte was preparing to extinguish them as he always did at day's end.

"No, let us leave them lit tonight," Pietro said.

"Oh? But won't they die out during the night?"

"Possibly, but I'd just like to leave them lit, this once."

"All right, master. Are you going home now? You've had a long, busy day."

Pietro didn't answer but stood gazing at the tall god in the torchlight.

"I will watch the temple," the acolyte assured him. "You go take your rest."

"Yes. Yes, I will."

He started to walk out, but turned again for one last look.

Even earlier than yesterday, Pietro climbed the stairs of the temple of Dagon. The acolyte was sleeping on a stone bench by the entrance.

"Wake up!" Pietro called out playfully.

The acolyte stirred and rose on one elbow.

"Sorry, master."

"It's all right. I'm here, so you can go home now."

The acolyte stood and Pietro entered the temple, touching the talisman, entering the inner sanctum and taking the oil lamp from its stand as he did every morning.

The torches had gone out as expected, so Pietro began lighting the two torches on one wall as before, then turned and again stopped short when he saw the space where the image of Dagon should be was again empty!

He rushed over and saw the image again on the floor, but this time its head and hands were broken off!

The Hebrew god was undisturbed. Pietro nearly fainted.

❧ 27 ❧

Hadassah cared for her household and prepared food for her husband's mother and brother as before, but it was as if she were a shell; a ghost. Nothing that happened could change her expression. Her mouth was a straight, gray line on her thin, young face. Her laughter, which had rivaled the sunshine, had not been heard for some time.

Another week had passed after the Philistines occupied the town. It appeared her husband, Eldad, would not return from the battle of Eben-ezer, like so many others. And like so many other women in their highland village, she wore the black wool head covering of a widow, as she was expected to do for some time, perhaps even for the rest of her life.

She had been a young wife so much in love with her husband, anticipating their life together. Now she would be seen as a childless widow, dependent on others for her sustenance.

Except she was hiding something, though it couldn't be hidden forever.

One day, she came out of her house carrying a clay jar to perform a chore that was her lot every day. Harried and tired, she let herself into the goat pen beside the house, intending to milk the goat. Then she sensed someone looking at her, so she turned to see Jacob standing at the corner of the house, staring at her. Slowly he backed up where she couldn't see him.

She sighed and sat down to do her milking.

❧

"My son Jacob is willing to do his duty," Hadassah's mother-in-law said one day, when Hadassah had begun preparing the evening meal.

"What? What duty?"

"To give Eldad sons. It is the duty of a brother to give the oldest sons if he dies without descendants. Jacob is willing."

Zemirah was talking about Levirate marriage where, when a firstborn son died childless, a younger brother would impregnate the widow to continue the line of the firstborn. Hadassah had heard of it, of course, but it hadn't occurred to her that Zemirah might invoke it. She had been focused on her grief.

She knew she would have no choice; in their culture, it was Jacob's choice to make. She shuddered as she thought about letting Eldad's brother into her bed.

"He's willing to take you as his second wife after your days of mourning have passed," Eldad's mother finished her thought matter-of-factly. "After a year, he and Ophrah will move into the main house with you."

"Eldad will return. You'll see," Hadassah said curtly, and walked away.

From that moment she began considering fleeing to her father's house in Beth-Zur in Judah. She began by hiding a pita in her shawl during the evening meal and secreting it in her bed chamber. She spent idle moments plotting the best day and time to escape, but before she could leave, something happened that changed everything.

Late one afternoon, as Hadassah swept the stone house's upper floor, a chore she performed endlessly and now joylessly, she saw through the window a man coming down the street outside the walls of the family compound. He had long hair and a dirty beard. He looked like a beggar, walking with a slight limp, with clothes worn and tattered, carrying a ragged bedroll. She sucked in her breath when he came through the gate of the compound and walked toward her front door.

She ran downstairs to bolt the door, but she was too late. He didn't knock! He opened the door and came in. Their eyes met, hers shining with fear and his, dark and inscrutable under matted hair. She thought she could perhaps fend him off with the broom. Then he spoke.

"Hadassah!"

Her eyes now widened and then closed as she sank to the floor. Eldad ran to catch her before her head could hit the packed-earth floor.

When Hadassah awoke, she embraced her husband who had come back from the dead and then arose to lavish all manner of food upon him, for she thought he must be starving. Zemirah came in, rejoicing in the return of her son. Then Jacob came to hear what happened and they all sat around the family table.

"We thought you were dead," Hadassah told him. "We couldn't find out anything. What happened?"

Eldad looked at his family and wondered how much he should tell these women he loved. Slowly he began to tell of the battle, with its unbelievable carnage, and what happened after; how he awoke from unconsciousness and crawled away from the battlefield.

He showed them the deep, jagged scars on his leg.

"I was found by a farmer near the battlefield. His family took me in and helped me recover. I spent many days in his son's bed with fever, most of the time unable to respond, so the farmer had no idea who I was or where I was from."

"Praise Yahweh!" Hadassah cried and she threw her arms around him and they wept together. He didn't want to ever let her go.

"We must do something to thank the farmer for saving your life," Hadassah said.

"But, why did Yahweh abandon us?" Jacob asked. "I mean, all those men killed and the Ark taken as well?"

"I certainly don't know," Eldad answered. "I'm not a prophet or a priest."

"Or king."

"What will become of us?" Ophrah asked. "The Philistines have ejected Kenan from his house and they have levied taxes on all of Mizpah."

"All of Benjamin, in fact," Jacob added. "I pray taxes are the worst of it."

That night, after the rest of the family had gone to their homes, Eldad limped to the bed and sat down, raising his tunic and rubbing the scar where he had removed the arrow. Hadassah came and examined it lovingly.

"It will heal," he assured her.

"Yes, and I have news that may speed its recovery."

Hadassah took his hand and put it on her abdomen where he was able to feel the growing of new life inside her. His face lit up. He pulled her close and kissed her.

"You are really having a baby?"

"I only hope I can give you a son!" she exclaimed.

"Any child of our love will make me overjoyed and I will love him or her supremely."

⋘ 28 ⋙

Eldad plunged the hot metal into the water and listened to the satisfying hiss as it rapidly cooled. It was good to be back in his shop. The sickle he was forging was nearly finished and it would not be a moment too soon, as he had orders from two farmers in need of sickles to finish the wheat harvest.

He brought the sickle blade out of the water, laid it on his hammering stone and used a bronze hammer to pound out the fine inner edge, flattening the bronze edge to the thinness of a sycamore leaf. Once more into the fire and a final careful hammering, then back in the water and this blade would be complete, ready for attaching a handle and sharpening.

Eldad was turning to hang the finished sickle blade on a line so it could cool, when two men entered his shop. They were Philistine soldiers.

"Smith!" shouted one of the soldiers in a Canaanite tongue with a thick accent. "Put down your tools, Hebrew dog! The new governor of this province has decreed that you will not make any weapons or tools!"

The man smiled an evil smile, wearing the bronze mail of a soldier over his green tunic, but he had the air of a street thug who enjoyed cruelty. The man with him smiled menacingly too.

"No more of these either," the soldier said, taking the brand new bronze sickle blade and snapping it in two under his foot.

"You can't..." Eldad protested.

"And you must not sharpen the blades of the farmers either." With that he drew his iron sword and hacked several times at the wooden axle of Eldad's grind wheel, splitting it so it fell to the ground, useless.

"You cannot do this!"

"And why not? There is no army in Israel and no champion to lead. I am Enbol, and I will be coming to visit you regularly. You will obey the laws of your Palusata masters and pay the tax when it is demanded of you."

"How will I pay taxes when you take my livelihood?"

"If you do not pay, we will take what we will to fulfill the debt. Do not think you can easily turn us aside, smith. We will be back."

And the two men left the shop, looking back at Eldad contemptuously.

When they were gone, Eldad retrieved the bedroll he had brought back from battle from a hiding place in his shop. From it he withdrew the Philistine sword of iron, the one he had taken from the battlefield. He turned it over in his hands, admiring its craftsmanship. A look of determination came over his face.

<h1 style="text-align:center">❦ 29 ❦</h1>

It was night in Mizpah. All was quiet, except for the occasional stirring of an animal. At Eldad's family compound everyone was sleeping. All but one, that is.

The door to the forge was closed and the curtains were closed to prevent the light from spilling outside, because Eldad was busy making tools and weapons the Philistines had forbidden. He had wrapped his hammer in rags to muffle it, though he worried it would not be enough.

Then he heard something outside. He went to the window and pulled back the curtain slightly so he could peek out into the courtyard. He could see nothing, but he heard something again, like pottery breaking, so he went to the door and stepped out, continuing to listen. He walked over to the compound wall and heard something scrape against it.

He went to the gate and opened it as quietly as possible. Outside he found a very drunk Phanuel, throwing rocks at the wall and breaking pottery.

"Phanuel! Stop it!" Eldad whispered. "Get in here!"

Eldad went and pulled Phanuel toward the gate, but he resisted. Eldad looked down the street and saw a Philistine soldier, silhouetted in the moonlight.

"Come on! You're breaking curfew! The sentries are making their rounds."

Eldad pulled Phanuel through the gate against his will and closed the gate after him.

"What do you know about it?!" Phanuel snapped.

"I know what they'll do if they catch you. What are you doing out so late?"

"You! You were there!"

"Where?"

"At Eben-ezer. I thought you were dead."

"It took a long time for me to heal."

"I didn't see what happened to Asaph. But I saw what they did to Jedediah. They split his head!

Phanuel drew his hand down in front of his face as if to split his skull.

"I didn't know about Asaph either," Eldad answered. "But I saw the giant kill the shepherd."

The men were silent for a moment.

"Why didn't Yahweh help us?" Phanuel asked. "We had the Ark."

"I don't know. Perhaps Samuel will hear from the Lord."

"All those good men dead. Now we're under the heel of these uncircumcised pagans and no one to care."

"Come, let me make a place in the forge for you to sleep. You can't go home until morning."

"All right."

Eldad led him into the forge and arranged some straw on the packed-earth floor where Phanuel could lie down.

"You have always been such a good friend," Phanuel said as his heavy eyelids closed.

Eldad looked at his friend who had not spoken to him since he returned the flawed sickle, not knowing what to expect from him in the morning.

❦ 30 ❧

King Methusia was bored as he sat on his throne listening as two Ashdod subjects argued their grievances. Soldiers stood on either side of the throne and others were in the room, some nobility, some commoners, waiting to be heard.

"But everyone knows where my eastern boundary is," one petitioner asserted. "It has been thus since my father built the wall."

"There is nothing that says where the boundary should be," argued the other. "I only know where the wall is NOW."

"Is there no land deed?" King Methusia wondered idly.

"Why would we need a deed? Everyone knows. He obviously moved the wall!" the first man insisted.

King Methusia squirmed as if sitting on something.

"The only thing that is obvious is where the wall IS. THAT is the boundary," insisted the second man.

"Enough! I am not well," King Methusia interrupted. "Come before me again tomorrow and it will be decided."

The two subjects did not ask what the king meant, but withdrew, bowing. A courtier came forward solicitously.

"Your majesty, you are not well? What is wrong?"

"I don't know. Let's go to my room."

The king and the courtier went through a door behind the throne as those in the room murmured their curiosity.

The courtier followed the king into the room, which was a private room with an office space and a bed, so the king could work or rest as needed near the throne.

"Are you in pain, majesty?"

"Yes, it came on this morning."

King Methusia took off his royal robe and pulled his tunic off his shoulder, freeing his arm, which he raised, revealing red sores in his armpit.

"They afflict my privates as well."

"Oh, your majesty! I will call for the physician immediately!"

"If you must."

The courtier hurried down the street to the central marketplace and climbed the steps to the temple of Dagon.

"Hello! The king has a message for the high priest," he called out to whoever might hear, not willing to enter the temple unbidden.

A young priest appeared at the doorway.

"The high priest, Pietro, is ill. He is not here."

"Him too? When did he fall ill?"

"Last night. An acolyte is also ill."

"How does their illness present?"

"They have soreness and tumors under their arms and in their privates."

"The king has the same illness. I fear it is a plague."

"What shall we do?"

"Pray to Dagon that it spreads no further. I will inform the king."

The people in Ashdod's marketplace parted and moved away from the route being traveled by four priests of Dagon, who were carrying a body in a shroud. When they came to the temple of Dagon, they carried the body up the stairs and laid it on the stone platform. One of them uncovered the face. It was the high priest, Pietro.

In the street, other bodies were being borne out of the city gate, some carried by men, others in carts. The men who bore Pietro's body watched and covered their noses and mouths with kerchiefs or folds of their clothing. One of them winced and grabbed his underarm, then looked at the others, who slowly moved away from him.

❦ 31 ❧

King Maoch of Gath was not one to question good fortune so cheaply won, but he could not help but wonder at the brevity of time the king of Ashdod wished to keep the Hebrew god. It had been taken to Ashdod from the battlefield at Aphek with great pomp and ceremony, but now the messenger had reported that King Methusia wished not to keep the honor for his city, but to share it with all the Palusata after only a couple of months, which was very much out of character.

Perhaps Methusia wished to smooth over Maoch's feelings from past injustices. Or perhaps he hoped to promote Ashdod by building a reputation for generosity, as if the city, centrally located in the land as it was, might be looked upon as the benefactor, and therefore the senior, of the other four city-states.

Maoch could not divine Methusia's motive, but he would accept the gift nonetheless. He rode at the head of his personal guard as they escorted an oxcart on which to transport the Hebrew god, the spoils of war.

"Where is King Methusia?" Maoch asked the small contingent of low-level Ashdod servants that met them outside the city, dressed only in in threadbare loincloths. The Hebrew god, a small, curious box covered in gold and with two beaten-gold, winged figures atop it, sat on a flat rock as if it had been hastily brought there and abandoned. *What an odd image of their god this is,* thought Maoch. He had never seen a god like this.

"We are to tell you that the god is yours to take. Take it now!" shouted a thin, young man who was spokesman for the pitiful band of laborers standing some distance away. Their charge complete, the ragtag men ran off toward the city gate.

How odd it is, thought Maoch, *that Methusia has not turned the transfer into a pageant.*

Instead, the luminaries of the city were nowhere to be seen and the emissaries from Gath were not even invited into Ashdod, but were told to take the golden box from the stone on which it sat outside the city.

If Methusia thinks to curry favor with Gath through this gesture, he has a strange way of showing it.

"Load it onto the cart," Maoch gave the obvious order to his men. Several soldiers dismounted and approached the heavy golden box, beginning to try to pick it up. Suddenly one of them, named Aji'id, screamed and jumped backward, holding a bleeding thumb. Maoch saw two rats run away from the box. The men watching from horseback laughed heartily at Aji'id's fear of the little creatures. Angrily, Aji'id threw a stone at the fleeing rodents. The rats had been behind or under the Hebrew god. But some of the soldiers looked at one another, unsure if this was an omen.

"Load it onto the cart and let us be gone!" Maoch repeated impatiently. This whole episode was giving him a sour feeling.

"We can't go into the city?" Adji'id asked.

"It would appear we will die awaiting the invitation," King Maoch answered.

"But I was looking forward to a night by the sea," Aji'id said. "There's a beer hall with a view of the water I was going to visit again."

"I guess we just load it up and head back. We won't be able to go very fast with this burden. We'll probably have to camp on the way, but the wild country will be more hospitable than this place!"

❧

The next morning, they broke camp before daylight to continue the journey, which would have taken a third of the time if they had not been slowed by the oxen pulling the cart carrying their prize. The men mounted up after an improvised breakfast and prepared to go on to Gath.

"Where is Adji'id?" asked the captain of the guard. The soldiers looked at each other. No one knew. When they broke camp in the darkness none had seen him. They returned to the place they had camped and saw that there was still a bedroll on the ground. The light was just beginning to show over the eastern hills.

"Adji'id!" called the captain. The man stirred but did not raise his head. His face was flushed and covered with sweat.

"Adji'id is stricken!" one of the soldiers said. The others looked at one another.

"Come, let us carry him to the cart," directed the captain.

"What is it?" asked King Maoch, as he rode up on his horse, obviously ready to be on the way.

"Adji'id is sick," replied the captain.

"Let him lie in the cart," Maoch said solemnly.

Too many ill omens accompany us on this journey.

"Come, let us ride. We can be in Gath by midday."

Before they reached Gath, the situation had worsened. Aji'id was deathly ill and two others of the cohort were complaining of fever and sores which made it difficult to stay in the saddle. Maoch realized the two men were the ones who had helped Aji'id lift the god onto the cart. Whether these men were merely having pains in sympathy for Aji'id's rapidly deteriorating condition, Maoch could not tell.

When Gath was in view, one of the men fell from his horse and had to be laid beside Aji'id in the cart with the Hebrew god. They entered Gath and were glad to be rid of the burden in the cart.

❧

Soon the story spread of how the soldier Aji'id had carried the Hebrew god and he and others had fallen sick. Later it was reported that Aji'id had died and there were rumors that the golden god of the Hebrew was the cause.

As more and more citizens of Gath fell ill, the plague of rats spread also and general panic set in. Maoch now heard that the sickness was epidemic in Ashdod and had even caused the image of Dagon to topple to the floor of his temple and shatter to pieces! The king could not avoid the conclusion that the golden box he had brought from there was to blame.

"Cursed thing!" he said to no one in particular as he sat in his court. "I will send it away."

"What, lord?" asked the captain of his guard.

"The god of the Hebrews!"

"Where would you have it taken?"

"To Ekron. Today!"

❦ 32 ❦

Ekron was the Philistine city closest to Gath, so the Ark was shortly left in the keeping of the king of that city, whose name was Kogn, but word had already reached Ekron that possessing the god of the Hebrews brought a curse, so he was already thinking of how to rid himself of the hot potato.

But before he could formulate a plan that would both solve the problem and save face, citizens of Ekron began to fall ill, and soon an ad hoc committee approached the king and demanded something be done. Messengers were sent to the other city-states, Gaza and Ashkelon, but their lords wanted nothing to do with the cursed thing, so it stayed in Ekron for several weeks.

The plague spread to Gaza and Ashkelon anyway.

"I will consult with the other kings," Kogn told the representatives of the citizens of Ekron, and he immediately dispatched messengers to the other four city states, urgently requesting a high-level conference.

Since all knew of the horrible disease that befell any city that hosted the Ark, the five kings hastily gathered in Ekron as soon as Kogn's messages arrived. And so, barely a month after the Ark arrived in Ekron, the five lords of the Palusata sat at table in the hall of Kogn.

"But it is the great prize of our victory over the Hebrews and conquest of the hill country," protested the king of Ashkelon, one of the two cities which had not yet experienced the full wrath of the Hebrew god.

"It is plain to see the god brings a curse," insisted Kogn. "Everywhere it has been, the people are afflicted with horrible illness, tumors and death."

"And yet we have this illness in Gaza also," said Kittim, the lord of that city. "Perhaps it is not the Hebrew god that brings the curse."

"It is indeed a cursed thing," said Methusia, who was one of the few who had recovered from the plague and whose city of Ashdod had been ravaged by the curse the longest. "We took it to the temple of Dagon and in the morning, he had fallen. We thought it coincidence, but it happened twice. We need to banish it!"

"And that is just what I believe we should do; send it back to the Hebrews." Kogn had been hatching a plan for a while.

"But that will be admitting the Hebrew god is more powerful than our gods!" Maoch of Gath protested.

"We should allow the gods to decide," Kogn declared. "What say you, priest?"

Kogn directed his question to a couple of priests of Dagon who had been quietly observing the lords of the Philistines argue about the disposition of the Ark. All eyes were on them as they murmured to one another briefly, then the chief among them stood and spoke.

"Put the god on a new cart pulled by milk cows which have never drawn a cart, and will desire to return to their calves to be milked. If the cows return home in our land we can conclude this terrible plague is not because of the Hebrew god, but because of natural causes, but if the cows go on up the road to Beth-Shemesh of the Hebrews, then we will know that the curse has fallen on us for possessing the god of the Hebrews and we must return it to end the curse!"

The five rulers of the Philistine city-states looked at one another. "Does this test sound appropriate?" Kogn asked.

"I believe this would establish the reason for the curse," Maoch answered. "We would know if it was a curse of the Hebrew god and it would rid us of the curse.

"I agree," Methusia said, and the others nodded.

"Good. If the cows do not take the god to Beth-Shemesh, we might then still cast it into the sea to be safe, but either way we would see the curse end," Kogn joked bitterly.

"Let us do one thing more," the priest suggested. "Let us make five gold rats and five gold tumors and put them in a chest on the cart with the god as an offering to the Hebrews."

"An offering!" Kittim said, incensed. "We should give them gifts?"

"Give them anything if they will take it back!" Methusia said. "In fact, make rats and golden tumors in number matching our five cities and all our outlying towns as well. They MUST take it back!"

❧ 33 ❧

"Father, I'm tired," nine-year-old Ammiel complained.

"It's only the ninth hour," Ammiel's father, Joshua, answered without pausing his sweeping movements with the scythe. "We have at least four hours of daylight in which to work. The barley will not harvest itself."

He held the two wooden handles of a bronze-bladed scythe, repeatedly swinging from side to side, felling the slender stalks of golden grain so they lay in neat rows on the fertile ground.

Ammiel frowned and continued raking the felled barley into piles which would later be tied into sheafs for threshing. The sun was very hot on the sloping plain to the west of Beth-Shemesh in Israel's tribe of Judah. It would be another week at least before they would finish the harvest.

Joshua glanced back at his son to see if he was keeping up, when he noticed something on the road to the west. He straightened his aching back and shaded his eyes from the afternoon sun, squinting toward the approaching figures.

A cart was being pulled by oxen and, some distance behind it, many riders on horseback, following at the cart's slow pace.

"Ammiel, run get your brother! Have him bring the ax!"

The road came out of Philistine land. In fact, Joshua's field was on the very border between Judah and Philistia. This looked to be a military escort of some kind. Joshua had no weapons, but his scythe and his oldest son with an ax might dissuade them from entering his land.

The cart continued to approach and Joshua noticed that no one was driving it. The oxen were bellowing as if in pain –

or as if needing to be milked – yet they continued moving on the road. The company following the cart had seen Joshua now, but they made no menacing gesture. Rather they waved in a hesitant, almost plaintive way, then stopped at the border of his field while the cows continued to pull the cart as if driven by a goad in unseen hands.

Fourteen-year-old Jobab, Joshua's oldest, arrived now with the ax and Ammiel close behind. Joshua motioned for Jobab to lower the ax. He did not want to be seen as threatening until he knew the purpose of these Philistines. The father and two sons watched as the cart grew closer.

It's – it can't be! Is it the Ark of God?

Joshua knew the Ark only from descriptions given by local priests which they had only heard from the high priest, because he was the only one allowed to see it. It had been seven months since the army of Israel had been destroyed at Eben-ezer and the Ark had been taken by the uncircumcised Philistines. But now, here it was!

The riders were close enough now that Joshua could see that they were nobility, accompanied by a military guard of about 50 mounted men.

As Joshua and his two sons watched, other farmers from adjoining fields were drawn to the curious site of the Ark on the cart pulled by two bellowing cows. Suddenly, the two cows pulled the cart to the side of the road and stopped, while continuing to bellow pitifully.

"Come my sons. This is a momentous day," Joshua and Jobab began running toward the cart, but Ammiel held back, the memory of the last time he saw Philistines still fresh.

The other farmers approached as well, but Jobab arrived first, pausing a short distance from the Ark. The riders still hung back at the border of the land, but Joshua saw the crowns on the heads of the five lead riders, their ornate robes and behind them, riders bearing the banners of the five walled cities of the Philistines. His eyes grew wide and the assembling farmers gasped with him as they realized that the Philistine rulers of all five city-states were before them.

As if satisfied, the Philistines wordlessly turned their horses and galloped away, down the road to Ekron, apparently eager to return to their cities.

When they were gone, the men from the fields jumped and danced for joy at the miracle of the Ark's return.

"Take the Ark to the stone," Joshua called out, gesturing to a high outcropping of rock near the road. "We must build an altar and sacrifice to Yahweh!"

In no time at all, the Ark had been lifted from the cart and placed on the highest part of the rock, the cows were unhitched and butchered for sacrifice. Jobab used the ax to cut up the yoke and the cart for the fire. Word spread and all of Beth-Shemesh and the surrounding area came to worship Yahweh for returning the Ark to them.

The celebration and worship continued into the night with the local Levites coming to marvel at the miraculous return of Israel's treasure, containing the golden charms, half of which looked like rats or mice, but they were not sure what the others represented. It was a great deal of gold.

The Levites erected a tent for the Ark and built an altar, not far from where the cows had stopped. They began official rituals, with morning and evening sacrifices. It appeared Beth-Shemesh would be the new center of worship for Israel.

Then one of the Levites fell ill. The fever was accompanied by sores in the groin and armpit. Other citizens of Beth-Shemesh became sick and some died as well. Some said it was because they had looked upon the Ark. Now they began to understand the meaning of the curious golden objects the Philistines had put into the Ark.

After a town council, a messenger was sent up the road to Kiriath-Jearim, where there was a priest in the line of Aaron's son, Eleazar, to request that they take the Ark to their town.

Abinidab had served as priest in the hill town of Kiriath-Jearim for many years. Situated at the junction of Judah and Benjamin, it was an ideal place for many Israelites to worship. He was a priest in the line of Aaron's son, Eleazar, unlike the priests who had been at Shiloh, who were descended from Aaron's other son, Ithamar.

Abinidab gave strict instructions to the Levites charged with bringing the Ark up from Beth-Shemesh. They were to carry the Ark on poles, covered with a drape, and walk it all the way up to Kiriath-Jearim. That was the directive of the Law. This way Kiriath-Jearim would escape the plague.

When the Ark arrived, Abinidab conducted a ceremony with sacrifice, also according to the Law, and consecrated his young son, also named Eleazar as it happened, to be the administrative priest for the Holy Place they would construct to house the Ark.

❦ 34 ❦

Samuel – prophet, priest and judge – heard the news of the return of the Ark gladly. He had grown up sleeping a few cubits away from it. It was the glory of Israel; a glory which was lost, but now was restored.

Shiloh lay in ruins and Eli and his scoundrel sons were dead, but there were survivors to the priestly line. The Philistines had advanced into the hill country and destroyed the city. He now must go and see if anything could be salvaged from the Tent of Meeting and the 400-year-old equipment for its ritual worship, now that the Ark had been miraculously recovered and worship was being conducted at its new home in Kiriath-Jearim.

Perhaps there was hope in Israel after all.

Zedekiah, the Levite of Nob, led the way as the prophet and his apprentice, Jabal, followed on the mountain road from Ramah to Shiloh in Ephraim.

They arrived to find the city a charred ruin. Mud-brick walls lay shattered in piles of rubble. A few blackened, smoking timbers and mountains of ash were all that was left of the rafters of the village's roofs. Grass and bushes had already begun the inevitable reclaiming of the land.

They passed through the town and went out the eastern gate where they could see the sanctuary site a few score cubits away. The white cloth of the courtyard was torn and scorched where it had burned. Many of the pillars were pushed over. Surprisingly, the Tent itself was still standing.

They made their way around to the east where the opening into the courtyard had been. They respectfully entered through the gate, even though there were many places in the linen wall that were burned and they could have walked right in.

"The altar!" Zedekiah shouted. "It's still here!"

Samuel came into the courtyard and took hold of the horn on one of the corners of the large bronze-plated Altar of Sacrifice and knelt briefly before rising, looking around and moving forward.

"They must not have had a way of taking it with them," Samuel said.

"The laver! They just tipped it over," Zedekiah shouted.

Samuel caught up and they looked at the heavy bronze bowl and its base, lying on its side.

"They damaged it, but it could be repaired," Samuel commented. "Let's see the inside."

"Why didn't they burn the Tent?" Jabal asked.

"Perhaps they didn't have time," Samuel proposed. "Or maybe they were loathe to destroy our holy place."

Zedekiah doubted the Philistines would have hesitated to destroy the Tent, since they had taken the Ark. Maybe even they knew that, without the Ark, the Tent had little value.

The pair reverently passed through the opening, having to push aside the veil that was partially, apparently violently, pulled down.

Once inside, their eyes had to adjust to the darkness.

"They're here!" Jabal cried.

"Why didn't they take the candlestick?" Zedekiah strained to raise the solid-gold, seven-branch menorah, which had been knocked to the floor.

"Perhaps because it's so heavy," Samuel supposed. "It doesn't appear damaged."

Likewise, the table of shewbread sat askew as if it had been kicked, but it remained upright.

"They did take the vessels," Samuel said.

Zedekiah saw that it was true. The jars and utensils used for managing the sacrifices and drink and meal offerings, as well as the dishes for the shewbread were all gone.

"They must have been travelling light," Samuel said. "Praise Yahweh they did not destroy or take everything!"

"What shall we do?" Zedekiah asked.

"We should recruit men to remove and preserve the tent in case the Philistines come back," Samuel answered.

"Where should it be taken?"

"Eventually we should again unite the Ark with the Tent. 'Where?' is the question. Maybe we take it to Nob, the new home of the heir to the priesthood."

❧ 35 ❧

Hadassah had not known pain like this before. The midwife was talking to her non-stop, but it did not dull the pain as she squatted near the fire pit in the center of the ground-level room of their house.

The baby was coming, but it could not come too soon for Hadassah. She let out a groan that started as a low guttural cry and ended in a high-pitched scream.

"Keep pushing, Hadassah. I see the head," the short, stout midwife shouted.

The bedclothes lying on the hard, earthen floor under her were soaked and she looked down at them as she bowed her head and obediently pushed with what energy she had left. She had been in labor for hours and was weary beyond anything in her memory. Knowing that the baby was possibly near birth was all that kept her going now.

"It's coming! It's coming!" the midwife shouted. "Push, Hadassah, push!"

And she did. With one more great effort, she pushed with all the strength her weary body could muster and she felt the life within her slide between her legs. The midwife caught the baby, covered with the red and white, slippery fluid of her womb. Hadassah sank back exhausted as the midwife held the baby upside down to clear its airway, giving it a slap on its backside.

For a long moment Hadassah listened, then the baby cried. It continued crying loud and long and to her it was the sweetest music she had ever heard. The pain and exertion of moments before was forgotten as she worked to raise her head to see the young life in the arms of the midwife.

"You have a son," she said, laying the naked infant on his mother's breast.

Hadassah cradled the boy in her arms and looked at his face, thinking she had never seen anything so beautiful.

There could have been no prouder father than Eldad in all of Israel. His firstborn was a son: a son who would carry on his name after him; who would follow him in his trade.

Eldad would have been pleased if Hadassah had given him a daughter as well, but to have a son as firstborn was what every man wanted.

"We shall name him 'Jeriah.' It means 'Taught of Yahweh,'" Eldad announced.

"It is a good name," Hadassah answered, smiling down at the baby's angelic face.

❧ 36 ❧

"They stole my barley harvest! I had just gathered it into sheaves and they came and held my sons at spearpoint while they loaded it into carts and took it away!"

The old man spat the words in a hoarse whisper. He was not the first to tell such a story as the men of Mizpah listened. Eldad was there, as were other merchants and craftsmen of the town and the elders of the council.

The curtains were drawn and just one oil lamp in the middle of the room held back the darkness and cast long shadows on the walls.

"One of the soldiers eyed my daughter and said the most vile things to her. I've sent her away to my sister's house in Beth-Horon," said a shepherd from a nearby village.

"I'm from Bethel of Ephraim," said another man. "I came to sell my pottery. The Philistines are in Ephraim, too. Shiloh has fallen and been burned, and the Tent is abandoned."

"We had heard that," said Kenan, the head elder, nodding. "The Ark has been returned, but the Philistines discourage the worship of Yahweh."

The men talked longer, but solved nothing. How could they, without a champion to lead them? Soon they were dismissed and began leaving.

"Eldad," said the chief elder.

"Yes, lord?" he answered turning away from the door.

"The others on the council would like to invite you to join the council of elders, as a probationary member."

"Lord, I – thank you!"

"Two of our number were at Ebenezer, but did not return. You have experienced much at the hands of these oppressors," he said, looking down at Eldad's leg, which still caused him to limp a bit.

Kenan turned away and Eldad left the meeting, feeling blessed, but then he remembered: tomorrow was the day the soldiers would come to collect taxes.

His eyes narrowed as he bitterly thought how he might resist them.

Hadassah left the house to go to the stone oven in the courtyard where she was baking pita for the family's breakfast. Eldad was already at work in the forge and would break when she called him to eat. She retrieved the bread and returned the short distance to the house.

The family owned a goat, which provided its needs for milk and cheese, and sometimes enough for taking to the market to trade. Milking the goat was a regular part of Hadassah's daily routine. After setting the flat bread on the table, Hadassah took a clay pot by its handle from a shelf and went outside, entering the goat's small pen, on the opposite end of the house from the smith shop. She took a stool from a hanger on the wall and set it near the goat, which was tied to a fence post.

She had not been milking long when she caught the sound of men talking in the forge. She didn't think much about it because men were always coming and going for tools they had ordered from Eldad. Then suddenly she heard a loud crash and angry voices, one of which belonged to her husband. Without thinking, she ran to the open door of the forge. She stopped in the doorway when she saw who it was.

Two Philistine soldiers turned to see her when she appeared in the doorway. One of the men stood over her husband with sword drawn. Eldad was on the dirt floor, along with a table the soldiers had overturned, scattering tools and raw metal bars.

"What's this?" the one with the sword asked when he saw Hadassah. "Dagmol, if the smith won't pay the tax, we should teach him a lesson!"

The other man laughed as he leered at Hadassah and started toward her. She turned to run but was caught by the leering man, who dragged her back into the shop and pushed her to the ground. He unbuckled his belt and let it, with his sword in its scabbard, fall to the earthen floor, then reached and took hold of Hadassah's skirt, raising it almost to her chin, exposing her. He then raised his own tunic and began lowering himself over her.

Hadassah screamed in panic and rage, but she was powerless to stop the burly soldier.

❧ 37 ❦

"Stop! I can pay!" Eldad cried out in protest, trying to rise, but the sword's point stopped him and he fell back.

Then Eldad saw Enbol was distracted, watching Dagmol and Hadassah, so he slapped the flat of the double-edged sword that was holding him down as hard as he could. It swung away and he rose quickly, swinging a fist, hitting the Philistine's ugly jaw.

The soldier fell back and dropped his sword, which Eldad immediately retrieved.

"Stop!" Eldad shouted, holding one soldier at bay with his own sword while looking at the other standing over Hadassah. The man hesitated.

"Go to Jacob, Hadassah!" Eldad shouted. She wasted no time, but rose and, straightening her clothing, ran from the shop to the home of her brother- and sister-in-law.

"Now, take your cursed taxes!" Eldad fought his rage, as he kept the sword pointed at Enbol, who was still lying on the floor. He went to a box on a lower shelf of his workbench. From it he took a bar of silver and threw it on the floor before Enbol.

"Out! Out of my shop!"

The man picked up the silver and stood. For a moment Enbol didn't move, but looked over at Dagmol whose sword was in its sheath, lying on the floor.

"All right, we are going," Enbol said. "But, my sword. Hand it over."

"You'll get it when you're outside my gate."

The other soldier picked up his belt and drew his sword. "This should be a lesson, smith," the other brute said. "Be sure to have the tax money ready next week."

Dagmol then swung his sword into a shelf by the door, breaking it and causing finished implements to crash to the packed-earth floor of the shop. Both men laughed and left as Eldad kept the sword pointed at them.

When they were out in the courtyard and the soldiers were backing toward the gate, apparently calculating whether they should try to take Eldad, Jacob ran out of his house, brandishing a thick piece of wood as a club. This made the Philistines' decision for them and they went out through the gate.

Eldad was tempted to keep the sword, but he knew that would bring reprisals, so he went to a part of the wall far from the gate and threw it over for the soldier to retrieve. He then ran to his brother's apartment and entered.

Hadassah, weeping with the shame of it all, jumped when he entered. "I am sorry, my love," Eldad cried. "I should have just given them what they wanted. I objected to the tax, but I was only stalling. I had no idea what they would do."

"Are you all right?" Hadassah asked through her tears.

"I'm fine. Are YOU all right?"

She didn't answer as he embraced her tightly. Eldad saw that his mother was there, and she was frowning.

"Mother! What brings you to the forge?" Jacob asked.

He and Eldad were working; Eldad hammering a bronze serving tray. Jacob was stoking the fire in the forge when Zemirah entered.

"I must speak with Eldad," Zemirah said.

"What is it, mother?"

"I have decided. You must take a second wife."

"What?!" Eldad laid down the hammer. "Why? Hadassah has given me a son! Who knows how many more she may give me?"

"Hadassah is disgraced. The Philistine uncovered her."

Eldad's anger prevented him from immediately responding. Finally he spoke.

"She is not disgraced. What happened was not her fault. If anything it was my fault!"

"No matter, I will find a suitable second wife for you."

"But I love Hadassah and she has given me a son! I don't need another wife!"

Zemirah didn't continue the conversation, but walked out the door. Jacob watched Eldad's reaction.

He threw the tray he was working on across the forge.

Later than night, Eldad and Hadassah were preparing for bed. He moved to embrace her, but she moved away.

"Please don't come near me!" she cried.

"What's wrong?"

"I don't deserve you."

"But I love you."

"I - I just can't right now."

"You don't want me to sleep in my own bed?"

"Please understand."

Eldad turned and left in a huff, taking a blanket as he went downstairs to sleep.

❦ 38 ❦

Eldad, covered in sweat, exited the forge and got a dipper of water from a clay jar near the door. As he drank long and eagerly, his mother entered the courtyard through the front gate with a man and, hanging back behind him, a girl.

"My son, you know Ehud, the tanner."

"Yes. Shalom, Ehud."

"Shalom," Ehud replied.

"Ehud's daughter, Tzipporah, is willing to become your wife," Zemirah began, pointing to the young girl. "She just became a woman and could bear you many sons."

Eldad looked at the terrified girl, realizing she might be only 13 years old, and then at her father.

"I would be proud for you to take Tzipporah," Ehud said. "Yours is a great family in Benjamin. You need only pay the bride price..."

"Mother!" Eldad whispered harshly, pulling Zemirah aside roughly. "Did I not tell you I love Hadassah!"

Then he turned to Ehud.

"I'm sorry you have been troubled. My mother has made a mistake. I don't want another wife."

Tzipporah hid her face and Ehud grew angry.

"Why do you embarrass me this way?" Zemirah cried.

Eldad turned and had started to go back into the forge when Jacob appeared in the doorway.

"What disgrace is this?!" Ehud bellowed. "Come, Tzipporah."

He took her arm and started toward the gate.

"I'll take her."

All eyes turned to Jacob.

"What?" Eldad said, glaring at his brother.

"I will take Tzipporah as wife," Jacob said, ignoring Eldad as he stepped forward to face Ehud. "Ophrah has given me a daughter, but that was almost seven years ago. Eldad should not have the only son."

Tzipporah's face showed panic and embarrassment.

"Ehud, allow my other son to save my honor." Zermirah pleaded. "Let Jacob take your daughter."

"But he is not the firstborn."

"We will double the bride price," Jacob offered.

"We will?" Eldad challenged.

"That way it equals the price for the firstborn," Jacob continued.

Ehud stroked his beard for a moment and looked down at Tzipporah, but not to learn her opinion, Eldad realized.

"Very well. Jacob, you and I will visit the head elder tomorrow to seal our contract."

"Until tomorrow," Jacob said, shaking Ehud's hand.

Ehud turned and took Tzipporah out the gate as Jacob, Eldad and Zemirah watched.

"Be glad your brother was here to salvage our family's honor!" Zemirah spat at Eldad.

She stormed off to her house and Jacob looked condescendingly at Eldad as he returned to the forge. Eldad then saw Ophrah looking out the window of her and Jacob's house. He could see her eyes were red and wet until she disappeared behind the curtain.

After the engagement period agreed upon by Jacob and Ehud, Jacob paid the bride price and brought Tzipporah home with him. They did not have a wedding feast, for this was Jacob's second wife and his father, who ordinarily would have made all the arrangements, was dead.

Jacob entered his house, holding Tzipporah's hand. Ophrah and Talia sat on mats on the floor, mending clothing.

"I have taken another wife," Jacob announced. "This is Tzipporah. Tzipporah, this is Ophrah, my first wife, and our daughter, Talia."

Ophrah and six-year-old Talia looked at Tzipporah with wide eyes.

"Tzipporah and I will sleep here tonight," Jacob continued. "Ophrah, fetch some bedding, please. Tomorrow we will arrange a permanent place for her."

Ophrah got up from the mat. "Come Talia. Help me with the bedding."

They went upstairs. Tzipporah was on the verge of tears. Jacob embraced her and stroked her back, attempting to comfort her.

"Welcome to your new home, Tzipporah. Tonight I will make you my wife and tomorrow we will divide the household responsibilities between you, Ophrah and Talia."

Hadassah was already in bed with baby Jeriah asleep beside her when Eldad entered. He looked at them, then gathered a blanket and pillow and left the room.

Only one oil lamp illuminated the room as Eldad came down the stairs to the main room. He spread the blanket on the floor and lay the pillow on it, then extinguished the oil lamp and lay down. Moonlight was the only light as he wrapped the blanket around him to sleep.

Hadassah was putting away clothing. Two-year-old baby Jeriah lay on the bed, napping. Eldad came up behind Hadassah and started to embrace her, but she pulled away.

"Why do you continue to pursue me? I am disgraced!"

"You are my wife and I love you! It's been almost two years. Haven't I proven my love?"

"Even your mother tells me I must leave the household, for I am dishonored."

"Forget my mother, my love. Only I am to blame for what happened to you. Don't let others tell you what I should think of you. I love you and always will."

He took her in his arms made strong like the bronze and iron he forged and held her close until her body relaxed and she dissolved in tears. With a gentle hand, he turned her face and kissed her deeply and long.

❦ 39 ❧

"They say it's for taxes, but they take what they want!" exclaimed one of the men in a sharp whisper.

"It's the same for us all. Do you think you've been singled out?" said another.

Eldad listened to the back and forth. He had been told he would soon be initiated as a full member of the council and had already related how Hadassah had been almost raped. Sadly, others had been raped in Mizpah. Each member of the council had a story of mistreatment at the hands of their Philistine oppressors.

The council of elders had to meet in secret because the Philistines didn't allow meetings of the elders, regarding the system to have been superseded by the Philistine governor. They were meeting in a darkened barn some distance outside Mizpah. The only gatherings allowed by the Philistines were gatherings of worship and sacrifice.

"The wheat harvest was taken last year," Kenan said, stating what everyone knew. "Every sheaf, taken as 'taxes.'"

"Other towns in Benjamin report the same treatment," the first man said, repeating something else everyone knew. "No doubt the same is true in Ephraim."

How can we be delivered? Eldad wondered.

Jeriah's pounding rang like a bell in the smith shop as he used a rock to beat a scrap of bronze. Now two years old, he was imitating his father, while Eldad worked at the forge.

Eldad glanced over at his son proudly, then turned back to his work. Another few years and he could begin teaching

Jeriah their family's trade. In the meantime, Jeriah loved sitting on the floor and "working" with his father.

Eldad plunged the bronze spoon into the liquid in the clay cooling jar and held the tongs as the steam rose, then raised the large serving spoon and examined it. It was finished, he decided, and he took it to his cooling rack where he hung it with the other implements he was allowed to create by their Philistine masters.

"Jeriah! No!" he shouted, as he turned around again.

The boy was reaching toward the iron poker, one end of which was in the fire.

"Hot! Hot!" Eldad shouted as he ran to pull the boy away.

"Hot!" Jeriah said, imitating his father's tone and beating one hand against the other.

"You must not touch that!" Eldad said.

"No touch!" Jeriah said.

"That's right, 'no touch!'" Eldad folded his firstborn into is strong arms and held him close.

Over the months that had passed, Eldad had been able to mend his relationship with Hadassah, but he still worried about her. She always disappeared when there was any chance that a Philistine would be near.

This day, she came to the smith shop, surprising him as he worked and Jeriah played on the packed earth floor.

"What's wrong?" he asked instinctively.

"Nothing is wrong. I have news," she answered with a sly smile. "Jeriah will soon have a brother or sister."

"Oh, how wonderful!" Eldad said as he scooped up Jeriah, carried him to the doorway and embraced his wife.

"I pray it is a son," she exclaimed with the musical laugh Eldad had not heard for some time.

"No matter whether it is a son or daughter. It is a child of our love."

❧ 40 ❧

The prophet Samuel, or as some referred to him, "the seer," had come to meet with Zedekiah and Ahitub, who was now 12. They all sat on the floor around the table in Zedekiah's house. Raquel sat over to the side, watching and trying to keep three-year-old Ichabod quietly occupied.

"Ahitub, do you remember me?" Samuel asked.

"Yes, you are Samuel. You knew my father."

"And your grandfather, too. You know, don't you, that you are part of a very special tradition and, because your grandfather and your father and his brother died, you have a very important part to play?"

"I guess so."

"Zedekiah and your Aunt Raquel brought you here so you could play your part. Did you know you are very important?"

"No."

"You remember your grandfather, Eli?"

"Yes. He couldn't see."

"Well, he could see most of his life, but he lived a long time. Do you know that you are supposed to be a priest?"

"Because my father and grandfather were priests?"

"Yes, but more than that, because you are descended from Aaron. Do you know who he was?"

"Moses' brother?"

"Yes, and the father of the priesthood of Yahweh. There are two branches of the priesthood, one from Aaron's son Eleazar and the other from his son, Ithamar. Aaron's other two sons died in the wilderness, so only the descendants of Eleazar and Ithamar may be priests. Do you know whose descendant you are?"

"Ithamar?"

"You are a very smart boy, but you are soon to be a man, and it is time to begin your training."

Months were passing, and Ahitub's training was progressing well, but something else was progressing alongside it.

Samuel had seen it early on, but it wasn't a word from the Lord. It was actually plain to anyone paying attention, except the involved parties themselves.

As happens sometimes, when two people are falling in love, they themselves are the last to know, because their focus is elsewhere. Thus it was with Zedekiah and Raquel.

From that moment in Shiloh when he learned of Atarah's death and that Ahitub and Ichabod were orphans, Zedekiah had taken on Raquel and the two children as his own responsibility. Caring for them had been his main concern.

As for Raquel, she was so absorbed in caring for the two children of her brother- and sister-in-law she was just as surprised as he when one day, after bringing her something, Zedekiah lingered at the door and they looked at one another as if they were meeting for the first time. Before either of them knew what was happening, they kissed!

Afterward they were both embarrassed and confused and they agreed they should speak to Samuel, when he came for Ahitub's training.

"It's about time," Samuel said with a smile.

Samuel gladly gave his approval for the union and Zedekiah and Raquel began making plans to unite in marriage immediately.

Samuel insisted on preparing a feast. He and his wife brought enough food for all Zedekiah's and Raquel's family and friends in Nob to celebrate their wedding.

❦ 41 ❦

Eldad was too nervous to work, so Jacob was in the forge alone, fulfilling an order for door hinges. Eldad had Jeriah with him, because Hadassah was in labor. Zemirah had called the midwife and Ophrah to help and now they were all in the main room of the house, where he was not welcome.

He could hear muffled voices, but he couldn't make out what they were saying. Occasionally he heard Hadassah cry out in what Eldad realized must be contractions.

Jeriah continued to play in the dirt, unaware of the drama going on inside the house.

But to Eldad, it seemed like it was taking much too long.

Finally, after many hours, Ophrah emerged from the front door, covered in sweat.

"Eldad, you have another son! You can go in now."

Eldad scooped up three-year-old Jeriah and ran through the front door of the house.

Inside, he saw Hadassah, her hair soaked with sweat, but her face shining with a smile that lit up the room. She was holding the baby, who was asleep.

"I think we should name him 'Azel,'" Eldad said, one day after a couple of weeks had passed.

"You think he is noble?" Hadassah smiled as she held him to her breast, giving the baby the life-giving mother's milk.

"Yes, look at his face," Eldad said proudly.

"I suppose he does look noble," Hadassah said. "If we give him a name that means 'noble' perhaps he will be."

"Yes, I think he will."

Azel quickly grew and developed, learning to walk and talk even sooner than Jeriah had.

Unfortunately, he did not display the quality of nobility in his first year. In fact, he was quite a handful. Hadassah was surprised how different her two boys were: Jeriah was relatively quiet and quick to obey, but Azel was curious and always getting into things he shouldn't. He seemed to never miss an opportunity to test her.

Eldad had to step in on several occasions to administer the hand of discipline to the young child, but still Azel tended to do what he wanted.

Ophrah never had another child, but Tzipporah turned out to be fertile indeed.

The first child to be born was Elihu, a boy who took everything seriously. Jacob determined to begin his apprenticeship in the forge early because he demonstrated a level of competency at an early age; more than Jacob himself.

Elihu was barely a year old when Tzipporah was pregnant again. Jacob was overjoyed that the baby was another boy. He now could hold his head high with Eldad who only had two sons. He named the second son Shallam.

After two years, Tzipporah gave birth to a daughter.

Aisha, as she was called, became Zemirah's favorite, for she now had grandsons enough to ensure the legacy of the family name, so she could lavish attention on her baby granddaughter.

Ophrah silently bore the slight, because Talia was now almost old enough to be sought after by a husband herself. She didn't want to rush that process though, because when she married, Talia would go to live with her new husband, wherever the family might live, and Ophrah would be left alone for all practical purposes, with Hadassah as her only confidant and solace.

❧ 42 ❧

"How long O Lord?" Samuel cried out to God.

It was a prayer he prayed daily, but it had almost been twenty long years since the tragic battle of Eben-ezer and, in the hill country around Mizpah, the darkness had deepened into near permanent depression. Everywhere the people suffered under crushing poverty and deprivation. Efforts to prosper were repeatedly frustrated by their brutal Philistine overseers. Samuel sensed that despair was reaching a critical point among the people.

As the judge, prophet and priest of three mountain villages near to his home in Ramah, including Mizpah, he would often pray before the gatherings, his long hair tied in the middle of his back, with a gray mohair cloak about his shoulders. He would pray long, seeking God's plan to deliver Israel. He built altars in the towns in which he ministered, plus in his hometown of Ramah, and many of the elders of Israel gathered there to worship.

On a hill outside Mizpah, scores of men were laboring to carry and place stones. Samuel was there, overseeing the building project.

A raised, stone platform was almost complete. Stone steps were being built to allow access to the platform.

In the center of the high platform, on a smaller platform one-step higher, Samuel personally directed the stacking of stones for the altar. It was to have four walls with a firepit inside. The topmost stone on each corner was carved to resemble a horn, each oriented to the four directions.

Eldad approached, carrying a grate made of metal bars crossing at intervals of a palm's width.

"Lord Samuel, I have finished the grate you requested," Eldad said. "Made according to your instructions."

"Excellent! Thank you, Eldad," Samuel said. "Zedekiah, will you help Eldad put the grate in place?"

"Yes, lord," Zedekiah said, coming to take one side of the heavy grate. He and Eldad set it in place on the ledge that had been constructed for it on the inside of the altar's walls.

"Good, good," Samuel said. "Could you do something else for me, Eldad?"

"You need only name it."

"I need a couple of implements. A pair of pinching tongs with which to arrange the sacrifices over the fire and a poker to shift the wood below the grate. Can you do that?"

"You'll have them tomorrow."

"Good. Very good."

Samuel turned his attention back to the construction of the altar and Eldad descended the steps from the platform to return to the city.

After Kenan died a few years before, Eldad was appointed head elder, which surprised him, but he had accepted the appointment as a calling. In his new role, he interacted often with Samuel.

Soon the platform and altar were finished and Samuel began regular worship services in Mizpah. He also ministered in Gilgal, near the Jordan river, and in Bethel to the north in Ephraim.

He began a circuit from his home in Ramah of Benjamin, to these three cities. He would summon the people of the town and surrounding farms to offer sacrifices and then he would preach.

Eldad listened as Samuel spoke on one of his regular trips to sacrifice in Mizpah.

"If you will put away your Ba'als and Ashtoreths and worship only Yahweh," Samuel preached, much like he had many times before, "Then God will deliver you from the Philistines."

Eldad thought maybe Samuel was right. He and Hadassah had a teraph: an image of a local Canaanite god of fertility and harvest – a Ba'al, made of stone – that they had sometimes prayed to on behalf of the local farmers seeking a good harvest. His mother, Zemirah, had been partial to it before she died.

Abruptly, Eldad left the assembly, ignoring the looks of disapproval from the men who saw him leave.

Once home, he entered the front door as Hadassah came around the corner. Eldad said nothing, but went to the wooden shelf on which the idol sat. He picked up the statue that was about the length of his arm with a look of determination on his face. Hadassah watched, wondering, but did not ask his purpose.

He turned and carried the idol out the door.

Soon he was back at the place of sacrifice. He threaded his way through the crowd of men and boldly climbed the stone steps leading to the altar.

Samuel turned to see him approaching, carrying the heavy stone idol and seemed to understand at once.

Eldad walked up to Samuel as the men of the town watched and held the heavy teraph out to him. Samuel took the heavy statue with a knowing look and turned to Jabal, who accepted it from him wordlessly.

Samuel nodded to Jabal and he raised the stone statue of the Canaanite god over his head and with tremendous force, threw it down on the stone platform, where it shattered to pieces loudly.

Samuel looked out at the crowd of silent, dumbstruck men, then he turned and embraced Eldad.

Over the next several hours, other men followed Eldad's example and brought their cultic images to be destroyed.

❧ 43 ❧

Gradually the crowds at the altars Samuel had erected grew, until Samuel saw that Israel was reaching a turning point, at least in the towns he was serving. He saw a change taking place as he travelled his circuit from his home in Ramah to the three towns, Mizpah, Bethel and Gilgal, the last of which was across the watershed ridge almost to the Jordan river, near Jericho. People were turning to Yahweh.

And so he stood before them at the end of the well-attended sacrificial ceremonies in each of the three towns and said, "Let all Israel come together at Mizpah and I will intercede for you and the Lord will hear."

A day was announced and the word went out to all of the tribes of Israel.

The appointed day came and a large crowd gathered. Eldad was there, along with the other elders of Mizpah. Thousands of men came from surrounding towns, not just those that Samuel served. They gathered at the altar Samuel had erected in a field outside the town to accommodate the large number of people he expected to attend.

"We have sinned, O God!" Samuel prayed loudly.

"Yes…" answered the men in attendance.

"Amen…"

"Yes, Lord."

"We have sinned," Samuel continued, "by leaving you to worship other gods."

The worshippers murmured their agreement again.

Eldad looked around at the men in the gathering and realized that all the people present had begun to see Samuel, not just as a local judge and prophet, but as a leader of all Israel like Barak and Jephthah and Samson and Gideon had been in years past.

The people spent several days in Mizpah and rededicated themselves to the service of Yahweh, the God of Abraham, Isaac and Jacob.

❦ 44 ❦

"Lord, the Hebrews are gathered in large numbers," reported Enbol, now a captain of a company.

"How many are there?" asked Clamatos, governor for the Philistine occupation of Mizpah and the surrounding area. He was seated at the large table from which he conducted the business of the occupation.

"Perhaps thousands. It does appear to be a festival of their religion, but they are many."

"Come, bring your lieutenant. Let's see for ourselves."

The three Philistine warriors approached the field outside the town through a thicket of trees and watched the Hebrews from a distance, not because they were afraid, but because they wanted to watch what they were doing without being seen.

They were indeed sacrificing to their God; the presence of sheep and goats and blood on the altar made that obvious. "Still, it could be a ruse to mass for an attack," Clamatos stroked his black goatee. "Send word to Gath. King Maoch needs to know this. Perhaps he will take action."

Enbol saluted and the three men turned to leave. Enbol departed Mizpah a few minutes later for Gath on a fast horse.

King Maoch did indeed desire to take action. The king of Gath immediately ordered 1,000 soldiers to Mizpah. He determined he would ride at the head of the column himself, sitting proudly on a fine horse as the green banner of Gath fluttered in the breeze to his left.

Enbol rode beside him, to guide the king and his cohort to the outpost town of Mizpah. The veteran soldiers marched four abreast and were accompanied by a detail of cavalry and chariots, which was key to Philistine dominance on the battlefield. They were travelling to Ekron and beyond, north into the territory of Ephraim, then into Benjamin toward Mizpah. It was a long days' march which they had begun before dawn, but Maoch knew the hardened soldiers were well accustomed to this type of maneuver and would have no trouble attacking as soon as they arrived.

The detachment turned onto the small road that straddled the crest of a ridge and rose gently into the heights. Soon they had ascended some distance and could see down the slope in either direction to the brooks which ran out of the mountains all the way to the Sea, watering the fertile wadis as they went. Trees lined the banks of the brooks and dotted the hills.

It is a pleasant country, thought King Maoch.

Periodically they would have to put down insurrections such as this to maintain order. All conquered peoples tested their overlords' mettle. Today they would win a victory to the glory of Gath and the continued peace of the occupation.

Armies on the march are difficult to keep secret, so the elders of the village of Timnah sent a young man with word that the Philistines were on the move. He ran swiftly and arrived in Mizpah by mid-afternoon.

He gave the message to an elder who went to Samuel. Ahitub and Zedekiah were proceeding with the sacrifices.

As Zedekiah continued the worship, Samuel sent Jabal into the crowd, where he found Eldad and his son Jeriah, now a strong young man of 19, and told them to meet Samuel behind the platform.

"Yahweh has told me this is how He will deliver us," Samuel began. "Will you lead the way?"

"I will," Eldad replied. "What shall we do?"

"Here is what the Lord says…"

❦ 45 ❧

Meanwhile, Clamatos and his small garrison of soldiers rode out from Mizpah to meet the army from Gath and guide them to the site of Samuel's gathering to put down the rebellion that surely was brewing there.

"And so, what of the gathering?" asked King Maoch as the two columns met on the road.

"They remain, feasting and sacrificing to their god," Clamatos replied, reporting the most recent intelligence.

"Is there any reason to suspect a more rebellious reason for this meeting?"

"None, lord, although it is difficult to think they only intend to worship when it is so great a company."

"We will soon learn the truth."

Clamatos had been Maoch's adjutant, but was several years older than Maoch, and though he was a noble, he was not in a royal line, and so could not aspire to the role that Maoch played in life. To be a governor of an occupied province was reward enough for service to his city-state.

"A curious people, these Hebrews," Clamatos remarked, breaking the silence. "They rarely worship the gods of the other Canaanites: the gods of war and harvest and love; but prefer to worship one god who is everything."

"How can one god be for everything?" asked Maoch incredulously. "Such talk is nonsense. They must be atheists!"

"Perhaps. They are certainly a stubborn people."

"They will yet learn to bend," Maoch, said smiling. The governor returned the smile knowingly.

❦

The young boy had sounded the alarm when he arrived at the gathering place and the worshipers were panicking.

"Call on the Lord, Samuel!" cried an old man.

"Plead with the Lord to protect us!" said another.

Eldad knew that Samuel had been calling on the Lord for a couple of days, but now he again went to the altar and slashed the throat of a lamb, letting the blood flow to the ground as he raised the lifeless animal to the stacked-stone altar and cast it on the fire.

In the smoke and steam which rose from the roasting meat, Samuel stood with his hands stretched wide and his face raised to heaven. His eyes were closed and his lips were moving. Suddenly, as Eldad and the rest of the men watched, his lips stopped moving and he swayed a bit in the wind. Then he sank to his knees and clasped his hands together.

No one spoke or moved while Samuel knelt before the altar. For several minutes they were still, with no sound but the wind in the treetops. The wind picked up even more and a cloud obscured the setting sun. Then Samuel stirred and stood up. The crowd breathed in together and listened.

"Men of Israel. Hear what the Lord says," Samuel cried.

That was the signal. Eldad, Jeriah and several others Eldad had hand-selected slipped away from the crowd. The sun would be down soon.

"I see the smoke of their sacrifice," cried Clamatos, pointing to the field where the Israelites were gathered. It was twilight, but the smoke was visible as a lighter gray cloud against the darkening sky.

"Prepare to attack!" Maoch cried, and the order was repeated by officers down the column.

The men spurred their horses and began to gallop through the trees via the narrow path. The infantry hurried to keep up with the mounted men, but the charioteers struggled in the narrow space between the trees and gradually the chariots fell behind. The terrain was growing more and more difficult as the path ascended toward the height of the Watchtower.

The sky was growing darker and the space under the trees was darker still. On they went, toward the smoke.

Then it began to rain. Soon the smoke was joined by the gloom of nightfall and the storm. Their horses hesitated and some faltered as they collided with tree branches.

Suddenly there was a flash of lightning, momentarily blinding the soldiers, and rain began to fall in earnest.

"Forward! Attack!" urged Maoch, but the horses of the officers and cavalry were colliding with one another in the deepening darkness and it was no longer possible to tell what direction they should be going amid the trees. The infantry could not move forward because of the cavalry hesitating in confusion ahead of them. To the rear, the chariots were slipping on rain-soaked, stony earth and some were becoming stuck in rapidly forming mud.

⤜ 46 ⤏

There was a shout in the darkness as a soldier fell from his horse and lay motionless on the ground. Something whizzed past Enbol's face and he turned to look in the direction from which it came. Another cavalryman went limp and slipped off his horse with a choked cry. A spooked horse ran by in the direction from which they had come and collided with a rank of infantrymen in the darkness. Some men were knocked down and some were hurt.

Still it was eerily quiet except for the rain. Enbol looked back and sensed confusion among the soldiers in the darkness. More riders were being unhorsed and more objects were whizzing past.

Lightning lit the sky once more and was immediately followed by a loud thunderclap, but the brief, bright light only served to blind and confuse the soldiers further.

Suddenly a sword came out of the darkness and glanced against Enbol's breastplate. He reacted by pulling his own sword and slashing through the rain and darkness, but did not connect with anything. Even in the dark he knew the sword to be a thrusting, iron sword of the Palusata, not the bronze, slashing sickle-sword of the Hebrew. Then he was violently pulled from his horse and fell hard to the ground, being pelted with stones and struck with heavy clubs. Again he swung his sword and this time hit something. Momentarily whoever was attacking him backed off and Enbol sprang to his feet and began running in the darkness.

The pelting of stones from under the trees began again and he swung his sword wildly. He looked for commander Clamatos and King Maoch but neither of them were anywhere to be seen, if he could have seen in the darkness punctuated by blinding lightning.

The woods were now filled with the shouts of men and the neighing of frightened horses, reacting to the thunder. Enbol stood, continuing to swing his sword, but not seeing anyone to cut.

Are we fighting spirits?

He could hear other men running, so he ran again, running toward Gath, forgetting his station in Mizpah.

He stumbled when a stone struck him in the back of the head and he heard a voice say, "For Hadassah!" Then he felt a sharp pain in his back and all went black.

Eldad's sword – the iron Philistine weapon he had taken from the battlefield at Eben-ezer and kept hidden for more than 20 years – continued to flash in the night as rain fell and lightning disoriented the Philistine army. After using stones, Jeriah and the others took swords from the soldiers who had fallen and used them to pursue and kill more Philistines.

Each time Eldad used his sword, he thought of the men who tried to rape Hadassah and how they made it impossible for him to make a living for his family. He continued moving forward, looking for bronze breastplates shining in the rain.

Eldad retrieved the sword of one fallen Philistine and handed it to his son, who had thus far been pelting the Philistines with stones from the darkness. Jeriah took it, taking only a moment to test the way it felt in his hand, his bicep flexing as he swung it one way, then the other. Satisfied, he ran forward to hunt fleeing Philistines.

For several miles, the Israelites pursued the panicked Philistines, killing many of them. They chased them all night over terrain the Israelites knew well, much of it wooded, but with which the Philistines from Gath were unfamiliar. The darkness and lightning, rain and smoke, had produced the ideal circumstances in which Yahweh could confuse and defeat the enemy, just as Samuel had foreseen.

When they reached Timnah on the border of Israelite territory around midnight, Eldad, Jeriah and other men of Israel paused to rest. They had killed many Philistines, but others had run away in the darkness and escaped.

"We should return to Mizpah," Eldad said.

The others agreed. They had reached Beth Car, some distance west of Mizpah, and as long as the Philistines were fleeing, they had the upper hand, but, while they had routed the Philistine warriors from Gath during the night and the storm, other soldiers were in nearby Ekron and could counter-attack.

"Strip the bodies of their weapons and armor," Samuel said, when he caught up with the men, and they did so whenever they encountered a dead Philistine soldier on the long walk back to Mizpah. Along the way they found many useful items: from abandoned horses to fine iron swords to the bronze helmets, breastplates and grieves of the professional soldiers of Philistia. Later they found abandoned chariots, some with broken wheels.

These can be repaired, Eldad thought.

No longer would the Philistines' ban on the production of weapons and tools be observed in his shop.

❦ 47 ❦

When the weary men arrived back in Mizpah as the sun was rising, they gathered once again in the field of sacrifice and praised Yahweh for giving them the victory and for fighting for them in the thunder and rain. Representatives from all the tribes of Israel heard about Mizpah's vengeance on the cruel Philistines and gathered with them to worship and praise God for the victory over the next few days.

As the celebration continued, Eldad and other elders drew aside from the field of sacrifice.

"Now is the time," said one white haired man, continuing a conversation they had had many times before. "We may not have a better opportunity."

"Yes! We must move now," agreed another elder who came all the way from Naphtali to the north. "Samuel must inquire of the Lord."

"I too feel a king would enhance our national unity and security," An elder from Benjamin stated. "But will it preserve our devotion to Yahweh?"

"Indeed it would," the white-haired elder replied. "God through Samuel would select the king and the Lord's prophet would guide the him."

"But most importantly, the king would raise a well-trained army that would protect us," said a man from the tribe of Asher.

The gray-haired elders' heads nodded in agreement all around as Eldad listened.

❦

Samuel directed the men of Mizpah to stockpile the captured Philistine weapons and organize themselves into a kind of volunteer militia, taking turns keeping watch at the border of their lands. Because of this the Philistines would not return to the towns which Samuel served as judge for many years.

❦ 48 ❧

At twenty years old, Jeriah was tall and strong, serving in the militia rotation to patrol the border, which he did carrying the iron sword his father, Eldad, had brought from the Battle of Eben-ezer. He trained with the other men of Mizpah to serve defending their tribe if called upon to do so, while he worked with his father forging metal implements in the smith shop. The weapons they had captured from the Philistines were stored in a centrally located armory.

The Philistines had left them alone after they were driven from Mizpah, but Jeriah doubted their good fortune would last forever.

In recent months, Jeriah had built an apartment for himself adjoining his parents' house. He had fashioned the mud bricks himself and had cut the timbers for the rafters. Its wooden door opened directly into the family compound. There he would bring his bride, when he found one.

He was now sleeping in the new apartment, but today, he was preparing to leave for his turn at watch when his 17-year-old brother Azel appeared at the door.

"Let me come too," Azel asked.

"It may be dangerous," Jeriah cautioned.

"I am a man now," Azel insisted. "I should do my part."

Jeriah did not argue with his brother. He was indeed a man, having had his Bar Mitzvah four years ago and was now his full height and was strengthened by time in the forge.

"You will need a weapon," Jeriah said.

"I have my hunting knife," Azel said, pulling the knife from his belt. It was a short bronze blade he took on trips to hunt hart in the forest. "I need a sword or spear as well."

"All right," Jeriah answered. "We can get those from the armory. Does Father know?"

"I haven't spoken to him."

Jeriah and Azel came out of the apartment, walked to the front door of their parents' house and went inside.

When Azel told his father what he wanted to do, Jeriah could tell his father was reluctant, but also proud. His hair was no longer all black, but had strands of gray and he moved slower than he once did.

"You may go with Jeriah, son," he said. Then to Jeriah, "Train him well."

At the armory, Azel got a bronze-tipped spear and a wooden, leather-covered shield. In addition to the sword, Jeriah also carried a bronze hunting knife as a backup.

It was dusk when they arrived at their posting west of Mizpah. They were to cover a space of one mile, starting at the top of a ridge and passing down into a valley, then climbing the next ridge to the north, all the while keeping an eye on the territory to the west, whence the Philistines would come, if they came again.

"Look Jeriah!" Azel exclaimed, pointing to the south. "Is that a torch?" They had been walking for a couple of hours and it was now fully dark. The stars shown brightly above them, though the night was moonless.

"Yes, it is, but it's nothing to be concerned about," Jeriah answered. "That's the city gate of Gibeon. See how still it is? If we see many torches moving toward us, that is when we need to be concerned."

"Do you think the Philistines will return, Jeriah?"

"I fear they will. They are a warlike people. They will always be a threat."

"But they have not come back after the battle."

"Yes, they remain within their borders for now, but there are still places in Israel that are occupied. We are fortunate Samuel led us to drive them out of our homeland."

"Next time they come, I will help drive them out."

"Yes, you will be older next time."

"It was only a year ago."

"What do you mean?"

"Why didn't you or father call me to help?"

"You were only 16."

"I could have helped. Why did you exclude me?"

"We didn't exclude you. You were off somewhere with your friends."

"You spent time planning the attack, but you didn't tell me what you were doing."

Jeriah knew Azel wouldn't like the reason their father didn't include his brother in the plans for the battle.

"Father didn't want you to be in danger."

"Oh, but it's okay for you?"

Jeriah sighed.

"He didn't want you endangered, for mother's sake."

Azel stopped walking. Jeriah realized he would have to explain further.

"Mother can't have more children," Jeriah added.

Azel didn't speak for a bit, but finally did, shouting, "So will I never be able to defend our country? I will never be allowed to be a man?"

"It doesn't mean you won't be a man."

"But a man's responsibility is to defend his family, his tribe and his country. I'll have a family someday. Father went to battle and now you! But am I to be without honor?"

"No one said you would be without honor. In fact, no one has said you won't ever be able to go to battle."

"YOU just did. You just said I was the last child mother could have, so I had to be excluded from driving out the Philistines!"

Jeriah couldn't argue that, so Azel continued.

"I WILL be a man and defend our country!"

"Not if father says you won't."

"I will, too."

"Besides being your father, he is an elder."

"What if Yahweh tells me to?"

"Yahweh wouldn't tell you to go against those over us," Jeriah argued. "He puts those authorities in place."

"But the authorities don't always do the will of Yahweh."

Jeriah didn't know how to answer. Authority was authority, in his mind. And was that a backhanded swipe at their father?

"But they are still put in place by Yahweh," he argued. "If they fail to follow Yahweh, that's between them and Him."

They walked in silence for a while. To Jeriah, it was clear that Yahweh had ordained authorities over them and their role was to be loyal and support them. Azel finally spoke.

"If we had a king, he would defeat the Philistines."

"Perhaps," Jeriah answered. "Certainly, a king would unite the tribes and raise an army. But armies must be trained, clothed and fed. And defeating the Philistines would not be easier just because we had a king."

"But if all the tribes joined together..."

"All the tribes were joined at Eben-ezer."

Jeriah didn't have to explain. They had both heard their father's retelling of the story how he barely escaped with his life when so many did not.

"For now, Yahweh is our only King," Jeriah continued. "And Samuel speaks for him."

"Well, when we have a king, I want to be in the army that defeats the Philistines once and for all."

"I do, too," Jeriah said. "I do, too."

꧁ 49 ꧂

"She's been in labor five hours. Uncle Zedekiah is that normal?"

Ahitub called him uncle because he had married his Aunt Raquel, but the couple had raised him as their own son. Zedekiah considered his answer, since 30-year-old Ahitub's question might well be asked against the background of his mother's death in childbirth. They were sitting outside Ahitub's house while the women tended to his wife's birth.

"Labor can be much longer than that, but also shorter. It just depends. Have you thought of a name?" the Levite asked the young priest, about to become a father for the first time.

"Isn't the custom to wait until the child displays some characteristic on which to base a name?"

"Yes, that's right, but you can also have a name in mind in case the child fits it."

"Well, if it is a son, I had thought of 'Ahijah.'"

"That means 'brother of Yahweh?' How can he be brother to Yahweh?" Zedekiah laughed.

"Well, I just like the sound of it, and it could also mean 'Worshipper of Yahweh.'"

Zedekiah fell silent considering the idea of God as brother. It was difficult to think of him that way. As Master, as Lord, as King, yes, but as brother?

He looked at Ahitub, who had become his nephew when he married the widow Raquel, after the fall of Shiloh and the disastrous deaths of three members of the priestly family in one day, plus one of their wives, Ahitub's mother. He had grown to be a man, having long ago shouldered the responsibilities of the priesthood at the new religious center at Nob of Benjamin, now starting a family of his own with a young wife.

Ahijah. The name did roll off the tongue.

Then Raquel called from within the house: "Ahitub's son is born!"

Zedekiah and Ahitub jumped up to go and see how mother and child were doing.

❦ 50 ❦

Throughout the past several years, Jeriah had worked with his father in the smith shop. Together they became sought-after artisans in the making of bronze implements. Azel had begun his apprenticeship as well, and was showing great promise.

The battle of Mizpah ended the Philistine occupation that had prevented Eldad from making knives even for eating and preparing food, much less weapons. Now Jeriah and Eldad worked to perfect an iron sword which would be the equal those produced by the Philistines.

The only problem was, they had little iron. Mining operations within the territories controlled by the Israelite tribes were almost nonexistent. They were hunters, shepherds and farmers; the technologies of mining and the discovery of metallic ore deposits were foreign to them. The best Jeriah and Eldad could do was to trade for iron to use in making tools, farm implements and weapons.

But iron was expensive. Many times its weight in copper, tin or other soft metals was required to trade for it. It was on a trading trip to find iron that Jeriah's life was changed.

Accompanied by his brother Azel, he travelled north from Mizpah, along the watershed ridge which ran parallel to the Jordan River to the East, to Bethel. The mountain country was beautiful and at places they could see for many miles both east and west. This was the place where Israel himself had a vision of a ladder to heaven. "Beth-el" meant "House of God" and Jeriah thought the name fitting for this high sanctuary. Having some good fortune there in finding some hoarded iron tools for sale in the marketplace, he and Azel then went west to Upper Beth-Horon. While he would find no iron, he did find something of value.

They came into view of the little town, leading a pack donkey, along the rocky trail. They went first to the marketplace to try to find iron. It was there he saw her.

At a booth selling figs, pomegranates and almonds spread on brightly colored cloths on the ground, a slender girl of about 15 sat with her mother, who was bargaining with a matronly woman over a measure of figs. The girl turned and her eyes met Jeriah's. It seemed to him the rest of the world dimmed at that moment and the sun was shining only on her.

Her eyes were shaped much like the almonds she was selling, but were much darker. Jeriah realized he was staring as she lowered her head, then looked again at her customer.

"Azel, go that way and try to find something we can buy. I will go this way," Jeriah said, gesturing in the general direction of the booth where the girl was. As Azel walked away, leading the donkey, Jeriah went to her booth.

"I desire figs," he said, and she looked up at him as her mother continued to negotiate with the older woman.

Her face was soft and brown, glowing with health and youth. She had a small Ashteroth charm on her forehead, secured by a fine bronze chain tied in her lush, black hair, only a little of which was visible in front of the linen scarf she wore on her head.

"What can you trade?" her voice was lyrical and warm.

Jeriah stood still for a moment, simply looking at her, then realized he needed to answer.

"I, uh, have bronze bowls, spoons and knives," he said removing, sample items from the leather bag slung over his shoulder. He knelt down in front of where she was sitting and handed a couple of items across the figs on the cloths so she could examine them. He watched as she ran her slender fingers along the rim of a bowl, checking its craftsmanship.

"I'm Jeriah, son of Eldad the smith of Mizpah. What is your name?"

She looked up as if startled, not expecting the question.

"I'm Shelomith. My father is Eshban, the elder. He sits at the city gate," she said, stealing a glance at him. "I will take your bowl for a kab of figs."

"Agreed," Jeriah said. Then, seeing she was surprised when he didn't haggle, said. "You have treated me fairly, Shelomith. I may wish to do business with you again."

"Thank you, sir..."

"Jeriah of Mizpah," he smiled. "May Yahweh bless you today. And your mother."

"Thank you," she said, returning his smile, causing Jeriah to falter as he tried to rise, holding the clay jar of figs which Shelomith had given him.

Jeriah then continued down the row of booths but had a hard time concentrating on looking for iron as he remembered the warmth of Shelomith's smile.

Neither Azel nor Jeriah found any iron to buy in Beth-Horon, but on their way out, Jeriah saw a couple of elders at the city gate where it was customary for citizens to have their disputes judged.

"Wait, Azel, I have business with the elders."

Azel gave him a puzzled look, but took the donkey into the shade of the wall and squatted on the ground to wait.

"I wish to speak to Eshban. Which of you is he?" Jeriah asked the two elders.

"I am Eshban. What is your business?" The man was older than Jeriah's father, and was a bit heavy.

"I am Jeriah, son of Eldad of Mizpah."

"Eldad? I know your father. He is a smith and an elder of the town."

"Yes," said Jeriah, pleased that his father was already known to Shelomith's father. "I purchased some figs from your daughter Shelomith in the market. I would like to talk to her again, if you will permit me."

"What bride price can you pay?" Eshban said.

Jeriah was surprised by the abrupt question. Apparently, her father was eager to marry Shelomith off.

"I will consult my father, but you may be sure we are a generous family."

"Hmm," answered Eshban. "We shall see. Because I know your father is honorable, you may see my daughter again if you come tomorrow, at the sixth hour. Come meet me here and I will take you to my house, where we will have the midday meal. Agreed?"

"Agreed. Yes. Thank you."

With that, Eshban turned away to other concerns and Jeriah understood he was dismissed.

51

Shelomith turned out to be more difficult to talk to than Jeriah had imagined, although it may have just been because they were sitting in her home with Eshban, both of his wives and the other six children. All six were younger and displayed attitudes ranging from being in awe of Jeriah to whispered, mischievous ridicule.

Shelomith's mother, wife number one, had been with her at the market. She was outwardly stoic, but Jeriah could see that she was proud of her daughter and maybe a little impressed with him. Eshban on the other hand was opaque and preferred the occasional question about Eldad's business to anything more personal.

They all sat in the middle of the stone house on woven mats around a central fire pit, eating the midday meal prepared by Shelomith and her mother.

"Shelomith, where do you get what you sell in the market?" Jeriah asked, trying to get her to open up.

"We have a field in the valley over there," she said gesturing to the west. "We have several healthy sycamore and pomegranate trees there."

"The figs are very good," Jeriah replied, woodenly. He hated the sound of his own voice at that moment.

"The field has always produced well," Shelomith's father put in, just before filling his mouth with boiled mutton and following it with wine from a clay jar.

Jeriah would see Shelomith twice more, but she was mostly behind her mother or father and Jeriah talked to her father about business and farming and the bride price.

Finally, the day came when Jeriah told Eshban his offer for Shelomith. Her father considered the amount Jeriah had named as his bride price only briefly before agreeing to it. Jeriah was a little surprised, because he would have paid much more, if only he had it to pay. But Eshban agreed and gave permission for Jeriah to marry Shelomith, at the end of the engagement period established by the couple's fathers.

Finally the day came. Jeriah paid the bride price, and his family went to Beth-Horon for a celebration for the union.

When the celebration of the two families ended, Jeriah carried Shelomith's meager belongings out of her house and arranged them on his donkey, the weight evenly distributed. Shelomith said goodbye to her family, her father only slightly less stoic than usual and her mother weeping tears of joy to see her oldest daughter begin her new life. Then joined Jeriah and, as he led the donkey away, Shelomith turned and waved to her family. When they were out of site, she smiled and slipped her hand into Jeriah's and laid her head on his shoulder as they walked along.

He couldn't think of anything better in his whole life.

And finally, alone on the road, they were able to talk, and Shelomith proved to have a lot to say.

When they arrived at Mizpah, Jeriah took Shelomith to his family compound and his apartment that now he and Shelomith would make their own.

At twilight, the family ate the evening meal and, afterward, Jeriah took Shelomith to their apartment where she went before him to the bed chamber. She finally called Jeriah to come to her. He entered the room, where she stood naked in the light of a single candle. After a moment of rapture seeing her full beauty for the first time and the sweet aroma of sweet-smelling oil, Jeriah took her to his bed and thus, they were married.

❧ 52 ❧

Gibeath ha-Elohim is certainly a backwoods town; even more so than Mizpah was.

Clamatos realized commanding the garrison would be difficult, since here in the highlands, chariots were useless and horses had trouble finding sure footing. That had been part of the problem in the defeat in Mizpah; their chariots mired in the mud and their horses slipped on rain-soaked stones. That, and the fact that the forest prevented the formation of a proper battle line.

Still, a year later, Clamatos was mystified by what had happened there, when the Hebrews had driven the Palusata from Mizpah. The Hebrews didn't even have weapons; at least not legal weapons. And yet they had routed a thousand elite professional soldiers from Gath. So spooked were his superiors by the experience that they had not gone back.

The storm and the outcome of the battle seemed to be more than met the eye; almost supernatural, though that made no sense, because most of the Hebrews were virtually atheists, only believing in one god. Ordinarily, his people would have returned with a much greater force and destroyed the town after such an uprising, but everyone seemed to want to forget it.

So, they had sent him to Gibeath instead and he supposed the people of Mizpah did as they pleased, ignoring the taxes.

Clamatos was a professional soldier, so he went where he was ordered, and would never complain aloud, except perhaps after several jars of beer with a Canaanite woman from one of the shrines which still survived at places like nearby Jebus.

The Hebrews were inconsistent about it, but periodically they instituted persecution of the local religions. In the local languages, this town's name, Gibeath ha-Elohim, meant "hill of the gods," though Clamatos was uncertain which gods the founders intended.

It had been three hundred years since the Hebrews had invaded and caused such havoc that the petty monarchs of all the towns from Hazor to Lachish pleaded with their lords in Egypt to help them. But the Pharaoh had not forgotten what the Hebrews had done to them as well, and Canaan was left to the ravages of the invaders.

Of course, Clamatos' own Palusata had been repulsed by Egypt a hundred years later and had invaded the southern coastline of this land, finally settling on the fertile plain by the Sea, displacing the people who lived in the Five Towns, known to the Canaanites and the Hebrews as Philistines. They now called Clamatos' Sea People Philistines as well, although he knew that their heritage lay far across the Great Sea.

At least this place was quiet. He knew of no meddlesome prophets here to stir up insurrection.

Clamatos commanded a larger garrison of soldiers than he had in Mizpah, so he was more of a bureaucrat now, with responsibilities beyond collection of taxes and policing the population, extending to overseeing infrastructure projects. That meant conscripting slaves to quarry and cut stone for buildings. His first project was to finish the barracks that had been started by his predecessor. The large, fortified building would house his troops and serve as his own headquarters.

Within a year, the love of Jeriah and Shelomith produced a son, whom they named Misha'el. With the passing of another year Misha'el was walking and into everything, his curiosity never satisfied. Jeriah was a proud father, indeed, but Eldad and Hadassah were just as proud to see that their legacy would be carried forward.

As he grew up, Misha'el would learn the smith's trade as Jeriah taught him all that he had learned from his own father. Together they would prosper, Jeriah believed, imagining the future, as they built a reputation for honest dealing and quality workmanship.

When Misha'el was two years old, Shelomith told Jeriah that she was again going to have a child. The whole family was excited that there would soon be another baby in the house, since Misha'el was no longer a baby at all.

A few months later, a baby girl was born and Shelomith declared her name should be Zaina, for what mother doesn't want her daughter to be lovely? Jeriah thought it was a perfect name; he didn't think any baby could be prettier.

Eldad and Hadassah doted on Zaina, because she was the first daughter to be born in their family in three generations.

Samuel rose from his knees and drew his grey, mohair cloak about him against the early morning chill. He daily spent time in prayer; it was the source of his strength and spiritual insight. He had always had a genuine, close connection to the one true God and had often heard His voice. Sometimes it was actually audible. Other times it was merely an impression, but a clear impression, to be sure. Today, he was surprised by the word he received.

Internally he had argued with Yahweh, which was rare, but this word was surprising and not a little distressing. He did not often feel like resisting God's will, but he was thoroughly conflicted about this.

Nonetheless, after taking a crust of bread from the cutting board and kissing his wife, he left by the front door, descended the stone stairs of his modest home and trudged up the dusty path toward the altar.

He was joined halfway by Jabal, his faithful student and helping hand, now well into his thirties.

"Come with me. I have a word from the Lord."

"Yes, Master," said Jabal with a quizzical look.

The impression Samuel had received today concerned a man who would be coming to see him. He began walking toward the city gate, trusting that God would let him know who the man was when the time came.

❧ 53 ❧

Donkeys were grazing in the valley under the leafy bows of the gnarled olive trees, but the men on the ridge could not see them. They continued walking the other way.

"How long are we to search for them?" asked the shorter of the two.

"I cannot disappoint my father," said the other, his voice heavy with concern.

"But soon your father will be more worried about you than the donkeys, lord."

They continued walking, getting farther and farther from home with each step. It was the second morning of searching for the valuable pack animals.

Kish, father of the taller man, was an elder of the tribe of Benjamin and a farmer of some note. He counted on these animals and although his lanky son was married and had children of his own, the old, wealthy farmer was the patriarch of his branch of the tiny clan and he didn't allow anyone to forget it.

As the men continued to put distance between themselves and their home in Gibeath ha-Elohim, they began to despair of ever finding the animals. Then the tall one had an idea.

"We are near Ramah. The man of God lives there."

"And he will be sacrificing," his servant added. "He can tell us where they are."

"But we have nothing to offer the man of God. Our food is gone." Indeed, their stomachs confirmed the fact the journey had been ill planned, but it was customary to offer a gift.

"I have a small silver piece," replied the loyal servant, fingering the square ingot, worth about three hours' wages. "Let us offer it to the seer."

Samuel sat on the flat rock by the large sycamore that marked the entrance to Ramah of Ephraim as people came and went on their various errands. He had sent Jabal on to the place of sacrifice to get things ready for today's worship.

God had only told him that the man he was to meet was of the tribe of Benjamin and he would be tall. He had only been sitting for a few minutes when he saw him.

Immediately he had the familiar impression of God telling him this was the one. There were perhaps 20 people on the road going and coming into Ramah, but this man stood out. He was taller than any of them. His head was well above the heads of all the other men.

Standing from his resting place on the rock, Samuel stood waiting as the man approached. He was a striking man, whose face had a noble look to it. His beard was dark and lush, showing evidence of grooming, though he had obviously been travelling for some time. He wore a wool cloak, died red, over a white linen tunic, turned gray on the hem with the dust of many miles. His gait was surprisingly graceful for such a tall man. His eyes met Samuel's.

"Sir, I am looking for the prophet. Could you tell me where the seer's house is?"

"I am the prophet," Samuel began, "go on ahead to the place of sacrifice. You will eat with me today and, in the morning, I will tell you all that is in your heart."

Then inspiration hit him again. "Oh, and Saul son of Kish, do not worry about the donkeys you have searched for the past three days. They have been found."

Saul's eyes grew wide.

❧ 54 ❧

There were perhaps 50 men seated at tables under goat-hair tents a short distance from the altar. This noon communal meal was a customary part of the weekly worship ritual, which had just ended. They spoke in hushed tones over their roast lamb and leeks, as they glanced furtively at the imposing stranger sitting cross-legged on the rug at Samuel's table.

Samuel watched Saul closely as they talked. The man certainly was striking. The people would probably be pleased with him. Samuel did not know his family, even though Gibeath was not that far from Ramah. Samuel rarely went that way, because he knew he could encounter soldiers from the Philistine garrison there. He suspected that some of them might know that he was behind their defeat at Mizpah. It would not be difficult to find it out.

Samuel could see why God had brought Saul to him. He appeared to be about 30 years old and his demeanor was humble, almost shy. It seemed he was a sincere worshipper of Yahweh and the seeds of leadership were definitely in him.

"Jabal, please fetch my horn of holy oil," Samuel asked his apprentice as the meal drew to a close. "I will walk a while with Saul as he begins his journey home."

Jabal was up and out of the tent and back in no time at all with a small, hollow bull's horn, closed on one end and stopped with a wooden plug on the other. Samuel took the horn by the leather thong attached to each end and hung it from his belt, saying no more about it.

"That will be all today, Jabal," Samuel said. "Thank you for your faithfulness."

Jabal bowed slightly to Samuel and to Saul and his servant, then turned and began walking toward his home.

Samuel, Saul and his servant walked toward the road out of town to the south, passing the flat rock and into the hill country which Samuel knew so well. When they had gone perhaps two miles and Ramah was long since obscured by the hills and trees, Samuel turned and spoke.

"You may go on," he said to Saul's servant. "Your master and I have business to discuss."

When the curious but obedient servant passed beyond a bend in the road, Samuel turned to Saul.

"I have brought you out here away from the prying eyes of Israel and hopefully from the spying eyes of the Philistines and their sympathizers," he began. "The Lord has shown me much concerning you today."

"Concerning me?"

"Yes. He has shown me that Israel is to have a king."

Saul's eyes widened in confusion.

"You are to be Israel's king," Samuel said, directly.

"But, sir, I am the least of all Israel, of the least of the clans from the least of all the tribes of Israel," Saul protested, his voice shaking. "I, I cannot! God would not..."

"Yahweh's ways are not our ways. He will choose whom he will to be king, and He has chosen you," Samuel said, without betraying how distasteful it was to say what he had been given to say. "Now kneel before me, Saul son of Kish. You who are the least in Israel shall be the greatest."

Saul obediently knelt and Samuel took the horn from his belt and, removing the wooden plug, he poured fragrant olive oil onto the top of Saul's bowed head, where it ran in shiny streams down his sunburned forehead and temples.

"This oil is God's Spirit. Has he not anointed you with power to lead His people?

"Today you will see God's power," Samuel continued. "When you leave me, you will encounter two men at Rachel's tomb near the border of Benjamin. They will tell you the donkeys have been found and now your father worries about you, saying 'What shall I do about my son?'

"Then you will reach the great tree of Tabor, where you will meet three men going to worship God at Bethel: one will have three young goats, another three loaves of bread, and the third a full wineskin. They will give you two loaves of bread, which you will accept.

"Next, when you are approaching Gibeath ha-Elohim, you will meet prophets in procession on the road from the high place. They will be prophesying with musicians preceding them playing lyres, tambourines, flutes and harps.

"Then the Spirit of the Lord will powerfully come upon you also, and you will join them in prophesying. You will never be the same, for you will then be empowered to do what God would have you do as king."

The prophet paused.

"But do not act unless I have given you what the Lord has given me."

Saul arose after his anointing, his mind reeling from what Samuel had done and said. They said goodbye and Saul started down the road south the short distance toward his home in Gibeath.

Almost immediately he met the two men, whom he recognized as herdsmen of his father's cattle.

"Saul, so glad to have found you!" one of them said. "The lost donkeys are found and now your father worries about you, saying, 'What can I do to find my son?'"

"I'm going home now, so he shouldn't worry," Saul answered, remembering what Samuel had said.

The first sign has been fulfilled.

The two men, having delivered the message from Saul's father, now walked with him. Just ahead, Saul could see the Terebinth of Tabor. Would Samuel's prediction prove true again? Saul did not see anyone on the road yet.

Then, around the curve in the road, a goat came, then another, then the rest of the flock, followed by a man driving them. Behind him came a man with a bag slung over his shoulder and a third man carrying a wineskin.

The second man saw Saul and ran up to him.

"I am to give you these for your journey," he said, taking two loaves of bread from the bag and holding them out for Saul to take, which he did.

For a moment he couldn't speak, then finally said, "Thank you" and the three men continued on their way.

These signs have been fulfilled just as Samuel had said they would be!

That meant he was indeed to be anointed with God's Spirit to lead Israel. There was one more sign to be fulfilled.

He was nearing home now, where Samuel said he would meet a company of prophets. The sun was now low in the west and the shadows were long.

He heard them before he saw them. Music floating through the air; the sound of plucked strings, smooth notes of a flute and the clink-clink of tambourines. He saw women first, in flowing robes, dancing on the road and rhythmically hitting tambourines. Then came the prophets and the musicians walking and playing the flutes and lyres.

As Saul watched them approach, Saul felt something come over him like he had never felt before. Suddenly he began to speak words he was not intentionally saying.

"The Lord is great and greatly to be praised!

"Let us worship the Lord on his throne, for
He is the King of heaven.

"The Lord will fight for his people and make
them victorious.

"The Lord will smite their enemies
and bring them low."

For some time, Saul prophesied as the prophets also praised and prophesied. Finally, Saul fell silent and the prophets also stopped.

"What has happened to the son of Kish? Is he now a prophet?" one of the herdsmen asked the other as they were about to continue toward home.

❧ 55 ☙

Now that Mizpah was free of its Philistine oppressors, Samuel's gatherings grew larger as Israelites from many of the tribes gathered there to worship. When they came together, the household of Eldad invariably offered hospitality to Hadassah's kinsmen from the villages of Judah to the south.

"You should say something, Eldad," asserted Hadassah's second cousin as the men sat on the rooftop after the evening meal provided by Hadassah. "You are a chief elder now, and there is talk throughout the land."

Jeriah, now a man of 24, listened for his father's answer.

"But we as children of Israel have never had a king," Eldad argued. "We are ruled by Yahweh."

"And we would still be ruled by Yahweh, because a king would have to listen to the prophets. But a king would be able to defend us against our enemies. Why did Yahweh allow the Ark to be taken by the Philistines?"

"Would a king raise a standing army?" Jeriah broke in.

"Of course, cousin," the man said. "It is too much to expect shepherds and shopkeepers to defend our borders. Even now, Philistines are in our midst at Gibeath ha-Elohim."

"And the Canaanites pollute our people with their sacrilege," admitted Eldad.

"Exactly," the kinsman agreed. "A king would drive out the wicked Amorites and Hittites, as well as the Philistines."

"I will talk to the other elders at the festival," Eldad said. "I'm sure the topic will come up."

Jeriah sat quietly alongside his father.

A professional army in Israel? It was an intriguing idea.

❧

Thousands were gathering into the small town of Mizpah. The surrounding hills were already dotted with tents, because there were only a few inns in the town, so most of the worshippers brought their accommodations with them on the backs of donkeys. White smoke from hundreds of cookfires rose into the sky as the sun slowly descended to its evening destination.

Samuel had arrived in Mizpah two days before the festival would officially begin. Though both prophet and priest, he did not personally perform priestly rituals anymore, except offering sacrifices at his weekly gatherings. The duties of the Lord's Tent in Nob were now performed by Ahitub, even though the Ark was still not there.

Samuel was seen as the de facto leader of the fragile nation, if it could even be called a nation. The tribes from east of the Jordan River, Reuben, Gad, and half the tribe of Manasseh, were represented in the growing encampment, but at times they had been seen as foreign by those on the west side of the river. And more concerning to Samuel was the ill-concealed feeling by members of the tribe of Judah that their great numbers and walled cities like Hebron and Lachish somehow made them superior to the others.

To make these unruly clans unite in the worship of Yahweh was Samuel's passion, but there were so many obstacles. Some of these very people gathering here would go home and burn incense before their home shrines to El, Baal, Dagon, Astarte and many other gods and goddesses of the Canaanites and Philistines.

Such two-faced apostasy led to the battle of Eben-ezer and the oppression that followed, Samuel thought bitterly.

Samuel sensed he was being watched, so he turned and saw a small group of men turn from looking at him to looking at one another again. He wondered what it meant.

❧

The households of Kish and Ner, the sons of the late Abiel of Benjamin, traveled together from their home in Gibeath ha-Elohim. They, with thousands of others, were going to Mizpah to sacrifice to Yahweh as Samuel had requested.

"What bothers you, cousin?" asked Abner, Ner's son.

"What makes you think something is bothering me?" Saul retorted with an irritated tone.

"You haven't spoken two words this entire trip," Abner replied, shifting his weight on his donkey's back. "Your mind seem to be elsewhere."

"What of it? I have growing responsibilities," Saul said. "Perhaps you should look to your own."

"I hardly think the weight of the world is on your shoulders. Yes, you will someday inherit your father's household, as will I mine, but today we should rejoice. We go to the feast!"

"We go to sacrifice," was Saul's answer, and he gestured to the sheep their children were driving along. Saul's oldest, Jonathan, was his pride; a strong, dashing young man. He stood tall like Saul himself as he walked along, driving the sheep before him.

He will be king after me!

It was the first time a thought of the kingship had brought him joy.

The weight of his secret pressed on him, for Samuel had made him promise not to tell anyone he had been anointed with the holy oil. But soon all Israel would know that he was the chosen one.

Saul's two other boys were Ishvi, who preferred to be called Abinidab, and Malchishua, the youngest of his sons, and as fearless as he could be foolish. Saul's wife carried the baby, a girl named Merab.

⚜ 56 ⚜

Eldad made good on his word to speak to the other elders as they arrived in Mizpah about the need for Israel to have a king, but he needn't have made the effort. It was the topic uppermost on everyone's mind. The battle at Mizpah that had displaced the Philistines from the area convinced everyone that what was needed was a strong government, similar to the nations which lay round about the 12 tribes and periodically threatened them.

Eldad and the other elders of the tribe of Benjamin stood together near the front of the crowd, along with the elders from the other tribes. The families of their tribe stood behind them as they waited for Samuel to begin.

On arriving in Mizpah to prepare for the assembly, Samuel had encountered requests and even demands that he appoint a king at almost every turn, but he couldn't share what the Lord had made him do in anointing Saul. Now he had to go through the motions of a public selection of a king, though God had already chosen him.

He didn't fully understand why Yahweh had told him to anoint a king. He had done everything he could to unite the confederacy of tribes around the worship of Yahweh, but to now give in to the people's desire for a human king highlighted Samuel's failure.

After the people gathered and the rituals were completed, Samuel called the assembly together to address the issue that was on everyone's mind. The people stood expectantly before the altar, where Samuel stood leaning on his staff, his long gray beard blowing in the breeze.

Gary L. Ivey

"You have asked for a king," Samuel began in a strong voice that could be heard throughout the crowd. "But you do not know what you are asking for. A king will take your sons for his army and your flocks for his table. He will even take your daughters for his harem and your gold for his palaces."

Eldad looked at the elders to his right and left and saw frowns on all their faces. He looked at the altar once again. Samuel continued to recite a litany of woes that would come to Israel with the creation of a monarchy. Finally, Samuel concluded his speech with a surprising statement.

"However, God told me that in asking for a king, you are rejecting Him, not me, and I am to give you what you ask."

For a moment the crowd was silent, then as the meaning of Samuel's words sank in, a cheer erupted.

Samuel motioned for the Elders to come forward and join him on the platform around the altar. At his instruction, each tribe selected one representative to cast lots to determine who would become Israel's king. To his surprise, Eldad was selected by the elders of Benjamin to represent the tribe.

It was an involved process, requiring that each of the tribes be eliminated by the casting of lots. Representatives from two tribes at a time stood before Samuel, who held a flat stone in his hand, on which was inscribed an Alef, the first letter of the Hebrew alphabet, on one side and a Bet on the other side. The representative of one of the tribes was to call Alef or Bet, then Samuel would cast the stone to the platform and how the stone landed would determine which tribe went forward.

One by one, tribes were eliminated. Dan was eliminated, then Reuben, then Ephraim, then Judah. There was a collective mumbling from that tribe's delegation, and Eldad knew that there were many in Judah who assumed God would choose a king from their midst.

Gad, Simeon and Manassah fell next and the casting of lots continued, with Benjamin surviving several one-on-one lots. Finally only Naphtali and Benjamin remained.

Eldad looked on nervously as Samuel cast the lot between them. It was in favor of Benjamin! The elder from Naphtali descended the steps, leaving Eldad and Samuel on the platform.

"Yahweh has chosen the tribe of Benjamin from which to draw his king," Samuel proclaimed, and Eldad thought he saw Samuel wink at him. "Blessed be the name of the Lord."

"Blessed be the name of the Lord," came the answer.

"Now we will cast lots for the clans of Benjamin," Samuel told Eldad. "Let the elders of Benjamin come forward!"

Eldad's fellow elders climbed the stone steps to join Eldad at the altar as the rest of the Israelites looked on. The process of casting lots began again, this time with two clans at a time casting, one of which was eliminated. One by one the elders representing various clans walked back down the stairs to join the people after their clan was eliminated. Eldad's clan was eliminated early and he descended the stairs to stand with the rest of the elders. The last clan left standing was the clan of Matri.

Saul could take no more. Matri was his own clan. He had thought perhaps he still might escape the responsibility of kingship through the process of the lots, but it was clear that the hand of God was in it and Samuel's word would be proven true. In a sudden fit of panic, he mumbled something to his silver-haired father and hurried through the crowd.

When he was free of the throng, he ran to find a place where he could be alone to think. In the middle of the camp was a compound where pack animals and the excess baggage of the encampment was kept. He bent low and slipped under the rope which defined the space and threaded his way through the stacks of goods the thousands of people had brought with them. He found a wooden crate and sat down, cradling his head in his hands.

I didn't ask for this.

He couldn't imagine what God saw in him that He would choose him out of all the distinguished men of Israel.

I can't take the pressure.

He hadn't been there too long when Abner rounded a corner and stood before him.

"My cousin, why do you hide here among the baggage?" Abner asked, watching Saul's reaction closely. "Did you already know the lot was for you?"

Saul raised his head with a look that must have betrayed his thoughts, for Abner immediately knelt to the ground.

"My king!" Abner bowed his head as he knelt. He was not as tall as Saul – nobody was – but he nearly prostrated himself for a moment, which surprised Saul, for he had never known his cousin to defer to him in anything.

"Samuel seeks you," Abner said, finally rising. "You must go to him. All Israel seeks you now."

Saul paused a moment before standing.

"Let us go and see what God will do."

❦ 57 ❦

Jeriah felt bad for Samuel.

He had been watching the drawing of lots, standing beside his father. The final lot had fallen on the household of Kish of Benjamin, specifically on his son, Saul. Yet, when Saul was called for, he was nowhere to be found. There had been commotion around the altar and finally Samuel had whispered something to the elderly man Jeriah guessed was Kish. Kish had then spoken to a younger kinsman who immediately ran off.

For several minutes the men of Israel had simply stood in their places before the altar of Mizpah, not knowing what else to do.

"Father, do you know this Saul, son of Kish?" Jeriah asked.

"No son," said Eldad, "The name is not known to me."

That was somewhat surprising, since as an elder of the tribe, Eldad had met most of the influential Benjamites; and it was the smallest tribe, after all.

Presently the man Kish had sent away returned, and with him was apparently the man Saul, the man who would be Israel's first king.

Jeriah watched him as he approached the steps before the altar. All the people watched silently with growing anticipation. As Saul climbed up the stairs and turned to face the crowd, a spontaneous cheer erupted; partly because the people were glad to be getting a king, but mostly because the man before them truly had a kingly bearing. Indeed he towered over Samuel.

"Do you see, O Israel, your king!" Samuel exclaimed. "There is no one like him in Israel!"

"Long live the king!" the people shouted.

"Long live King Saul!"

From his vantage point at the front of the crowd and the honored place for the tribe of Benjamin, Jeriah thought he saw a brief look of fear pass over Saul's – King Saul's – face before he smiled a big, disarming smile and raised his fist, eliciting another cheer from the crowd.

Sixteen-year-old Jonathan watched in amazement as his father, his own father, was declared to be king of all Israel right then and there. The lots had fallen surely on his clan, so it appeared now his father's house would lead all Israel. Jonathan was not even sure what this would mean, since Israel had never had a king. He knew of kings of other nations which surrounded them, but had not observed them enough to know how a king's son should behave.

As the men of Israel continued to rejoice and cheer, Samuel invited the entire households of Kish and Ner, sons of Abiel, of the clan of Matri, to stand on the platform with Saul. Climbing the hewn stone stairs, Jonathan felt a bit foolish, so he waved to the crowd, which made them cheer louder, and he felt even more sheepish.

Some in the crowd were not cheering, however.

"Can we do no better than this Benjamite bumpkin?" loudly complained Othnal, elder of Hebron in Judah, to his fellow elders from that tribe, after the coronation ceremony had ended and the crowd was dispersing. "Are there no champions in all of mighty Judah that could lead us?"

"What does this Saul have to recommend him, besides the fact that he is unnaturally tall?" asked another elder.

"Are we really going to be ruled by this fellow?" chimed in another elder from Judah.

"Are there no prophets in Judah to anoint a proper king?" Othnal groused.

"Do you not fear the Lord?"

The question came from an elder from another tribe. Othnal didn't know him.

"The identity of the king was decided by sacred lot," the man continued. "I should think that would mean something."

He stalked away and Othnal frowned as the elders of Judah broke up and went to break camp before returning to their homes.

This is not how the king should have been chosen, Othnal thought bitterly.

Gary L. Ivey

❦ 58 ❦

Achim Ben-Hasem stood upon the city wall looking into the distant haze on the eastern horizon. The city stood at the edge of the high plateau of Gilead, where some of the best pasture land in Israel stretched up and away from the Jordan River to the east, second only to Bashan to the north. Beyond the fertile plateau to the east and south, the terrain became desert which stretched for thousands of miles.

Achim wore a brightly colored cloak with a bronze clasp that identified him as an elder of the city of Jabesh Gilead of the eastern half tribe of the tribe of Manasseh. He was Jabesh's youngest elder. Achim swelled with pride as he strode along the wall. Jabesh was one of few fortified cities east of the Jordan that the Israelites could call their own. Indeed it was the Jewel of Gilead, standing high as it did above the Jordan valley.

Behind him the bleating of sheep and the hawking of merchants filled the air above the market where goods from distant Persia to the East and as far away as Tarshish in the West were bartered and sold after arriving on the backs of camels, donkeys and slaves.

The Jordan River made a bright line of demarcation between the three tribes east of its banks — Gad, Reuben and the eastern half of Manasseh — and the rest of Israel. There was a ford just below the Sea of Chinnereth, but during the spring it was often too deep and treacherous to be able to pass. So the trans-Jordanian tribes went their own way in terms of clothing styles, dialect and culture. The other tribes occasionally questioned their loyalty to Yahweh, but while it was difficult for them to travel to some of the feasts, their devotion was no less. They took pride that their inheritance was given to them by Moses himself, instead of Joshua like the other tribes.

Then something on the Mahanaim road caught Achim's eye. An obviously exhausted young man was running as fast as his spent legs would take him toward the city gate. As he ran, Achim could see he was turning and shouting something to the men and women working in the barley fields at the side of the road. As soon as the people understood what he was saying they dropped their tools and began running like startled cockroaches from under an upturned urn. Finally Achim understood a name in what the man was saying.

Nahash.

It was the name of the king of Rabbah, the Ammonite capital to the south and east, on the edge of the Great Desert. For weeks they had heard rumors that Nahash was moving with a vast army. Now perhaps the threat had reached Jabesh Gilead. Achim looked to the horizon beyond the Mahanaim road and did indeed see a distant cloud of dust, confirming his worst fears.

He ran down the mud-brick stairs from the top of the wall just in time to see the young man enter the gate and fall to the ground in front of the first man he encountered. After a few short words from the exhausted runner, the man turned and sounded the alarm.

"The army of Ammon is upon us!"

Immediately all those within earshot began running in all directions, women shrieking and men calling out, repeating the warning as they hurried toward their homes. Before many minutes had passed, people who lived in the surrounding hills began crowding into the city, carrying as much of their valuables as they could and making their way to the marketplace, where they would pause until they could find lodging.

Achim found himself swept along by the crowd as he made his way home to check on his wife and young son.

"Achim, what is happening?" exclaimed his wife when he arrived, holding their son close.

"The Ammonites are marching."

"They're coming here?"

"It appears so. I have to go meet with the other elders of the city. Stay here. I'll be back soon."

Achim gave each of them a hurried kiss and left to make his way back to the marketplace, where he was certain he would find the rest of the elders.

Panic had thoroughly taken over the city of Jabesh since the dust cloud appeared on the horizon. Now the ranks of soldiers could be seen descending the Manahaim Road, their banners flying and a corps of men riding camels, which seemed to augment the fear in the town's population even more than the infantry.

Achim arrived in the marketplace in time to see a heated argument between Ezer, who sold beef in the market, and a man Achim didn't know.

"I and my family will not stay, only to starve in a siege!" Ezer exclaimed, gripping the reins of the family donkey. "We will go to my uncle in Bashan."

"It's too dangerous!" the man argued. "You and your family won't survive."

"We go to Bashan!" Ezer insisted and he pulled the reins on the donkey which was packed with hastily assembled belongings. "Come, family!"

Two wives and eight children of varying ages followed, their eyes wide and several with tears flowing.

Achim followed as they made their way to the gate of the city. There, others who had also apparently decided to flee joined them and they formed a small caravan which slowly made its way out of the gate and turned north. Achim bounded up the stairs to the top of the wall to watch the slowly moving band of refugees attempt to escape the Ammonites' advance.

"Close the gates!" cried Zedeq, the top-ranking elder of the city. Achim and the other elders were together on the east wall looking toward the approaching army with growing dread. Three guards rushed down the nearest steps to execute the order.

Achim looked again at the small caravan, now cresting a rise on the road to Bashan. Suddenly, riders came out of a nearby stand of trees, coming toward the refugees with their camels at full gallop. The little band saw them and ran screaming in all directions.

Helplessly, Achim and the others watched as the Ammonites cut down their fellow citizens; some being slashed with long, curved swords, some being trampled by the camels. All were eventually dead: men, women, and children. The terrifying warriors from the East even killed their donkeys.

Jabesh was a walled city but really had only a small formal militia to guard the walls. The militia members were scattered thinly on the wall, armed with everything available from their arsenal, nervously watching the approaching mass of fighting men. They were being joined by the merchants and shopkeepers of the town, each carrying whatever weapons they had.

Now we will either be overrun or suffer through a siege, Achim thought.

As night fell, the army of Ammon drew up just out of bowshot and began to set up rows of tents facing the eastern and southern walls of the city. Scouts and skirmishers remained to the north and west toward the Jordan, marauding over the scattered, now deserted farm houses.

"Riders coming!" someone on the wall shouted. This caused a renewed panic as everyone searched the twilight for the attack they feared was inevitable. But only a single torch showed in the near-darkness, revealing just three horsemen approaching the Manahaim gate.

"Men of Gilead!" began the spokesman in a Canaanite dialect known to the Israelites. He wore an oddly shaped headdress with a sun medallion. "The great and gracious Nahash of Ammon sends greetings and informs you that you do not need to die. You need only surrender and submit to Ammonite rule. Your men will each have your right eyes gouged out as surety of your continued loyalty."

A collective gasp went up from all those on the wall.

"Who brings this challenge?" Zedeq shouted in the Canaanite tongue.

"I am the mighty Heshak, Captain of the host of Ammon. Do you see this host? It will overrun you and kill you and your sons and ravage your women. Your cattle we will take to add to our wealth. Only surrender to avoid this fate."

On the wall, the elders huddled, knowing their situation was desperate.

"What are we to answer?" one nervous elder asked.

"What CAN we answer?" asked another bitterly. "To defy is certain death and to agree is to be maimed."

"Unless," Achim said, "we can get word to the rest of Israel to come and help us. Israel has a king now."

He and the other elders had been in Mizpah for the casting of lots, so they knew the identity of the new king.

"But the Ammonites are already here. It will take days before anyone, even the king, could come to help."

"So, let us ask for time," Achim answered.

"Why would Nahash give us time?" Zedeq asked his youngest elder.

"The Captain has spoken of Nahash's benevolence in offering to let us live after our eyes are gouged out. Let us test his benevolence, and while we wait, let us send messengers across the Jordan to appeal to our brothers to help us."

"The same tribes that once massacred us?" the oldest of their number reminded them.

The bitter elder did not need to remind his fellows how the rest of Israel attacked Jabesh because the city had failed

178

to fight in the civil war against the Benjamites in the days of their grandparents. After decimating the tribe of Benjamin, an army of 12,000 Israelites attacked Jabesh and killed the men, taking their daughters as brides for the men of Benjamin so the tribe would not be completely wiped out.

Zedeq was obviously unhappy to have that horrible history recalled at such a time as this.

"Still, if no one comes to help within the time allotted, we will be no worse off than now." Zedeq said. "Agreed?"

The elders looked at one another desperately and most of them nodded. Zedeq turned and looked toward the torch in the gathering darkness.

"We appeal to the manifest patience and benevolence of our Lord Nahash," he shouted, "that we be allowed one week to send messengers throughout Israel for someone to help us. If no one comes to help, we will surrender to you. Will the gracious Nahash grant this request?"

After a brief pause, the answer came: "I shall propose this to the great Nahash. You shall have the answer tomorrow."

At that, Zedeq looked at Achim: "Send your messengers. Choose them well. They must be cunning and swift, and persuasive as well when they arrive."

"Yes, lord," Achim said and he hurried away, already beginning to compile a list of those he might call upon for this vital mission.

❦ 59 ❦

Heshak was amused that the dance had begun once again. In a way, he hoped the doomed rulers of Jabesh would refuse the offer of servitude after partial blinding, for it would allow their warriors to demonstrate once again their prowess in battle, the walls of the city notwithstanding. It was his part to deliver the reply to King Nahash. The king was often unpredictable, so Heshak couldn't be sure what his decision would be. He and his deputy approached and bowed low before the king.

Nahash sat on his sedan chair, which slaves had borne countless miles on this campaign after leaving the Ammonite capital in Rabbah. He wore the colorful cape of a desert chieftain and on his head was a white keffeiah with a thin band of gold which had an emerald set over his forehead. He was in his forties with gray beginning to shade his temples.

"They wish to appeal to the tribes across the Jordan? What do you suppose the tribes will say?" Nahash laughed heartily. Then with a wave of his hand, he said to Heshak, "Give them their week. What difference could it make? Our soldiers could do with the rest."

"As you wish, your majesty."

Heshak walked away with his deputy. When they were out of earshot, the young deputy spoke.

"Sir, why do we wait? We could overwhelm this insignificant river town and be on to the next tomorrow."

"My loyal aide and friend," Heshak began, "When you have lived longer you will know the value of waiting until the time is right. In his wisdom, Nahash sees that the fear inside the walls will grow as the days go by and our victory will be assured, whether the Gileadites choose to fight or submit. Not only that, but waiting will make our forces more effective. They will be rested and eager to move forward. Tonight they will rest. Tomorrow there will be feasting and games of chance and skill. The next day, impatience will begin within the ranks and by the end of the week, the men will be eager to storm the walls."

"But will the rest of Israel come to help them and we will have to fight them as well?"

"Years ago, before either of us were born, all of Israel attacked this city and killed almost everyone. There will be no one to help Jabesh."

"I bow to your experience, lord," said the deputy.

Heshak bid good night to him and went into his tent, which had been pitched for him by the king's personal contingency. He sat down heavily at the table and pulled the stopper from a jar of beer. It had been a long day.

On the other side of Jabesh, men dressed in black mohair robes emerged from a well-hidden cave opening surrounded by willow trees fed by a spring that provided water for the city. In the dark, they followed a trail they knew well through the thicket that spread from the banks of the Jordan and now hid them.

Achim watched from the mouth of the cave as the men filed by, then fell into line behind them. He had decided to accompany them to bear the message himself. They made their way quickly and silently to the river and then would follow it to the north where they would ford at Beth Shan. There they would acquire donkeys to carry them to Gibeath ha-Elohim, where they would appeal to the new king.

Whether they would survive to complete their mission, Achim could only pray. Even if they reached their destination, could an army be gathered and reach Jabesh in just a week's time? Israel had no standing army yet. Even though it was Achim's idea to send the messengers, he knew there was only a slim chance that the king would be able to respond, much less raise a large enough army to defeat the vicious Ammonites.

It was ironic, Achim remembered, that the Ammonites were distant relatives of the Israelites. Like the Moabites, the Ammonites were children of an incestuous union between Abraham's nephew Lot and his daughters. It happened after the fiery destruction of the Cities of the Plain, when his daughters thought all life had been erased from the world and the only way for humankind to survive was for them to have children by their father. So they got him so drunk he didn't know what he was doing and were each able to become pregnant. Moab was the first to be born and the second they named Ben-Ammi, whose descendants were the Ammonites besieging Jabesh.

But the one-thousand-years-ago family connection made no difference now. Their situation was desperate, so Achim and the others crossed the Jordan River to plead for help.

The events of the past few weeks had been like a dream to Saul. As he drove the team of lumbering oxen pulling the plow, he was surprised how little urgency he felt. He had been inaugurated as king of Israel, but since Israel had never really been a cohesive nation, much less had a central government, he wasn't entirely sure what form his monarchy should take.

He did know that there was still much work to be done at his home in Gibeath, however. His father had made sure he understood that. Saul might be king, but Kish was still patriarch of the clan, that was certain.

Suddenly Saul was startled to hear the sound of mourning coming from the town. He could hear the sound of women crying and men wailing. He stopped goading the oxen and began running from his field at the edge of town. He was met by nearly 50 people who were casting dirt into the air and wailing as if their hearts were breaking.

"What happened?" Saul exclaimed, "Has there been an accident?"

It took a while for him to get a coherent answer.

"Nahash the Ammonite has besieged Jabesh Gilead," answered a man dressed in black. Saul did not recognize him. "I am Achim, an elder of Jabesh. Nahash has demanded that we surrender. We are to have our right eyes gouged out and live in servitude if we submit. Else, he will kill all our men and destroy the city."

Saul looked far away as the information sunk in. Jabesh was under siege. There was a particular bond between Gibeath and Jabesh, although the memories were anything but pleasant. In the days of Saul's grandfather, the men of Gibeath had commited a crime so heinous that all of Israel had turned against them.

A Levite and his concubine had stopped for the night in the city and the woman had been gang-raped by the men of the town and left dead in the street. After her husband recovered the body, he cut it into 12 pieces and sent them by messenger to each of the tribes, demanding that they come to his aid to avenge her humiliation and death.

The civil war that followed nearly ended the line of Benjamin forever. Outnumbered as they were, the Benjamites were overrun and slaughtered. When the elders of the other tribes realized that the heritage of one of Jacob's sons might be cut off, they looked for a solution to revive the tribe. That's where Jabesh came in.

Of all the clans and all the towns of Israel, only Jabesh failed to send volunteers to fight in the civil war against Benjamin. For this, the army that had annihilated Benjamin turned north and east, to attack Jabesh, thoroughly defeating the town and killing most of their men.

To solve the problem of the survival of Benjamin's tribe, the men of Israel then took 400 young girls of Jabesh to be wives and bear children to the few surviving men and the young boys of Gibeath and the other towns of Benjamin.

Saul's grandmother was one of those young girls from Jabesh Gilead.

Gary L. Ivey

All of this came in a rush to Saul as he stood among the weeping townspeople with the emissary from Jabesh.

"Come with me!" Saul said to the puzzled crowd, and he began walking back to the field toward the pair of oxen still yoked to the plow. When he reached them he shocked the people into silence by taking a long knife from his belt, which he plunged into one of the oxen and pulled up, cutting it open. It fell with a shrill cry and Saul walked around to the other ox and killed it as well.

"I will avenge Jabesh!" Saul said, holding the bloody knife over his head. "You men will be my messengers throughout Israel! We will send them a message they cannot ignore."

With that he began butchering the oxen.

"Take a piece of ox carcass to the elders of each tribe and tell them if they do not immediately assemble an army for their tribe I will make them like these oxen, so help me God!"

The people of Gibeath who had moments earlier been wailing in grief stood in stunned silence watching Saul carve up large sections of the animals with blood dripping from his hands. Though they had known him for years, never had they seen him take command of a situation like this. Never had they seen him step out of the shadow of this father. Never had they seen him act with such singleness of purpose.

"God's Spirit is upon him," one of them said, to which the others nodded.

The chilling symbolism of cutting up the carcass and sending the parts by messenger to other tribes was not lost on them either.

❧ 60 ❧

The messengers who took the butchered oxen parts to the elders of the tribes electrified the population. The message was that all who could respond to come to the aid of Jabesh would gather in Bezek near the Jordan in two days.

When Saul arrived at Bezek, accompanied by his cousin, Abner, and several thousand men of Benjamin, they found the little town in the highlands west of the Jordan River crowded with men who had come from deep in the south of Judah and Simeon to the borders of Philistia, up through Ephraim, western Manassah and Issachar. Runners appeared periodically announcing that hastily formed armies were marching from the northern reaches of Zebulun, Naphtali, Asher, Dan and even Reuben and Eastern Manassah from the other side of the Jordan. Saul sent back word of welcome to each of them.

As they prepared to march from Bezek, there was a feeling of power in the air. The men cheered when Saul and his son, Jonathan, rode by and Saul raised his sword in answer. Every hour brought more volunteers joining with the host of Israel. Soon they were ready to march to the ford of the Jordan below Beth Shan.

Eldad, Jeriah and Azel had ridden their donkeys with the men of Benjamin. As an elder, Eldad was an officer for Mizpah. Jeriah carried the Philistine sword his father had brought back from Ebenezer and Azel was armed with a kophesh from the armory. They were proud that the king who was calling forth the volunteer army was of Benjamin.

Gary L. Ivey

The night before they were to march, Eldad was summoned to meet with Saul and the other elders, who were to be his field counselors. The general staff was rather meager and Saul relied on the elders who knew the men from their tribes to quickly form a chain of command. Two elders, Erek from Judah and Jerubel from Ephraim, were appointed commanders, second only to Saul.

Erek was from Hebron and was a big man, given to sweeping hand gestures and over-the-top storytelling. He was an ideal leader of men. Jerubel, the head elder of Bethel, was characterized more by quiet strength. No one doubted his commitment or resolve, In his own way, he also won loyalty from the men he commanded.

Under the bows of a tree, Saul and his hastily assembled staff were joined by the messengers from Jabesh Gilead.

"As near as we can tell, we number nearly 300,000," Saul began. There was a collective gasp that went around the circle. Eldad could hardly conceive of such a host.

"Our brothers from Jabesh risked their lives to bring us the information about the army of Nahash. We outnumber the Ammonites greatly, yet we are untrained and untried, and we have marched many miles to get this far."

Saul turned to the spies from Jabesh.

"You must return quickly and take this message to your brothers: 'Before the sun is hot tomorrow you will have your deliverance.' Go now, and may Yahweh go with you."

"Thank you Lord, and may Yahweh be with you all," Achim said as he and the others bowed before Saul, then filed away from the assembly and disappeared into the night.

"And now, though we have numbers on our side, we must be wise to ensure victory. The army of Nahash is well trained and equipped," Saul continued. "Here is the plan I intend to execute to ensure victory."

Eldad and the others were impressed by the decisiveness and wisdom of Saul and his strategy. Eldad again swelled with pride that Saul was from Benjamin.

Word had reached Nob almost immediately, being only three miles from Gibeah where King Saul had declared that Jabesh Gilead would be saved. Ahitub, now a man of 35 and the high priest, rode his faithful donkey to join the gathering army for the crossing of the Jordan River.

In his saddlebag was the ephod, which Zedekiah had rescued from Shiloh when he helped Ahitub, his newborn brother, Ichabod, and his aunt Raquel escape as the Philistines were destroying the city.

It was not lost on Ahitub that his father, uncle, grandfather and mother had all died because of a battle like the one he was travelling to now.

While the officers met, the men slept, but shortly after midnight, trumpets sounded and the men roused to be told they were marching.

Jeriah mounted his donkey. As the thousands of men fell in, the officers directed them into three columns, with four tribes represented in each column. Saul commanded the center column, including the men of Benjamin. Gradually the two ranking generals, following the plan Saul had outlined, led their outer columns north and south respectively, so about a mile separated the three columns when they reached the river.

Since it was harvest time, the river was shallow and could be forded at several places, unlike the spring, when the melting snows of Mt. Hermon would swell the river and make it virtually impassable.

Well before dawn, as the vast army divided into three parts, Jeriah understood Saul's strategy: They would attack the Ammonites from three directions before dawn when they would be least expecting it.

It is a good plan, Jeriah thought.

❧ 61 ❧

Scouts from the northern contingent, led by Erek of Judah, encountered the first Ammonite sentries to the north of Jabesh after crossing the river and quickly killed them. They were drunk, drowsy or asleep, so none were able to escape or even sound an alarm. The advantage of surprise was complete. From there they moved rapidly into position to attack the Ammonite camp to the east of the city. Erek was amazed at the feeling of power that riding at the head of 100,000 men gave him.

"Men of Israel, be strong and swift," Erek called as his column reached the edge of the waking Ammonite camp. The men ran forward, throwing torches against the mohair tents which ignited quickly and Ammonite soldiers came running out, having been awakened from a dead sleep, some of them with clothing burning. The Israelites cut most of them down quickly. Others escaped and began running in all directions in panic. A few turned to fight but Israel was too numerous and immediately killed them. Then the Israelites drove further into the camp.

Nearby someone cut a line that tethered the camels and soon they were stampeding through the camp, trampling soldiers and pulling down tents, sometimes pulling a burning tent along and setting fire to other tents.

Erek dismounted his donkey to help roust the occupants of one tent and killed two Ammonites who ran out of it in short order. Two more ran away in terror and confusion. Erek's armor bearer threw a spear that caught one of them in the back and he fell.

Heshak rolled over in his linen bedroll and opened one eye to see that the first gray light of dawn had just made the tent wall visible. It would be several minutes before he would need to rise. He ran his hand along the soft profile of the dark, still-sleeping, slave girl whom he had enjoyed so much the night before. She was Edomite he supposed, part of the entourage of slaves collected in their conquests who now bore their burdens, fought alongside them in some cases, and gave them pleasure in others.

Today was the last day of the week that the mighty King Nahash had given to the men of Jabesh to pray to their god for someone to come to their aid. Tomorrow Heshak would once again ride to the wall to learn their decision: whether they surrendered or fought hardly made a difference to him, since there was little doubt of victory either way.

He would spend the last idle day tending to a few clerical duties for the king and use the rest of the time drinking good Ammonite beer and watching the games of the enlisted men.

Then he heard a noise, followed by excited shouting. He opened his eyes wondering what it meant. It was much too early for the games to have begun. Nahash had given the army leave to sleep late one more day.

There was more shouting and running outside his tent. He rose, stepped over the rousing girl, and parted the tent flap to see soldiers who had obviously just rolled out of bed themselves running by, some with weapons, some without.

"What's the meaning of this?" Heshak demanded of one of the soldiers.

"We are under attack!" the breathless soldier replied.

Heshak exited his tent to get a better look at the tumult. The noise was growing and more and more men were running by, some with blood streaming from wounds. In a distant part of the camp Heshak could see smoke ascending, as if tents were burning.

"Who is attacking us?" Heshak cried.

"Israel!" was the answer from a running man.

Heshak took a moment to grasp what the man had said. Israel had no government and no army. It was hardly an idea that had any form at all except in the minds of some of the members of the loosely affiliated tribes.

How could "Israel" be attacking them? *Is Jabesh even part of Israel*, he wondered?

But there was no time to think about that. He needed to see to the welfare of the king.

Jeriah and Azel, part of Saul's contingent under the direct command of their father, rode their donkeys down a tent row in the southern part of the Ammonite camp, severing tent ropes with their swords as they went. Behind them, other men of Benjamin on foot set fire to the tents and killed the Ammonite soldiers who escaped them. They had killed or maimed hundreds now.

Suddenly Jeriah's donkey brayed and fell, throwing him over. Jeriah rolled to a stop and looked back at his mount, on the ground continuing to bray in pain, an arrow protruding from its chest. Jeriah then looked ahead and saw the naked Ammonite soldier who had shot his donkey, preparing to shoot again, aiming at him on the ground.

Then another donkey jumped over Jeriah and the rider cut down the Ammonite. It was Azel, swinging his sickle sword, first slashing through the bow and then landing a fatal blow to the neck of the Ammonite.

Azel came over as Jeriah got to his feet.

"Are you all right?" Azel shouted over the din of battle.

"Yes, I'll be fine. Go ahead. I'll continue on foot.

Azel gave him a nod and turned his mount to continue further into the camp. Jeriah picked up the Philistine sword and ran forward, continuing to chase down bewildered enemy soldiers.

❧

Heshak found total panic and confusion around the tent of the king when he arrived. The soldiers of his elite guard were trying to get him to mount a camel, but others of the general staff were arguing that he should be disguised and spirited away on foot. The king himself was apparently in denial, because he was arguing with both proposals.

But it was all moot, because the parade ground around the king's tent was suddenly full of confused Ammonite soldiers in various stages of undress, some of them lashing out at each other, inflicting wounds and death on their own comrades. Others were knocked down and trampled in the panic. It was soon impossible to move as the soldiers were coming from all directions and crowding into the square.

Heshak's panic was complete when he saw the soldiers of Israel coming behind the panicked Ammonites with bloodlust in their eyes. He looked at Nahash and saw to his dismay that he was wearing his crown. It was too late.

Saul's plan called for Jerubel to take his southern contingent to pursue the Ammonites who were fleeing into the desert. Erek and his column would mop up what was left of the eastern camp. But Saul and his troops had captured the Ammonite king and he would now deal with him.

The Ammonite soldiers who had crowded into the central parade ground had been stripped of their weapons and were seated on the ground with scores of Israelites standing guard. Saul dismounted his donkey and, accompanied by his armor bearer, Eldad and another elder of Benjamin, he walked to the center parade ground that had been created in the camp layout to where his men guarded a handful of men they had identified as the king and his general staff.

"King Nahash," Saul addressed the man wearing the crown, kneeling with his hands tied behind him. "I am Saul, king of Israel. You have dared to threaten a city in my protection. For that you will pay with your life. Do you have anything to say?"

"King of Israel? I did not know there was such a thing," the bewildered Nahash replied. His tunic was soiled with dirt where Israelite soldiers had pushed him to the ground, but the crown was still on his head.

"Now you know, and you will feel his blade."

With that, Saul swung his sword in a wide arc and beheaded him. A collective cry rose from the remnant of the Ammonite army around them. Saul bent over the lifeless head and removed the crown. He looked at it a moment and then placed it on his own head. The Israelites cheered and cried, "Long live King Saul! Long live King Saul! Long live King Saul!"

Then the cry suddenly changed.

"Where are those who said, 'Shall Saul reign over us?'" cried one man.

"Yes," answered another nearby. "Let them be brought so we can put them to death!"

The rejoicing crowd grew suddenly ugly as they called for the heads of those who had grumbled against Saul in Mizpah. Othnal, elder of Judah standing nearby, tried to slip away, but it was too late.

"Here's one! This man did not honor Saul!" said a man nearby as he seized Othnal by the arm.

"Kill him! Kill him!" shouted the frenzied warriors.

"NO!" came a shout heard over the confusion. It was the king. "No one else of our number will die today. Nothing will happen to spoil the great victory Yahweh has given us!"

The man released Othnal's arm. Othnal looked at Saul and bowed his head ever so slightly, then hurried away.

❧ 62 ❧

Some of the men under Erek's command went about setting up their own camp while the rest thoroughly finished cleaning up the charred remains of the Ammonite tent city. They scavenged what they could as booty.

It became apparent that the Ammonite army had been travelling with significant riches captured from other cities they had conquered. Included were all manner of jewels and precious metals in the form of everything from tools to jewelry to shrines of a variety of deities. Moreover, there were textiles of exotic design and great herds of cattle, sheep and goats.

Then there were the slaves: a few men – probably many had been killed or worked to death – but many more women and not a few children.

Erek detailed a thousand men to assemble the slaves who survived the battle and sort out who the slaves were and where they came from. Those from Israelite towns would be freed. The fate of the others would be determined by the men of Jabesh.

When Erek reported to Saul with his lieutenants at his side, the body of Nahash still lay in front of his tent and Erek laughed loudly when he saw the crown on Saul's head. Saul stood over the body talking to men Erek didn't recognize.

As Erek listened to the conversation it quickly became apparent that the men were the elders of Jabesh.

"Bless are you, O king, anointed of Yahweh!" said Zedeq, first elder of Jabesh, as he bowed low. He was respectful, but unable to conceal his giddy joy at the rescue that Saul had affected. Achim and the others bowed as well.

"You are our brothers, men of Gilead," Saul replied. "Bone of our bone, flesh of our flesh; we are all Jacob's children."

The next day, 100,000 exhausted men under the command of Jerubel marched back to Jabesh, covered in dust and blood, bearing the captured weapons and armor of the Ammonite soldiers they had run down and killed. They brought no prisoners; all they had found, they had killed.

The camp of Israel spread over many acres on three sides of Jabesh and the people of the city attempted to lavish gifts on the victorious soldiers, but they were so numerous the citizens and their bounty were swallowed up.

The riches of the Ammonites more than made up for it, however. The captured armaments Jerubel brought back were assembled with the wealth left behind in the camp and it was truly more than anyone of Israel had ever seen. The flocks and cattle the Ammonites had driven with them made for sumptuous feasts for the multitude of Israelite volunteers and the residents of Jabesh as well. Saul reserved a percentage of the wealth to himself and his kingdom, but appointed the elders of the tribes to distribute the rest for the benefit of the warriors.

For two more days, the men rested and feasted while cleaning up the field of battle. Then, Saul called the elders and officers to assemble. Eldad of Mizpah was among the elders that assembled, as was Zedeq and Achim of Gilead and Erek and Othnal of Judah and Jerubel of Bethel.

"God be praised for this victory," Saul began in a loud voice, since there were several hundred gathered before him. "And thanks to each of you for your response to my appeal. The people of Jabesh have given us their thanks," he nodded to Zedeq. "However, this will not be the last time our enemies will encroach upon our borders. As the anointed King of

Israel, I ask that you convey to your men the need for us to raise an army; a small, professional force that would undergo training to enable them to fight against the best armies of our enemies and can be swelled by volunteers when dire circumstances present themselves.

"This time, we had overwhelming numbers and complete surprise. We won't always be so fortunate.

"Give your men leave to go home with their share of the booty, but first convey this need to them and if there are any who wish to join me in Gilgal in the Spring, we will organize and assign commissions there."

"Let us go to Gilgal now!"

Saul was startled and looked to see who spoke. It was Samuel. *When did he get here?*

"Let us go to Gilgal now and reaffirm the kingship!" the prophet cried, smiling broadly.

Gilgal was a site that had deep meaning for all Israelites who knew their history and believed God's promise to make of them a great nation. Gilgal had been the base of operations for Joshua when Israel had crossed the Jordan River and attacked Jericho and then had claimed the land of promise. It was where their nation had been born. And now with the inauguration of the kingdom, it would see a new birth.

As he rode along on the road south to Gilgal after fording the Jordan near Jabesh, Saul realized this would be the third time he had been declared king: first, secretly outside Ramah, then when the lots were cast in Mizpah, and now he was to be confirmed after the historic victory at Jabesh.

He only hoped at last he would FEEL like a king.

❧ 63 ❧

Azel picked up a small stone and threw it as hard as he could. It bounced before hitting the large boulder he had been aiming for. Frustrated he, kicked another stone loose from its place, embedded in the sandy soil. He picked it up, tossed it in the air and caught it a couple of times, evaluating it as a stone for throwing.

He was bored. He was a veteran of the battle of Jabesh and was old enough now that he was patrolling the western outskirts of Mizpah alone. Many years had passed since the Philistines were driven away.

Jeriah was wrong, Azel thought. He had said that the Philistines would come back, but they had not. It was true that they still held some territory, notably Gibeah, the king's own city, but Mizpah was still free.

Azel threw his stone, which was heavier than the other one. This time, he hit the boulder, finally. He supposed he should continue on his assigned patrol route, so he picked up his spear and shuffled along toward the boulder at which he had been throwing the rocks.

He reached the boulder and climbed atop it, pausing to look around. He was about to hop down to continue his circuit, when something caught his eye. It was smoke on the horizon to the west; or was it dust? Yes, it was dust, swirling in the air like a windstorm in the Negev.

He squinted into the afternoon sun, but couldn't tell anything. What could be creating such a dust storm? Then he realized, it could only be caused by many horses.

He jumped down from the boulder and began running in the direction of the dust. He needed to know for sure what was causing the dust storm before sounding an alarm. He skirted a line of trees to avoid being seen, moving as fast as he could with his spear in his left hand.

Soon he thought he had gone far enough, so he crouched behind a farmer's stone wall where he could see down the road to Gibeon.

It took a couple of minutes, but then Azel could see riders' bronze helmets reflecting the sun.

Philistines!

He froze for a moment, finding it hard to believe his own eyes, then he remembered what he must do. He stood, but keeping his head down, he ran as fast as he could in the direction of Mizpah.

But then he heard hoofbeats behind him. He turned to look and saw Philistine cavalry had started forward at a gallop. He stopped behind a tree to avoid being seen as they went past.

The rest of the column continued at its previous pace. *So, the cavalry is the advance party*, Azel thought. I can't outrun them. How can I warn Mizpah?

Then he realized he was now between the Philistine cavalry and the main force. Impulsively he ran further into the trees where he couldn't be seen, then turned and again ran as fast as he could toward Mizpah.

Hadassah was at the market as she had been so many times, but now her head covering hid her hair, still long and beautiful, but now graying. She was focused on dickering with a merchant over a leg of lamb for the family, when she was startled by a scream nearby. She turned to see what it meant and was horrified to see horses and riders entering the market. Next, she recognized the uniforms.

Philistines!

Then she screamed also, as did the many other men and women in the marketplace.

The riders crashed into some of the booths in the market and slashed at the wooden and cloth shelters, causing some to fall, but they didn't stop, because it appeared they knew where they were going.

Panicked, Hadassah looked desperately for a place to hide, but then she realized the Philistines were not bothering the people. Instead they went directly to a building at the edge of the square.

The armory! Hadassah thought. *How do they know where the armory is?*

One of the Philistines dismounted and used a battle ax to split the wooden door of the small building and break it apart. The people of Mizpah looked on as the Philistines pulled the precious weapons from the armory and stacked them, several of their number facing outward with swords drawn to ensure no one would be so foolish as to interfere.

Eldad was working in the shop when his sister-in-law entered and shouted, "The Philistines are here!"

"Where?"

"The market."

"How many?"

"I don't know. I heard it in the street."

With that she hurried away to her house.

Eldad knew if the Philistines were already in the market, there was no way they could get to their weapons. Then he remembered: *Azel is on sentry duty. How did the Philistines get here without him warning us?*

Just then, Azel appeared, carrying his spear.

"Father, the Philistines…"

"Yes, thank Yahweh you are safe!"

"They were on horseback. I couldn't get here to warn anyone in time."

Eldad was trying to think of what to do next, when three Philistine soldiers burst through the door, swords drawn.

"On the ground, smith! Now!"

Eldad obeyed and sat down on the packed earth floor with his hands outstretched. Azel slipped to one side and laid his spear down behind a workbench.

"You must surrender any and all weapons you are working on, now!" the soldier said. The other two began looking around at anything that was in the shop. One of them then noticed Azel.

"Hey! Who are you!"

"He is my young son and apprentice," Eldad said.

"Go, sit beside your father."

Azel went and sat down.

The soldiers had collected a few knives and axes, as well as a couple of unfinished swords.

"Smith, we have seized your town's armory and now, once again, you will not make weapons or sharpen the tools that are brought to you. We will once again install a garrison here, so we will do that for you. We will check on you periodically to be sure you are obedient."

The soldiers left with their sacks of weapons and sharpened tools and with them, many hours of Eldad's toil and the money he would have made from them.

When they were sure the soldiers were gone, Eldad and Azel stood up.

"You were wise to so quickly hide the spear," Eldad said.

"And do you still have the Philistine sword, the one you brought from battle?"

Eldad closed his eyes. "I left it in the armory!"

❦ 64 ❦

Azel once again raised his hand and put it on his mother's shoulder to steady her. She was mounted on the family's donkey as they slowly made their way south toward her family's ancestral city on the road that traversed the watershed ridge; the highest point between the Jordan River and the Great Sea. They could see great distances both to the east and the west.

He was thankful that the new occupation by the Philistines did not prevent them from travelling, though their oppressors never missed an opportunity to add difficulty to the most mundane activities.

Hadassah was quiet and had her head down, her face mostly covered by the shawl she always wore over her gray head. Azel knew she was weary. She was getting older and the years of hard, domestic labor had taken their toll.

This trip was tiring for her, but important. She would see an elderly aunt and her surviving siblings and cousins who lived in Beth-zur, where Azel's mother had been born.

They were deep into the tribe of Judah territory now, having passed Jebus on the border of Benjamin hours ago and were now well beyond the little village of Bethlehem. They must reach Beth-zur before nightfall, but Azel knew he couldn't push his mother to go faster than they had been.

Beth-zur was not as far as Hebron, the most important city of Judah. Azel was thankful for that. Presently, Azel saw the village he believed must be Beth-zur, the sides of the houses turned gold by the setting sun.

Azel sat on the ground, leaning against the family compound wall with his male cousins of Beth-zur, whom he had just met for the first time, as they waited for the women to bring the noon meal. After arriving last night, Azel and Hadassah had bedded down in the home of his mother's sister and, this morning, Azel had simply waited while the others went about their work; the men at their tasks in the fields and the women caring for children and preparing the noon meal, to which extended family had been invited.

His mother was more animated than she had been on the trip, now catching up on the news with her cousins and two younger sisters. Azel did not know these relatives.

His attention was then drawn to some more women coming into the compound through the gate carrying jars of meal, oil and wine. There was one who captured Azel's attention immediately. She was young and slender and moved quickly. She greeted Azel's mother's aged aunt with a smile and a kiss and then went to help with preparations for the meal. Azel could not stop seeing her smile.

"Who are these women?" Azel asked the cousin sitting beside him, his mother's nephew.

"They are our cousins from the line of your mother's aunt," he answered. "There were four generations that came in just now."

"So, the youngest is our Aunt's great-grandchild?"

"Yes, that is Dani. She is the daughter of Shallum, your cousin, twice removed, I believe."

Azel chose his next words carefully. "Is her father here?"

"Not yet. He is likely still in the fields, but he will be here when the food is served. I can promise you that!" Azel's cousin laughed.

Azel continued to watch as they waited. Every so often he caught a glimpse of Dani as she energetically and cheerfully worked alongside the women who were in her family. He determined that he would introduce himself to his cousin, twice removed, Shallum, to ask if he could meet Dani.

Azel felt like he was flying, for his cousin Shallum had agreed to allow him to talk to Dani. As he looked into her dark eyes, he felt like he might lose his composure and embarrass himself. They talked most of the afternoon while the women talked and laughed, getting reacquainted with Azel's mother, while the men returned to the fields.

"I am apprenticed to my father as a metal smith," he said in answer to her question about his occupation.

"My father and brothers are all farmers," she said looking away shyly, then back at him with her big, brown eyes. Azel felt the strength leave his legs and he feared he might fall.

"What is it like in Mizpah?"

"Not too different from here, except that Mizpah is very high." Again he felt foolish. Of course Mizpah was high. The word meant "watchtower" after all!

They talked until Dani's mother called her that it was time to go home to prepare the evening meal for her father and brothers.

Azel almost felt dizzy as he watched her go through the gate. He turned to see his mother watching and smiling. She came over to him.

"You seem to be taken with my cousin's granddaughter," she said, with a knowing look.

"Yes," Azel mumbled.

"She is a fine girl from a fine family," Hadassah said, watching her son's eyes closely. "Perhaps you will see her again before we leave."

"Perhaps. That would be good," Azel said, not really knowing what he said. He had already determined he would find a way to do just that.

❦ 65 ❦

Azel did see Dani again, along with her father. Then he and his mother returned home to Mizpah. Two months later, Azel returned to Beth-zur and, after spending two weeks with Dani's family, he reached an agreement with her father on the bride price and he and Dani rolled up her meager belongings in a blanket and together they set out hand-in-hand on the road toward Mizpah where they would make their home.

They would have to stay with Eldad and Hadassah while he readied an apartment for Dani in the family compound, but Azel did not want to wait to bring Dani home with him to make her his wife.

When Azel and Dani arrived in Mizpah, they were surprised to learn that Hadassah was sick. She had taken to bed with a fever.

Dani immediately went to work to keep the household together: fixing meals, going to market, cleaning and mending. Azel was proud of her, but his mother's condition was worrisome.

As the days went by, Hadassah grew pale and thin. Efforts to get her to eat failed. Her face was terribly hot and Azel and Dani spent many hours swabbing her forehead with a wet cloth and trying to get her to take water, but nothing seemed to make any difference. Each day she was weaker than the day before.

❦

At night, when Azel and Dani had gone to their improvised bed in the common room of the mud-brick home, Eldad lay beside his beloved wife and told her of all that was going on and how he loved her and wished she would drink more water and eat more.

"You need your strength," he said, "and the water will cool your fever."

But Hadassah was barely responsive. She was unable to even raise her hand to take a cup of water from him, so he tried to pour it between her lips, but much of it spilled on the bedclothes.

He finally broke down and wept, desperate to do something, but not knowing what to do.

One morning, when Eldad awoke, Hadassah did not respond and her forehead was no longer hot, but was unnaturally cold. Eldad cried out so loud and long that Azel arose from bed and ran into his parents' bed chamber.

Eldad picked up her lifeless body from the bed and wept.

Eldad laid Hadassah to rest beside his mother and father in their family cave, where also lay his grandparents and great grandparents, though they had long ago been exhumed and their bones reburied in compact ossuaries, small stone boxes on which each of their names were inscribed.

Jeriah and Azel helped their father with all that had to be done and their wives and the wives of Eldad's brothers prepared food for the relatives that came to pay their respects to the mourning family.

Eldad still went to the forge each day, but the light was gone from his eyes. He was much slower than he had been and seemed devoid of any motivation.

❧ 66 ❧

Jonathan was surprised how little things had changed. With the passing of years, he was now a young man of 25. After the rescue of Jabesh Gilead, his father, the king, returned to farming as if nothing had happened. Meanwhile the Philistines remained in Gibeath.

"We still have work to do, son," Jonathan's grandfather, Kish, had once explained. "Saul gets only a small stipend from the tribes for now. We have to earn a living. It would be a shame for the royal family of Israel to be starving!" Kish had laughed long and loud about that.

Still, Jonathan was impatient. It did not help that the Philistine garrison in his own city of Gibeah made it almost impossible for Saul to publicly act as king. If only their professional force was assembled and trained, Jonathan lamented to himself, they could drive out the Philistines and his father could act in his rightful office as king of all Israel. But the Philistines had made sure that no smiths could operate nearby, not even to sharpen farm tools, much less produce weapons.

Jonathan scowled and swung a scythe through the ripe barley with unusual forcefulness, his frustration showing in every swing of the blade. The warm sun caused sweat to trickle from his long, black hair down his back, making the rough, brown tunic stick to his muscular body. His strong hands gripped the two-handled reaper tightly, his forearms taut and flexing as he moved rhythmically, swinging back and forth, back and forth.

Absent mindedly, he cursed the Philistines; little growls coming from deep in his chest with each thrust of the scythe.

Suddenly he was startled to see four horsemen at the edge of the field coming toward him. He squinted into the afternoon sunlit haze and was able to make out the horsehair plumes of Philistine helmets. Then he recognized the rider leading the others. It was Clamatos, the governor of Gibeah and commander of the garrison.

"Boy!" Clamatos shouted at Jonathan. "Help my men here. Men, gather this grain for the garrison. We need bread."

"No!" exclaimed Jonathan. "You cannot take our harvest!"

Clamatos turned toward him, as if startled by his impertinence. "Is that so? Men, can we take his harvest?"

The Philistine soldiers laughed and dismounted, taking goat-hair sacks from their saddles, which they began filling with the grain Jonathan had spent the day cutting.

Jonathan's vision clouded with fury and he gripped the scythe until his fists turned red and white under the grime of labor. He turned and watched as the smug Clamatos gave obvious instructions to his soldiers. Finally, it was too much.

With a red-hot anger which nearly blinded him, Jonathan lifted his scythe upward as he ran toward Clamatos' mount. With a great, deep cry, he brought it down with his full strength, point first into the governor's neck.

The startled man gave a choked cry as the shiny blade tore through his collar bone under the bronze ceremonial breastplate and severed rib from sternum, then pierced an artery near the heart. He was dead before his body clattered to the ground beside his terrified horse.

Without stopping, Jonathan then turned and ran toward the shocked soldiers, still holding their grain sacks. He swung the now-bloody scythe at the first one and decapitated him with surprising ease, but the force that was required made Jonathan fall sideways and he was momentarily stunned, giving the other two soldiers time to drop the sacks and draw their short swords. Jonathan stumbled away, found his footing and put his scythe between himself and them in a defensive posture, his sandaled feet planted far apart. For a moment they were at a standoff, the two soldiers unsure they wanted to pursue the fight with this fearsome young man who obviously knew how to use a farm implement.

Then without warning, one of the soldiers fell after something hit his head. The other soldier looked down at him in panic. The man had an arrow protruding from his cheek.

Jonathan looked up to see other members of his family coming on the run from the top of the hill. His younger brother, Malchishua, was drawing his bow once again and Jonathan's father was racing toward them with an ax; a very determined look on his face. Jonathan then lunged at the last soldier, who parried his scythe in a defensive move, but then turned to run, only to be cut down by Malchishua's arrow.

Saul trotted up to the scene and surveyed the four bodies. The last soldier stirred and moaned. Saul raised his ax and brought it down on the man's neck and he was still.

"We must sound an alarm," King Saul told his sons. "Things will be the same no longer."

Jonathan sank to the ground, suddenly very tired.

❧ 67 ❧

Saul and his family spread the word very quickly to the local men of Benjamin that the Governor of Gibeah was dead and they should strike the garrison.

About thirty men of Gibeah and the surrounding area gathered at Kish's farm near Gibeah and Saul told them how they would launch the assault.

"Cousin, remain at my side," Saul said to Abner, who nodded with a determined look. Saul gave the order to go into the town to attack.

The men were mostly armed with staves and sickles and axes, with a few swords, bows and slings, but they would have surprise on their side.

The men surrounded the barracks, remaining hidden on side streets until Saul's signal was given. The barracks were inside a rectangular wall with partially completed towers on each corner. The atmosphere in and around the barracks was casual. The gate was open. Soldiers were loitering inside and outside the wall; some working on construction, others washing clothes, playing games of chance or napping. Since the construction was incomplete, there were a couple of places where the wall wasn't finished. Saul had detailed men to attack those points as well as the gate.

Saul silently signaled the attack by making a chopping motion with his hand, which was passed along to the lookouts for the other units on the four sides of the barracks. Saul's men charged the gate and quickly killed the soldiers there, so they had no trouble gaining entry to the barracks.

Jonathan and his unit silently and quickly took out the men working on the wall on the west side and were quickly over the low, unfinished portion and inside where they surprised some men in the midst of a game of chance. Their weapons flashed and the soldiers were quickly dispatched.

On the other sides of the barracks, others were able to mount the walls and kill the few men standing guard there, then descend into the compound.

Confusion reigned as the totally unsuspecting Philistines fell with the fury brought by Saul and the volunteers. But there were some soldiers who were out of the barracks on patrol and, when word spread of the death of the governor and the fall of the barracks, those soldiers fled back to their homes in the five cities by the Sea.

Soon after Saul and his sons expelled the Philistines from Gibeah, word came from the west that a Philistine army was marching from Ekron to put down Saul's "rebellion." Even more disheartening was the word that men of Judah and Simeon from the western clans had been conscripted by the Philistines and were marching with them.

"How many are they?" Saul asked the weary runner who had brought the news.

"We counted 3,000 chariots and 6,000 men in the chariots, plus infantry like the sands of the seashore!"

"When will they get here?"

"They were barely a half day behind me!"

"We are not ready," Saul lamented. "We must withdraw."

"Let us just fight them Father," Jonathan pleaded. "God will be on our side as he was at Jabesh."

"Yes, Father, let us call the men together again," agreed Abinidab. "We can repel them. It is only Ekron."

"And our brothers of Judah and Simeon march with them," Saul mumbled, focused on the downside. "We must blow the trumpet and call all Israel to gather in Gilgal."

❧ 68 ❧

"It becomes clear why the Hebrews love their donkeys," said Ishnol, a Philistine captain, bitterly, as he and members of his company worked to repair another broken chariot wheel. It was the victim of one more sharp stone in this rocky, wooded wilderness. Already they had been required to chop through a fallen tree to clear the path for the chariots and replace broken wheels on two of them.

Each mile they travelled was made more difficult because of the terrain and the difficulty of driving the chariots up into the hill country and through the thick woodlands.

When Ishnol's men were finished repairing the chariot, a rider arrived and gave them good news.

"Captain, the king of Ekron has ordered you and your men to scout the territory to the south," said the rider.

"And what is to be my destination?" asked Ishnol.

"Micmash, to prepare the crossing of the gorge to Gibeath ha-Elohim."

The captain nodded.

"Men! We march south!" Ishnol shouted, and his men cheered, happy to be done with rescuing charioteers.

The captain didn't know the country very well, but he had a scout with him who knew the way, so they would have no problem finding the backwoods town of Micmash. He did know enough to realize that it was an important strategic approach to Gibeath, the place where the rebellion had begun. Ishnol also knew that the column of the army that would follow his advance skirmishers would be just one third of the total force, the King of Ekron having decreed that they should divide and move toward two other cities: Beth-horon to the west and Ophrah to the north.

He and his 24 men would be able to make much better time now.

The country was growing more difficult as they ascended into the hills. Joath paused to knock a pebble out of his sandal and dust off his feet. Knocking the dust off was futile since they had many miles to go, but it made him feel better.

Since leaving Ekron, the army had gone north and then moved inland where the land grew rockier by the mile and there were a lot more trees. They had recently split into thirds and Joath's column was marching for Micmash on the border of Ephraim and Benjamin.

It galled Joath to be marching with the Philistines, being an Israelite as he was, along with several hundred others of his fellow kinsmen from the clans of Simeon. They had submitted to the Philistines because their homes were so near the Philistine city of Ekron and the Philistines were so strong. It seemed expedient at the time and for a while it afforded them a measure of rest and relative freedom from harassment, but now it presented a real problem. It appeared the Israelite king had begun a real rebellion and Joath didn't like being on the wrong side of it.

Now the Philistines had come to collect on their alliance and Joath and his fellows were on the march beside Hittites, Amorites and Amalekites that had also been forced to fight with and for the Philistines. The Sea Peoples themselves were mainly officers and ruled their men with iron fists, as well as literal iron swords.

Joath's clan had felt alienated from the rest of the tribes of Israel, even before their now-regrettable alliance with the Philistines. The tribe of Simeon had been all but absorbed into the tribe of Judah, partly because they had no real inheritance of their own. The weakness of his tribe had been intentionally structured by none other than Israel himself, after his son Simeon had committed a great crime against the

Canaanite inhabitants of Schechem. As a result, the tribe of Simeon had no real territory to call its own.

"Is it true what they say, that your God fights for Israel?" a Canaanite man in the rank behind him asked Joath. The man wore a small image of a Ba'al on a cord around his neck.

"Our God has fought for us in the past, yes," Joath answered. "But He will not fight for me today, I fear."

"Why not?"

"Because, we fight against his chosen one, the one sanctified by lot and anointed to be king."

"So, will your God fight against us all, as in generations past?" the man persisted, his voice betraying fear. Joath knew he was talking about the conquests of Joshua and perhaps the past victories of Gideon and Barak against his people.

"I do not understand such things," Joath answered. "I am but a merchant who longs to go home in peace. Alas, that is not my lot."

"I fear to think what our lot may be today," the Canaanite answered.

Joath shifted the weight of his bedroll and the meager supplies it contained. From the Philistine captain he and his kinsmen had received a red tunic which identified them with the army of Ekron. Over the tunic was a breastplate made of small bronze scales like the scales of a fish. He also carried an iron sword and iron-tipped spear which were issued him by the Philistine captain and a shield which bore the same crest as the banner which fluttered above them.

They would have many more miles to trudge up into the Israelite hill country.

❦ 69 ❦

For the second time, Saul sent word throughout the land that all able-bodied men should report to muster for battle, this time in Gilgal. He also sent word to Samuel to come and offer sacrifices to ensure their victory.

Saul sent his second son, Abinidab, on to Gilgal with a small unit to receive the volunteers that would be arriving and to make necessary arrangements for a large encampment for several days while they gathered and prepared to march back to meet the Philistines.

The next day, Saul and his other sons led a contingent – only 2,000 men – from the tribe of Benjamin. They expected many times that number to assemble in Gilgal. The men went on the backs of their donkeys, by donkey-drawn cart and on foot, arriving in Gilgal on the second day, the same day the Philistine army was expected to arrive at Micmash.

Jeriah's donkey seemed to sense the urgency with which the small Benjamite army was moving toward Gilgal. He had answered the call of the trumpet and was riding to meet the rest of the volunteers. This time, Eldad and Azel remained at home to mind the forge.

But all along the way to Gilgal, others were moving also; some of them faster than the army. Men, women and children fled before the news of the Philistine advance, the word having panicked the people. Jeriah saw that some carried what baggage they could, but many simply ran from their homes and towns, stopping to hide in caves overnight, fearful that the Philistines would be upon them at any moment.

He thought about his family and wondered if he should have encouraged them to flee before he left to join Saul. Yet, his father would know when to flee and would know where it was best to go.

When the army arrived at their rendezvous in Gilgal, Jeriah noticed that many of the civilians who had been shadowing the army were not stopping at Gilgal or even at the Jordan River, but were continuing on to the territories of Gad and Reuben on the other side. There, he supposed, they hoped to be safe. Jeriah wondered at their lack of confidence in the army Saul was raising.

According to the scouts who returned to Gilgal, the Philistines were moving less quickly than the first messenger had estimated. For that, king Saul was thankful, but it didn't solve his biggest current problem.

"Where is he? We must be moving out!" Saul bellowed at no one in particular. Jonathan and Abner looked at one another, as did the other officers near Saul's tent. None answered, since the king had asked the question six times a day since they had arrived in Gilgal three days ago. And no one asked who "he" was. Saul and everyone else knew they dare not go into battle without offering sacrifice to Yahweh, and that was Samuel's responsibility. The altar was prepared and animals were tied nearby, but Samuel was nowhere to be found. The hours dragged on.

"Riders!" a sentry called. Saul exited his tent, hoping that Samuel was one of them, but it was only the messengers he had sent to Ramah to fetch Samuel. They halted their donkeys at a watering trough beside a well and dismounted. Saul ran over to them.

"Where is Samuel? I sent you to bring him," he shouted.

"Lord, the prophet said you should wait for him," one of the men said timidly.

"What? When will he come?"

The man shrugged.

Saul grabbed a clay jar from the lip of the well and smashed it against the stone trough startling the weary donkeys.

Is he making a point by staying away; that he is GOD's prophet and not the king's lackey?

Abner stood by Saul's tent as he returned, having watched the exchange with the messengers.

"What will you do?" Abner asked him as he stormed back to his tent. Saul stopped at the question but didn't answer.

"The response to the blowing of the trumpet was much less than for Gilead," the king said, finally. "The northern tribes did not respond at all and, except for a few hundred each from Ephraim and Judah, the army is Benjamite."

"It is the midst of the harvest," Abner said. "Perhaps this was all that could be mustered."

❦ 70 ❦

"They say the Philistine army is many thousands," a man from Ephraim whispered. He was seated with others of his tribe around a cook fire.

"Two groups of three left last night," another man said.

"Left? They deserted?"

"It's not deserting if you aren't a paid soldier," said the third. "We have a right to take care of our families and crops."

After a moment's reflection, the first man said, "I say we slip out tonight, before the second watch." He looked at the faces of the others in the firelight. "Staying here is suicide. Our families need us."

The men soon went to bed, but they only pretended to sleep. A few hours later, they stirred, gathered their belongings and quietly slipped past the other sleeping men, leaving the camp.

"You must do something, cousin," said Abner on the morning of the sixth day. "We counted 3,000 the first day, but during each night that passes, men are disappearing. Morale is very low among those that remain."

Saul merely grunted, but didn't agree or disagree.

"Samuel may not come," Abner continued. "He has obviously been delayed by some other mission for the Lord."

"I don't know," Saul replied quietly. "What if I forfeit God's blessing by moving ahead without Samuel?"

"Two more days and you will not have an army to lead," Abner said. "The men are demoralized. They worry about their homes. They must see action. You are the king; you should act like it! If the prophet will not respond when called, then you must go on without him."

Saul looked off into space for a moment, then stood up. "Assemble the men at the altar."

Saul conducted a relatively short service in which he personally slaughtered a lamb and set its body on the fire built on top of an altar of stacked stone. After he offered a prayer for victory, Saul ordered the men to prepare to march. Abner walked beside him as they went to his tent to supervise the packing of his equipment.

"What have you done?" Saul turned at the sound of the familiar voice. It was Samuel, arrived at last.

"Samuel!" Saul answered, surprised and not a little miffed. "When you delayed I had to act. We must march to meet the Philistines."

Samuel lowered his eyes and then looked at Saul through narrowed eyes under bushy, gray eyebrows. "For this act of disrespect," he said slowly, "Yahweh has rejected you from being king and selected another, a man after His own heart, because you have not done what Yahweh told you to do."

Saul's mouth opened but he could not speak. His face reddened. He just watched Samuel as he stalked off out of camp, then turned to look at his cousin. Abner scowled at the abrasive prophet.

"Has not my kingship been confirmed, not once but three times; the final confirmation right here at Gilgal?" Saul whispered loudly as Abner nodded. "Am I not acting to save Israel? Now Samuel says God has rejected ME?"

Then Saul turned and shouted, "We march to Gibeah!"

❧ 71 ❧

Jonathan commanded one of the companies, having been commissioned as a captain by his father. The company was only a few hundred now, after all the desertions.

Yet, we are servants of the Most High God. Jonathan thought, *Could not a thousand defeat a much larger force if God is on our side?*

Their scouts reported the Philistine army had gone north, then marched inland and was coming up into the high country toward Gibeah, but had also sent raiding parties in many directions. Pitifully ill-equipped, the men of Israel were also greatly outnumbered by the Philistines.

Saul's idea of a professional, trained fighting force was not yet realized and Jonathan worried that it might die before it could take form, and the kingdom would die with it.

Jonathan's company reached Gibeah ahead of the rest of the small army accompanying Saul, where they were relieved to find that the Philistines had not arrived so the town was still intact. It was largely deserted though, as the people had fled when word had come that they would be attacked.

Then they turned north, continuing on to the crest of a deep gorge that separated Gibeah from Micmash. The latter was hardly a town at all; only enough of a hamlet that it had a name. However, having grown up near there, Jonathan knew that the shape of the land would make it an ideal place to stage a battle.

The great gorge which separated Micmash from Gibeah was one of the many valleys that descended from the highlands of the watershed ridge to the Great Sea, but it was uncommonly deep and the walls of the gorge were particularly steep. It would prevent the Philistines from using their fearsome chariots and cavalry, unless they were able to take the pass that formed a land bridge nearby to the east. The high ground on the south side of the gorge north of Gibeah would be an ideal defensive position.

Jonathan only hoped they would get there first.

His hope was rewarded. When he and his cohort arrived, there was, so far, no sign of the Philistine army. His company made camp on the promontory on the southern edge of the gorge. To attack them, the Philistines would have to cross the ravine then climb the steep walls under the arrows of Israelite archers and the stones of slingmen.

As he stood looking across to the other side of the gorge, Jonathan liked their chances.

The next morning, King Saul's small force arrived at Gibeah and made the right turn toward Micmash. There they joined Jonathan's troops already in place. Shortly after Saul's contingent arrived, scouts came into camp reporting that a small advance column of the Philistine army was approaching on the road north of Micmash. The king, his sons and Abner met in conference. Compiling the various scouts' intelligence, they estimated they faced a total force of about 20,000, one third of which approached them now.

"Twenty thousand!" exclaimed Saul. "How can we meet such a force?"

"But Father, they have separated into multiple smaller forces which are scattered across the country. There are not 20,000 here now. And we have the high ground," Jonathan said. "Yahweh will be with us."

"Will He?" Saul shook his head, remembering the words of Samuel.

Jonathan was surprised at the change he saw in his father from the man who raised the army and attacked the Ammonites at Jabesh with such fury. He wondered what caused his father to go from such extremes of confidence and decisiveness to depths of despair and immobilization.

Two days went by without Saul issuing an order. Early in the morning, Jonathan and his officers went to the brink of the gorge and watched as a small Philistine advance party arrived on the other side and began making camp.

"Enos," Jonathan said to his armor bearer. "Detail some men to watch the pass. We must know whether the enemy knows about it and tries to come across to the east."

"Yes, lord!" Enos saluted briskly and strode off toward the camp.

❦ 72 ❦

Captain Ishnol and his small Philistine advance squad could see the army of Saul across the deep ravine which divided the towns of Micmash and Gibeah. He immediately summoned one of his men.

"Return to the king and tell him that we have arrived and have the rebels in view, but neither horse nor chariot can cross the gorge because the walls are too steep," Ishnol said. "We must either approach from the south or rely entirely on infantry. Go and be quick about it!"

The man saluted and turned to retrace his steps the way he had just come.

Ishnol knew one of the three main columns of the army was close behind them. The gorge between the two armies would set up a possible stalemate, with both knowing the difficulty they would have attacking across it.

"There is a rumor of a pass to the east," one of Ishnol's men said.

"Take me to see about it, once we have our camp set up."

The next step will be for the generals to decide.

"Father, we should attack before they can array themselves against us!" Jonathan pleaded.

"How can I attack when we are outnumbered so greatly?" Saul answered. "And we have few weapons. You and I have the only swords!" He was sitting slump-shouldered on a tree stump from which he had scarcely moved in two days.

Jonathan knew that, while it was true he and his father had the only swords, there were other deadly weapons being carried by the army, even if some were usually used for farming or hunting. Finally he turned and left, not knowing what to do, yet feeling that something must be done. He went to his tent, where his armor bearer and first officer, Enos, waited for him.

"Lord, what is the news?" said Enos.

"There is no news. My father is paralyzed. I don't know what to do."

"He will not lead us to battle?"

"He has lost his courage. He feels we cannot win." Deep down, Jonathan feared the Saul of Jabesh was the aberration; that his present vacillation and inaction was who he really was, but Jonathan had hoped Jabesh had changed him once and for all.

"So, what do we do?" Enos asked. "Can you lead your troops, even if your father does not give the command?"

"I dare not, but…. Enos, is God's hand weakened to act whether there are many or few?"

"No. God's hand is not weakened," Enos watched his commander curiously.

"Then let us go over to the Philistines. It may be that God will give them over to us."

"Just us?"

"Yes, God will help us."

"I am with you my Captain, in whatever you want to do," Enos said, swallowing hard.

"Then let us go."

❦ 73 ❦

The two men gathered their weapons and armor and slipped out of camp, going to the brow of the gorge. Enos followed as Jonathan went first, climbing down the steep valley wall. After several minutes, they arrived at the bottom of the ravine, where they threaded their way through thickets and tried to stay hidden as they crossed the small stream that was the *de facto* dividing line between the two armies. Then they started uphill and the going became more difficult, but the young men continued purposefully. As they began to climb the wall on the Philistine side of the gorge, Jonathan stopped.

"Enos, my brother, if they see us, and say 'We are coming down to you,' we will stay still and wait. But if they say 'Come up to us' we will go up to them and God will give them into our hands. That will be our sign."

Enos nodded, though his face betrayed his doubt that there would be any such conversations.

The two men began climbing through the bushes and around small scrubby trees growing from the cliff face, going higher, ever higher. From above them on the crest of the hill they could hear the voices of the Philistines setting up camp. Enos glanced at Jonathan, who returned his glance and turned toward the summit with determination.

When they were about halfway up, a sentry saw them.

"Hello there! Men of Israel, are you lost? Finally coming out of your holes?"

Jonathan and Enos heard others laughing nearby.

"Come on up you hill dwellers; we'd like to show you something!" and they laughed uproariously. Then the laughter faded away.

The two men looked at one another. That was the sign they had agreed on. They resumed climbing rapidly up the steep slope.

Jonathan reached the crest first. He pushed between two bushes and emerged in a clearing where a couple of dozen Philistines were erecting tents. Most of them were not paying any attention. Even the soldiers who had called out to them appeared to have forgotten and gone back to their tasks. Then one looked up from the tent stake he was bent over. His eyes grew wide as Jonathan drew his sword and raised it. The sword fell quickly and the man died without a sound.

Enos ran past and retrieved the sword of the Philistine Jonathan had just killed, swinging it upward into the neck of another unsuspecting soldier who turned at just the wrong moment. When he fell, there was a clatter of armor and three men nearby turned to see what the noise was.

Jonathan was immediately on the closest one and Enos was right behind, each of them quickly slashing at the man nearest him. The third man shouted the alarm and turned to run. He was armed only with a wooden hammer. Jonathan's sword caught the back of his helmet and he stumbled, after which Jonathan ran his sword through his torso.

Beyond the first row of tents several more Philistines raised their heads at the noise and saw the two wild-eyed Israelites coming toward them. Several of the Sea People turned and stumbled in their hurry to get away.

Jonathan and Enos, bloodlust fully activating them now, grasped Philistine spears where the soldiers had stacked them and hurled two apiece into the men in the next tent row, then rushed forward and cut down the men closest to them. They then met others who managed to access weapons. But the Israelites had adrenalin and surprise on their side and, in quick succession, disarmed and killed the tenth and eleventh men since they climbed out of the ravine.

Confused, Captain Ishnol turned to see several of his men on the ground covered in blood. Then he saw the two young Israelites, each running down a panicked Philistine soldier. Others of his company were running past him in terror. He looked fearfully toward the brow of the hill in the direction of the Israelite army and thought he saw others coming. He turned and began running with his men. A spear whistled past him and struck the man just ahead of him. Ishnol knew he must warn the main body, weary from their long march and unprepared to jump into a battle.

As his column approached Micmash, Joath heard someone yelling and looked up to see Philistine solders running toward them.

"The army of Saul is upon us!" shouted one.

Just at that moment, the ground began to shake and Joath lost his footing and fell. Most of the other men in his column fell to the ground as well. For 30 seconds they lay on the shuddering earth, unable to rise.

"It's an omen!" shouted the Canaanite man with the image of Ba'al when the earthquake subsided.

Joath sprang to his feet and drew his Philistine sword. "For Yahweh!" he cried and ran to his Philistine commander, who still lay on the ground, and ran him through. The man's eyes grew wide and remained that way in death.

The men of Simeon cheered Joath, their kinsman, and raised their swords. "For Yahweh and Israel!" they answered. They then turned their swords against the Canaanite conscripts, as well as their Philistine overseers. Panic and confusion reigned as Joath and his clan cut their way through the ranks of their shocked and disoriented comrades.

❧ 74 ❧

"The Philistines are melting away!" Jeriah shouted, pointing to the crest of the hill. King Saul raised his head from its downcast position and looked across the gorge.

Sure enough, the distant army seemed to be seething and moving in chaos, as if in a fight to the death with some unseen army. Saul's confusion lasted only a moment.

"Who is gone from us?" Saul shouted. "Muster the men and do a count!"

Abner turned and shouted, "Fall in. Count those present!"

"Fall in!" shouted each officer to his companies. Jeriah fell into parade formation with the others.

Because their numbers were so few, it didn't take long for the men to assemble in ranks and report. Of their revised number of 600 men, only Jonathan and Enos were missing.

"Attack, attack! We must not let this opportunity pass!" Saul cried, and surprised officers repeated the command. Their men began moving forward.

More orders were barked and soon the little army was moving rapidly in pursuit of the larger but panicked Philistine advance force. They descended the gorge and began the ascent, but there were no Philistines at the top to defend it.

When they reached the other side of the gorge, they saw scores of Philistine dead and wounded already on the ground and Saul discerned what was happening. Simeonites who had marched with the Philistines had turned against them and were fighting for Israel. Since the Simeonites were dressed in Philistine armor, confusion was the order of the day and it appeared to be every man for himself.

When Saul and the Israelite soldiers arrived, the Simeonites stripped off their distinctive Philistine armor and fell in with their Yahweh-worshipping brethren from Benjamin. In the rush of the moment, Saul had no way of knowing what had triggered the Simeonites' treachery against the Philistines, but he knew they had to take advantage of the situation while they could.

As Saul and his men joined the battle, the confusion among the Philistines increased exponentially, with no one fully knowing friend from foe. Every man lashed out against his neighbor and then ran in terror from the battle.

Saul and his men took full advantage of the rout, killing Philistines at will as more and more turned and ran. On and on they went, mile after dusty mile, running down the Philistines and killing them.

"Sire, the men are faint," said Abner, after they had chased the Philistines over several miles. "Let them stop to eat and renew their strength."

"No! We must finish them today!" Saul said. "Any man who eats a morsel before we have completely defeated the Philistines will be cursed."

Abner was stunned by the impulsive pronouncement, but turned his donkey to relay the order to the captains of the small companies.

❧ 75 ❧

Jonathan and Enos had pursued the Philistines for many miles and were now deep in a wooded area. Many of their own men were now visible to their right and left sides, doing as they were doing, cutting down the confused and fleeing Philistines. He was vaguely aware that the dynamic had changed because, after they had decimated the scouting party at the top of the gorge, the entire Philistine column that had been approaching had turned in confusion and was running. They had seemed to be fighting each other.

Exhausted, covered in Philistine blood and the dust churned by a thousand fleeing soldiers, Jonathan and Enos stopped to catch their breath by an old, dead pomegranate tree. Jonathan, desperate with thirst and weak from hunger, looked in vain for fruit on the tree. There was, however, a honeycomb in a hole in the trunk, and he scooped some honey in his hand and ate it hungrily.

Immediately he felt invigorated and he offered some to Enos, but just then one of his Captains, commander of the men from Ephraim, trotted up.

"Your father, the king, has forbidden any man to eat anything today until the Philistines are defeated," the Captain said with fear in his eyes. "Any man who eats will be cursed!"

Jonathan spoke his mind: "My father causes trouble for our country. See how my energy has returned and my eyes have lit up, just by eating a little honey? Wouldn't it be better to eat a little and be stronger for the battle? Our victory won't be as great because of this command!"

Enos and the Captain stood wide-eyed before Jonathan, surprised by his hubris, unable to answer.

"Let us go!" Jonathan said, and they continued their pursuit of the Philistines, now in full rout.

Hunger, thirst and fatigue had nearly prostrated Jeriah and the 20 or so men with him who had been pursuing the Philistines for hours now. Yet they pressed on.

The Philistines seem possessed of a sense of defeat and are simply like fruit for the picking.

Even in his fatigue, because of the king's decree, Jeriah chastised himself for using a food metaphor to describe their enemy. He could not remember being so hungry and thirsty.

Ahead of them, Jeriah saw the Philistines pausing and shouting to others, then continuing to run. Then Jeriah saw what had made them pause.

It was a Philistine supply train. Carts with large solid wood wheels, some pulled by horses, others by oxen, were laden with supplies for the army. Alongside the carts were scores of cattle, sheep and goats on the hoof. The cart drivers and the herdsmen saw the approaching Israelites and the shouts of their fellow Philistines convinced them to run also, so they abandoned their wagons and their animals.

To his surprise, Jeriah realized they were almost to Aijalon, which was about 15 miles from Micmash. The sun was going down. They had been running and decimating the Philistine army all day long. The realization caused him to collapse to the ground just short of the first wagon. The men with him paused and sat on the ground as well, breathing hard with sweat running down their faces into their beards. They were unable to move but, for now, sat looking at the wagons as if unsure they were really there.

Suddenly a man near Jeriah stood up as if re-energized.

"The day is ended, and with it the king's curse!" he cried and, running with his sword in hand, grabbed the closest sheep and slit its throat. The animal gave a short bleat and fell. The man immediately fell upon it, using his sword to slice open the carcass. As soon as he pulled back the skin he cut a piece of thigh muscle and put it into his mouth hungrily.

Jeriah was shocked, but other men soon joined the man from Ephraim and did the same, grabbing animals and butchering them on the spot. They then began eating the flesh raw, blood dripping down their arms to their elbows.

"Brothers, wait and let us drain the blood as the law says!" Jeriah shouted, jumping to his feet. "Do not do this thing! We can roast the meat soon enough!"

But the men did not even look up at him and continued to gorge themselves.

Saul and Abner were pushing ahead on their donkeys, continuing to urge the men forward in the twilight, when a courier ran up.

"Lord King, the men have captured a supply train! There are weapons and many flocks!"

"Take us there!" Saul replied looking at the fading sunlight. "Day is done."

"And the men are sinning against God by eating meat with the blood in it!" the courier added tentatively.

"Take us there immediately," Saul commanded the breathless messenger.

They didn't have to go far. When Saul arrived however, he was shocked by what he saw.

Several hundred men had gathered and were already finished eating, blood on their faces and hands. They had also found the Philistines' store of wine in one of the wagons, their faces bore the stains of the red wine.

Jeriah and a few men who would help him had built a bonfire which was pushing back the deepening darkness. They had slaughtered other animals, drained the blood and were roasting the meat. A few men had refrained from eating the raw meat.

"What is the meaning of this?" Saul shouted.

Jeriah looked up from the leg of roasted lamb he was finishing and washed down the last bite with a gulp of Philistine wine.

"Do you not know the law?" Saul demanded in a booming voice, causing all to look his way. "You have eaten meat with the blood in it."

Saul continued talking to those who had eaten the raw meat, but Abner came over to where Jeriah and the others were eating their roasted meat.

"Did you not eat the meat with the blood?" Abner asked.

"No, lord," Jeriah answered.

"We would have but he stopped us; those who would listen," another man said, pointing to Jeriah.

"What is your name?"

"Jeriah, son of Eldad, of Mizpah."

"Benjamite?"

"Yes."

"Have you been in battle before?"

"Yes, at Mizpah and Jabesh Gilead."

Abner looked Jeriah up and down, then said, "I'd like to offer you a commission as an officer in the new professional security force I – and the king – are going to set up once this emergency is over. Would you like that?"

"Yes, lord."

"Good. Come to Gibeah next month. I'll put you to work."

"Yes, thank-you."

Abner walked away and Jeriah sat down once more to finish his meal. Soon he heard more commotion over where Saul was.

"They're building an altar!" someone shouted.

Jeriah and the others who had roasted their meat watched as Saul gave orders and the men who had behaved like gluttons and broken the law of Moses brought stones and wood for an altar.

"He is calling on them to repent for their breaking of the law," Jeriah said to those nearby.

As they watched more and more men of the small army arrived and fires were built to roast the meat. There was no shortage of sheep, goats and oxen to be had for sacrifice.

Ahijah, the priest and son of Ahitub, arrived at the site of the supply train after everyone else and Saul had him oversee the sacrifices.

❦ 76 ❧

Once the men had repented and offered sacrifice, Saul stood and spoke.

"Let us not wait here, but pursue the Philistines during the night so we can plunder them until dawn and not leave one of them alive!"

"Do what you will," some replied.

"We will follow you, our king," others said.

But not everyone agreed. "Let us inquire of God," said Ahijah, the priest.

"Yes, son of Ahitub, great-grandson of Eli," Saul said, appearing a bit peeved at being interrupted, but relenting. "Let us inquire of the Lord. Shall I go down after the Philistines? Will God give them into our hands?"

Everyone looked and listened expectantly, but nothing seemed to happen. The priest, whom Jeriah judged to be about 25 years old, looked at a stone in his hand, as if expecting something to happen to give an answer, but no answer came.

Saul scowled. "I ask again, shall I go after the Philistines?"

Again, the perplexed priest looked at the stone in his hand, but there was no reply through the oracle.

"Gather 'round, those who are officers," Saul shouted. "Let us find out what sin has been committed today. As surely as the Lord who rescues Israel lives, even if the fault lies with my own son, he shall surely die. We will cast lots. Stand over there," Saul directed all the officers, "and I and my son Jonathan will stand over here."

Silence fell on those assembled as the bonfires threw long shadows in the night. Jeriah wondered why Saul had separated himself and his son before lots had been cast.

The priest cast the stones to choose between the king's house and the officers. The lot fell on the king's house, so all knew there was no fault in the officers.

The priest now cast lots between Saul and Jonathan. The lot fell on Jonathan.

"Tell me what you have done!" Saul bellowed at his son.

"I merely tasted a little honey with the end of my staff. And now must I die?"

"May God do the same to me if you do not die, Jonathan!" Saul said angrily.

"Lord king!" said an officer from Ephraim loudly. "Should Jonathan die? It is he who brought about this great deliverance in Israel today. Without him we wouldn't be talking about plundering and destroying the Philistines! Surely, as the Lord lives, not a hair of his head should fall to the ground, for he did this today with God's help!"

Others then chimed in and it was clear to Jeriah that if Saul moved forward to carry out his declaration of death for his son, there would be a revolt among the men, for Jonathan was very popular, especially now.

Saul turned, obviously frustrated, and said, "Then we go to our homes!" and he stalked off into the darkness. Abner belatedly followed him.

"I've been asked to become a full-time soldier," Jeriah told Shelomith when he was back home in Mizpah. "They want to make me an officer."

Shelomith didn't say anything at first, but just kept kneading the dough she was preparing for the oven.

"It's a great honor," Jeriah said, when Shelomith didn't say anything.

Then turning from her work, she said, "How can I be happy that you will be in constant danger?"

Jeriah didn't have a ready answer.

"But, I suppose you will do what you will do," she said, turning back to her work. "What about your father and the smith shop?"

Jeriah thought for a moment, then answered, "He has Azel and his brother Jacob. They will carry on without me."

Shelomith looked skeptical.

It would only take a little over an hour to walk the road from Mizpah to Gibeah. Jeriah's thoughts were of the future as he packed a goatskin shoulder bag with the few things he felt he would need to report for his induction into the standing army King Saul was establishing.

"When will you be back?" Shelomith asked the obvious question as she watched him preparing to leave.

"I'm not certain of my schedule yet, but I suppose I'll be on duty for a few days, then off a few days. I'll be able to come back then."

"Your children need you here."

"And you don't?" Jeriah smiled at her and drew her into his embrace. She appeared near tears.

"I'll be back soon. We won't go out to fight until spring. We'll spend the winter training and establishing the chain of command. A standing army is a new thing for Israel. It is a great honor to be asked to serve."

Shelomith said nothing and he could tell she was not impressed by his commission. Still he knew this was how he could best serve God and his country.

Moments later he embraced 12-year-old Misha'el. "My son, you are a man now. You must take care of your mother and your sister."

"Yes, Father."

"And Zaina," Jeriah said, throwing his arms around his 10-year-old daughter, "Do what your mother says and help her with running the house while I'm gone."

He then kissed Shelomith and held her close again, then turned and threw the strap of the goatskin bag over his shoulder, then pulled a leather thong over his head so his bedroll hung from his other shoulder. Inside the bedroll was his sword and hanging from the thong was his shield.

"I'll be back before you know it," he said, looking at his little family, not knowing if the words would come true. He then walked toward the gate of the family compound.

"Yahweh be with you, Father!" Misha'el called out.

"And with you," Jeriah answered, and for the first time, as he went through the gate, he felt a twinge in his stomach that he thought must be what homesickness feels like.

❦ 77 ❦

After Micmash, the elders of Gibeath ha-Elohim declared that it should now be called "Gibeath Saul" or just Gibeah in the Hebrew tongue. And so, it was. Abner was pleased.

Saul began building a courtyard to the north of his house, around the large Tamarisk tree. Its central feature would be a rustic throne where he would sit in judgment of all Israel.

The days were increasingly busy as autumn receded and winter came on. For the first time in many years, Israel was virtually free of interference by enemies on their borders. With Abner's counsel, Saul made good use of the peace to structure a government based loosely on the monarchies of the nations around them, but with one big difference: Samuel still had great influence with the people as well as with the king himself.

Abner was perhaps the busiest of all. As the king's right hand, it was his job to carry forward the edicts of the king and to protect his interests, even when the king was unaware that his interests were threatened. If Saul wanted a building project, it was Abner's job to arrange for the stone cutters and carpenters that would be required, along with a complement of slaves that would do the literal heavy lifting to complete the project. Pack animals and raw materials were required for such projects as well. Abner, through declarations of taxation by the king, developed resources he could call upon for such initiatives.

While Jonathan and his brothers, as well as Saul himself, were in charge of training the professional soldiers of Israel's new army, Abner still served as the king's first and best lieutenant general in charge of supply and support. As such, while Saul and his sons concentrated on the specifics of training men to defend the nation, Abner was free to pursue ancillary projects that he considered necessary to the success of the king.

One of those ancillary projects took Abner deep into Israel's underbelly.

"I can promise you two pieces of silver for each valuable piece of intelligence you bring me," Abner whispered. He had come to Hebron of Judah for this meeting.

The sun-wrinkled man frowned. He was of the tribe of Judah and sat cross-legged on the ground across from Abner. They had met in the marketplace in the city of Hebron, then left to find a secluded place in a wooded ravine to conduct business. Abner had brought a jar of wine to sweeten the deal, and the man was taking full advantage.

"Make it three," the man said, stroking his dirty beard.

Abner had anticipated this, although the man's worn clothes indicated that he had had no silver in his purse for some time.

"You negotiate well – what is your name?"

"Ze'ev ben-Yisachar, of Keilah."

"All right, Ze'ev ben-Yisachar of Keilah," Abner replied, purposely appearing sincere. "I can only go to three. Do not press me for more."

The man grunted his satisfaction. "How do I know you won't arrest me for – previous unfortunate behaviors?"

"Your service to the king will ensure that you and your family are unmolested."

The man squinted his eyes under bushy, black eyebrows and said, "How about a deposit?"

Abner had anticipated this as well, but was not about to open his purse too easily.

"You want to be paid before you have brought me any information?"

"You wish to retain my services, do you not?"

"Very well," Abner said, reaching inside his cloak for the bag tied to his belt right beside his dagger. "Here is one silver piece. I will pay you two more when you bring me information I can use."

The man snapped the small ingot from Abner's hand with obvious desperation. He might even have smiled, though in his hard, lined face it was difficult for Abner to be sure.

"I want to know if you hear any talk against the king," Abner told his new spy. "I want to know who it is and what they are saying."

"Of course."

"And if you hear anything of sedition; of rivals who might stage a revolt...."

"Of course."

Abner concluded the distasteful, but necessary, business and left the man while he was finishing the wine and turning the ingot between his grimy fingers.

Abner would play this little game many more times in his effort to protect his cousin. The power and wealth which would redound to his clan because of Saul's becoming king was bound to be threatened, of that Abner was certain.

And he intended to be prepared.

"Someone to see you, lord."

Abner looked up from the requisition list he was penning on a piece of vellum to see his aide at the door of his new office in the compound for the new government.

"Who? What do they want? I am very busy."

"He will only say he wishes to offer his services to the 'king's man.'"

"Very well," Abner said with a wave of his hand. He was bored with reports and correspondence anyway.

Through the door came a man covered in the dust of many miles, dressed in the loose, black robes of a desert nomad, with eyes, hair and beard as black as his robes. His skin was surprisingly light, however; almost ghostly.

"Who are you?" Abner demanded, suddenly wishing that his aide had stayed in the room.

"I am Doeg, of Edom."

Abner looked into the piercing, black eyes. "Why do you wish to serve King Saul?"

"Men such as yourself will sometimes have need of the services of men such as me," Doeg said mysteriously.

"What services?"

Doeg drew a long curved dagger out of his cloak.

"Wait!" Abner shouted. "What are you doing?"

Doeg laid the dagger on the table in front of Abner.

"A king has enemies. It is obvious. You may not know it yet," Doeg said with shocking coolness. "But you will need to deal with an enemy at some point. I can deal swiftly and stealthily to solve such problems."

"I have already established an intelligence network," Abner said, dismissively.

"Information is one thing. Action is another."

Abner shuddered internally at the coldness of the man's statement, but he didn't let it show. He paused before asking, "Why do you not offer your services to your own king?"

"Perhaps because," Doeg's eyes narrowed, "I am one of HIS enemies." And he laughed with such a wicked laugh Abner flinched in spite of himself.

Perhaps this desert rat could be useful.

❦ 78 ❧

The wind was chilly coming down the creek bed, but little Asahel barely noticed. He was too busy hiding from his brother and his uncle. He was the youngest of the playmates and was often left out when the other three were in a mood to torment him. Today they were playing Israel and Philistines and he was trying to find his brother and uncle – the Philistines – before they could attack him and his brother Abishai – the Israelites.

Asahel and his two brothers were only a little younger than their uncle because their mother, Zeruiah, was much older than he. With nine children in Asahel's mother's family, there were several years between the oldest and the youngest, their uncle, with whom they spent many hours.

They had learned recently though, that their uncle would have less time to be their playmate, since his father – Asahel's grandfather – had said he was soon to be a man must shoulder more responsibility.

Asahel climbed to the top of a familiar ridge and looked down into the next depression, then raised his eyes and scanned the next ridge. There he saw Abishai's head peaking from behind a boulder. Asahel tentatively waved to signal him. Abishai returned the wave and motioned to a knot of low bushes below. Asahel looked, understanding "the enemy" was hidden below them.

Abishai silently motioned to Asahel that they attack from opposite directions, so they descended toward the bushes.

Just as they prepared to attack the "Philistines" in their hiding place, Asahel and Abishai were ambushed from behind by the older boys, yelling loudly. The boys rolled in the dust, wrestling and punching, each making stabbing motions to try to vanquish his enemy.

Finally, it was the "Philistines" who were victorious over the "Israelites" and the older boys laughed with glee that their subterfuge had worked.

"It's not fair," pouted Asahel.

"Oh, don't be a baby!" Joab taunted.

"But he IS the baby!" their uncle said and Abishai joined in laughing with the two older boys, leaving Asahel to pout all the more.

After recovering from their war games, the boys loitered along the creek bed looking for shiny stones they could add to their collections. Each of the boys was learning to use the sling to fend off predators who might prey on the family's sheep and goats, which were scattered across the hills east of Bethlehem in Judah.

Joab knew it really wasn't fair that he and his uncle often sided against his two younger siblings in their games, but he didn't want to relinquish his position close to their uncle.

In his mother's family, their uncle was the youngest and was not paid much attention, but for Joab and his brothers, he hung the moon. No matter what the situation, their uncle could always make life sparkle. He had such a quick smile and creative imagination. No obstacle would stop him from doing what he set out to do, so the four playmates had countless adventures in the Judean hills.

Something new and exciting was always afoot when they were led by their uncle David.

❦ 79 ❦

The spring rains were coming and the farmers were sowing their seed, but for Samuel, it was time for a harvest.

The word of the Lord had come to Samuel once again, late in his life. So again, he journeyed from Ramah to the king's court in Gibeah, or Gibeath-Saul as it was now known.

It had been years since he had been to the king's court and he did not relish delivering the message Yahweh had given him, for it would result in many deaths and not a little danger for the king himself. His faithful man, Jabal, led his donkey on the short trip.

In Gibeah, Samuel was ushered into Saul's court, which was nearly finished after a 10-year construction project. Numerous courtiers were busy with the business of the king. There was now a proper gate into the court in the opening between two mud-brick rooms. There were rooms on three sides of the courtyard which was paved with stone and in the middle of the courtyard, before a tamarisk tree, was a stone platform and a simple, wooden throne with a few pieces of gold inlay. There was no roof over the throne, only a broad, colorful tent-top to supplement the shade of the tree.

Told to wait, Samuel stood leaning on his staff, looking like a pile of old gray straw and blankets, while Jabal got some water for the aging donkey.

Presently Saul came out of a room, sat on the throne and greeted Samuel. Samuel saw that he had aged as well.

"Yes, lord, what brings you to the king's house?" Saul asked perfunctorily, as if he saw Samuel every day.

"The Lord God would have you right a wrong."

Saul cocked his right eyebrow curiously.

Gary L. Ivey

"When Israel came up from slavery in Egypt, Amalek gave them no right of passage but opposed Moses on the way. It was I," Samuel continued, "who anointed you king, so now hear what Yahweh of Sabaoth says: 'You are to utterly destroy the Amalekite people; you are to leave nothing alive, not man, woman, nor sucking child; not goat, sheep, camel or ox.' Do you understand this command?"

Samuel could see Saul was at first shocked by the severity of his commission, but Samuel didn't need to remind the king of the stories told by the old men of the Exodus and Israel's encounter with the people of Amalek far to the south.

The Amalekites were desert people who roamed deep in the Negev on the Sinai Peninsula, sometimes raiding villages as far north as Beersheba in Judah. They were a wild and warlike people, covered in black, bushy hair, lacking the refinements of civilized cities and communities.

Samuel knew the king was remembering that, nearly 400 years before, when Israel had escaped slavery in Egypt, the Amalekites attacked them at Rephidim just north of where God gave Moses the Law. Moses had sat on a hill over the battlefield and, as long as he raised his arms in prayer to heaven, the battle went in Israel's favor, but if he wearied and lowered his arms, the Amalekites prevailed, so Aaron and Hur held his arms up for him.

In the end Israel won, but the Lord told Moses that God himself would always be at war with Amalek and that someday they would be wiped from the face of the earth.

"Someday" was finally here.

❧ 80 ❧

Never had Jeriah seen such a desolate landscape. It was so different from the familiar wooded hill country where he had grown up. There was virtually nothing growing anywhere on the mountain crags and sandy valleys over which they were travelling. He now understood better the stories the fathers told of the children of Israel, wandering in the wilderness.

Because that was where they were now.

Saul had raised a force of 200,000 to fulfill the word of the Lord to Samuel concerning Amalek. And now they were marching south, into the barren Negev, below Judah.

Jeriah rode a donkey at the head of his command, its numbers greatly increased by the influx of volunteers. Now 37 years old, he had served several years as a member of the small permanent army of Israel and had been promoted to Captain over a company of men from the tribe of Judah. On their second full day of marching, Jeriah was joined by his new second in command, who spurred his own donkey to catch up to Jeriah.

"Captain, may I ask you something?"

"Certainly... Tell me your name again?"

"Eliab. What is your trade?" He was a tall, strong young man, who had just been appointed Jeriah's lieutenant.

"I am a professional soldier now, Eliab of Bethlehem. But I apprenticed with my father, a smith of Mizpah."

"Did you forge your own armor then?"

"Much of it," Jeriah answered.

"The sword too?"

Jeriah drew the sword, so Eliab could examine it. "No, this I acquired on the battlefield."

"Is it Philistine?"

"Yes. I brought it back from Micmash."

"Micmash! I have heard the stories. An amazing victory by such a small force! I have yet to fight Philistines."

"Well, we can pray that Yahweh will keep the Philistines away from our borders for as long as possible."

"You have met them in other battles?"

"Yes," Jeriah said, "In several campaigns over the years."

Eliab was silent for a moment, in deference to his Captain, who was obviously a veteran with great experience.

"Have you seen this country before?" Jeriah asked.

"No, and I don't much like it."

"It is very different from home," Jeriah said, thinking of his family in Mizpah, no doubt worried about him, though with the passing years, they must have grown accustomed to his absences.

"Different from mine as well. Finding grazing and water for flocks would be next to impossible here."

Doeg shaded his dark eyes and scanned the shimmering horizon as he lay on his belly on a flat stone atop a high hill. He motioned for a couple of the men with him to be silent and continued scanning. They were a couple of miles ahead of Saul's army, scouting the desert for bands of Amalekites.

Doeg knew that the Amalekites would be living in a large, movable city of black tents, but there was no telling where they might be at the moment. Nomads like them could strike camp and move within a few hours, travel across the desert quickly, and then, just as fast, set up again in a new, unpredictable place. Doeg's own Edomite culture was not terribly different, so he knew something about their practices and could guess the rest.

Four men accompanied Doeg in his scouting party. Two were bronze-skinned Egyptians, who wore strange black paint around their eyes. Their clothes were different from the others as well and they often spoke to one another in a whisper in their language, while glancing at Doeg. He couldn't trust them, but they would be helpful should they need to go farther west.

One man was Israelite; Doeg didn't know which tribe and didn't really care. At least he didn't have to keep a wary eye on that one. The other was actually Amalekite, which was both good and bad. Good, because he could likely identify the clan when they found an encampment. Bad, because his loyalties might well be divided, although he swore he was an outcast among his people; something about a dalliance with the wife of a chieftain.

Once he was comfortable that there was no Amalekite hunting party within view and that they were not being watched themselves, Doeg ordered his men to get up and head down into the valley toward the next line of hills, where they would again look for signs and search the horizon for an Amalekite encampment that had to be out there somewhere.

Jeriah found he had a hard time staying awake in the heat of the desert, jogging along on the donkey, with its monotonous "clop, clop, clop, clop" on the baked earth. He jerked himself awake and reminded himself that he was a Captain now. He must set an example for the men in his command, most of whom were on foot, trudging along, covered in gray dust almost to their waists.

Suddenly, five men appeared on the horizon and Jeriah squinted into the shimmering distance. As they grew closer, he recognized the king's herdsman, the Edomite, Doeg. Saul had tapped him to lead the scouts, because he knew the country and the Amalekites. The men grew closer and Doeg shouted, "We have found their camp. Where is the king?"

"His column is to the East," Jeriah called out, gesturing to his left.

"Thank you," Doeg shouted, and he led the men away in that direction.

"Halt," Jeriah ordered, and his weary men stopped moving. "Eliab, follow the scouts to the king's corps and report back our orders."

"Yes, lord," Eliab said as he turned his donkey and rode to the East paralleling the scouts.

Jeriah then gave the rest of his men leave to rest.

❧ 81 ❧

Orders would come soon, Eliab reported back. The element of surprise was paramount, so they would not waste time setting up camp before attacking. Jeriah's company, which was part of Jonathan's column, was to march to the southwest and curve around an Amalekite village near a place known as Havilah, while Abinidab, Saul's second son with his first command, would mirror them on the East, forming a huge pincer that would close as Saul himself led the attack in the center.

Jeriah had confidence that the plan was a good one. He also had complete confidence in the righteousness of their endeavor. The Amalekites made regular forays into Israelite territory and had killed many of his people. They were his people, even though they were of Judah.

Eliab navigated the column, having been present at the debriefing of the scouts, so he knew where the encampment was. After perhaps an hour, they could see the blackness on the horizon that had to be their tents.

"Mount that hill!" Jeriah ordered his men and they obeyed. The hill was not terribly high and the sides were not steep, but when the order was given to charge, Jeriah reasoned it would be easier to charge downhill.

After they took their position on top of the rise, Jeriah halted the column again and they awaited the order to charge.

Their mission had been clear: leave nothing alive; not men, women or children or even livestock. Jeriah shuddered a bit at that, but reminded himself of the atrocities suffered by his people at the hands of the Amalekites.

Presently the signal came, a silent one this time instead of a blowing of trumpets. It was a bronze shield on the next hill, flashing short bursts of reflections of the bright sun.

"Forward!" Jeriah called out, and the men started down the hill toward the tent city. They had not gone far when someone saw them coming and sounded the alarm, running back to the square courtyard in the midst of the camp.

"Charge!" Jeriah shouted and the men shouted too as they began to run down the slope that would pour them into the camp. Soon Amalekite men came out of the tents with weapons, but before they could form a defensive line, Jeriah's warriors were upon them.

The Israelites crashed through the few Amalekites who stood against them and were soon running through the tents, slashing the ropes holding up the tents and setting them on fire. Men and women emerged from the tents, shrieking, not knowing what was happening. As soon as they came out, they were cut down by Jeriah's men.

In half an hour it was over. All the people, men, women and children, were dead and many of the tents were burned. Many of the men were now carrying out the order to kill the animals as well.

Jeriah's men turned to assembling the spoils that had not been destroyed by fire. The take would be huge, because the Amalekites were essentially pirates, they had booty taken from scores of towns and villages, including villages in the territory of Judah. Jeriah's men occasionally found something that they recognized as coming from one of their towns, and a cheer would go up.

Presently a commotion was heard about a hundred cubits away and Jeriah looked that way, curiously. He saw that King Saul had come into the center of the camp and some of his soldiers appeared to have a prisoner. Jeriah began moving toward them to see what was going on.

"The king!" said one of the men restraining the prisoner. "This is Agag."

"Are you indeed their king?" Saul asked. The bedraggled chieftain just scowled.

"Tie him!" Saul ordered. "We have much work to do." Then turning to the soldiers standing nearby, he said, "Kill the old and the sick of the flocks and herds. Save the best for our booty. And for sacrifice."

Jeriah wondered why Saul and amended his original order. He and his men did what Saul said. It took another full day to gather up all the booty and organize the columns for travel with all the wagons and livestock.

They continued South, deeper into the Negev. Over the next week, they would locate three other Amalekite villages, the last near Shur, deep in the wilderness of Sin. Each time they slaughtered men, women and children, as well as the old and sick of the livestock. Each time their wagon train filled with spoils and the flocks and herds travelling with them grew larger.

Finally, Saul decided it was enough, and he gave the order to return to the territory of Israel. The army with its booty went to Gilgal, which was the staging area for Israel's campaigns going back to the conquests of Joshua.

❧ 82 ❧

"What is the meaning of this?" It was Samuel, having travelled to Gilgal to meet the warriors. Jeriah was near the king's tent assisting as the temporary troops were being mustered out.

"Greetings!" said King Saul to the prophet. "I have fulfilled the Lord's command."

"Then what is this sound of the bleating of sheep and lowing of cattle in my ears?"

"Uh, the men took the best of the cattle to sacrifice," Saul answered. "The rest we completely destroyed."

"Hush and I will tell you what the Lord said last night."

Jeriah felt a chill of foreboding at the prophet's words.

"What did the Lord say?" Saul said, appearing sincere.

Samuel answered: "He said, 'Time was when you thought little of yourself, but now I have made you the head of all the tribes of Israel. You were anointed king of Israel and sent with strict instructions to destroy the Amalekites, that wicked nation.' Why then did you not obey the Lord?"

"But I did what the Lord commanded," Saul protested. "I went where the Lord commanded and have brought back Agag their king. The rest I destroyed. The men only saved animals that we might sacrifice to the Lord in Gilgal."

"Does Yahweh prefer sacrifice and offering to obedience?" Samuel replied angrily. "Obedience is better than sacrifice and to listen to His voice better than the fat of rams. Rebellion is as sinful as witchcraft and preferring the voice of men to His is as evil as idolatry!"

Samuel then raised his hand in solemn pronouncement: "Because you have rejected the word of the Lord, He has rejected you as king!" He then turned to leave.

Jeriah could hardly believe his ears. Does God condemn the king for keeping some cattle alive?

Saul was suddenly contrite, running after Samuel. "I have sinned! Please don't leave me; I beg you come back with me and I will submit to the Lord once again!"

"It's too late," Samuel said. "God has rejected you!"

, "No, please don't go!" Saul grabbed Samuel's cloak so firmly it ripped apart. All who were watching gasped and Saul then let go.

"Just as you have torn this cloak," Samuel said, "God has torn the kingdom from you and given it to your neighbor, to someone better than you! God has made his decision. He who is the Glory of Israel is not a man that he should lie; neither will He change his mind."

Then he turned to Abner.

"Bring King Agag to me."

Abner relayed the order and a couple of soldiers brought prisoner. The desert chieftain had been tied behind an ox and had fallen several times, so he was covered in dust, bruised and bloodied and burnt by the sun. Samuel strode forward to one of the men holding the arm of Agag and grasped his sword, pulling it from its scabbard. Before anyone could react, he raised the sword and brought it down with so much violence that Agag's arm was severed at the elbow.

He cried out in pain, but another swing of the sword in the old prophet's hand stopped the cry as it sliced mostly through the chieftain's neck.

As Jeriah and the others looked on, horrified, Samuel hacked at the bloody body of Agag until his head rolled away.

"Yahweh told you to save no person alive!" Samuel now turned once again to Saul, who, though he towered over the elderly prophet, drew back a step. The prophet, spattered in blood, flung the sword into the dirt and strode away, leaving Saul and his men to stand in stunned silence.

❧ 83 ❧

Most of the 200,000 who had fought the Amalekites at Havilah had long ago been mustered out to return to their farms and shops, but Jeriah and the other professional soldiers returned to Gibeath-Saul and remained there. With the reduction of the force to the full-time soldiers, Jeriah's duties changed. Rather than leading a company, he was assigned regular guard duty at Saul's court.

Over time, it became clear that Samuel would no longer come to Gibeath to counsel Saul and the king's mood turned sour. He mumbled and groused under his breath as he went about the duties of court. Jeriah worried about him.

One fall day, Jeriah was standing near the throne when Saul entered the court with his head down and a scowl on his face. He sat down on the throne with a flourish and stared forward. Those standing before the throne with various grievances or requests for the king grew quiet, unsure of what would happen next. Knots of men, elders of their tribes, abruptly ended political conversations.

Abner entered as well and sat at a table where he usually sat to conduct the business of the court. Jeriah stood to the left of the throne and another soldier, named Ephah, stood to the right, both with eyes straight ahead, each holding a spear.

Finally, Saul spoke: "Does my generosity mean nothing? I have given you all houses and lands and yet you betray me!"

A murmur flitted through the knot of people in the court.

What does the king mean by these words? Jeriah thought.

"Though I have defeated Philistine and Ammonite and Amalekite," Saul continued, "Still some of you plot against me. You seek for another to be king."

"No! It is not true!" said some, with fear in their voices.

"Who has told you such a thing?" others said.

"Oh, you sons of Benjamin," the King continued to rant, "I will find who is responsible. I will find who is disloyal. I..."

Suddenly the king's glassy eyes locked on a man over to his right and he shouted, "You! Stand before me!"

The man took a few hesitant, trembling steps.

"Why have you betrayed me?" Saul demanded.

"No lord, I have done nothing but serve you honorably!" the man protested.

"Seize him!" Saul shouted.

Jeriah realized belatedly that the order was directed at him. He took a step forward, then paused, looking at Ephah.

"Seize him now!"

Ephah moved to take the arm of the poor man, who turned wide eyes to look at him.

"Kill him!" Saul shouted.

Ephah's eyes grew wide, but then he moved to obey the order. As Jeriah watched, he let go of the man's arm only long enough to draw back and thrust his spear into the man's abdomen, then push hard to drive it further into his body, so the man doubled over and collapsed. The only sound he made was a choked, "Oof!"

Blood pooled under the man as the horrified onlookers stared at him dying on the floor, then looked up at the king.

"May this teach you a lesson," the king said loudly. "I will not tolerate any who would replace me!"

Then Abner came forward and motioned for Jeriah and the other soldier to carry the man outside. Jeriah joined his fellow soldier in picking up the limp body by the arms and dragging him toward the door.

Abner followed as they went out and directed them to put the body in a nearby ox cart, which they did. Ephah withdrew his spear from the man's body.

"I know his family," Abner said without emotion. "I will take him and break the news personally."

"Are there some who would take the kingdom from the house of Saul?" Jeriah asked.

"There are rumors, which I am trying to substantiate, that Samuel has anointed a successor to Saul; one not of Benjamin," Abner answered in a whisper. "Samuel's own words at Gilgal gave rise to the rumors, but my sources tell me the threat is real."

"And the king has heard the rumors?"

"It would appear so, although if I knew who had told him of them, I would have something to say to them!"

"What will you do?"

"I will neutralize the threat, of course."

Jeriah shuddered, because Abner's words contained threatening of their own.

"Both of you return to your posts," Abner said as he walked away, goading the ox forward.

Ephah returned to court to once again stand before the king, but Jeriah hesitated when he thought he heard his name being called.

"Jeriah!" It was the voice of his brother, Azel.

Then he saw him, running toward him. He was surprised at how mature he appeared, since he wasn't seeing him every day. He remembered hearing that Azel's wife had been with child, which must have been born by now.

"Azel, what brings you here?"

"Father is very ill. We don't know if he will survive."

Jeriah was shocked. Eldad was in his late sixties, but Jeriah hadn't thought he could possibly fall ill and die so soon. He looked around for someone to take his place before the throne.

❧ 84 ❧

When Jeriah and Azel arrived at their home in Mizpah, they found their wives and children and Eldad's brother and his family gathered around Eldad's bed. Jeriah quietly greeted Shelomith with a kiss on the cheek and hugged Misha'el and Zaina, silently marveling at how they were growing. Azel hugged Dani and stroked the cheek of baby Erel in her arms.

Eldad lay still and his eyes were closed. The family members parted to let the brothers come near.

"Father, it's Jeriah. I am here," Jeriah whispered.

Sixty-seven-year-old Eldad opened glassy eyes and looked at his firstborn. "My son," he said in a raspy whisper.

Jeriah took his hand and squeezed it. His father's hand, which had been as strong as the metal he had worked all his life, felt surprisingly weak.

"Now I can rest, because both my sons are with me," Eldad whispered.

"I love you, father." Jeriah stayed by Eldad's bedside for an hour, but his father didn't speak again.

Finally, Eldad's younger brother Jacob came forward and gently touched Eldad's arm, then held his hand in front of his brother's nose.

"He is cold," Jacob said, "and there is no spirit."

Jeriah's heart ached as he also put his own hand near his father's nostrils and realized he was not breathing. The women in the room began weeping. Jacob's sons, Elihu and Shallam, had tears running down their cheeks and Azel bent over to hug his father.

Jeriah and Azel, with the help of Jacob, Elihu and Shallam, buried Eldad in the cave with Hadassah and Eldad's parents. Jeriah stayed in Mizpah a week to help with arrangements.

Jeriah realized Azel would be the mainstay in the forge now, along with his cousins. Jacob had taken a lesser role, as Eldad had done some time ago.

Then Azel surprised Jeriah.

"I have decided to enlist in the army," Azel said one day, without any warning.

"What?! Who will mind the forge?"

"Elihu and Shallam are fully trained and uncle Jacob supervises. It is time I served my country. I have spoken to the elders and they have recommended me to lead a squad."

"Why didn't you come to me?" Jeriah said, trying to hide his disappointment. "I can put you over a company in my cohort. Abner lets me assign whoever I wish."

"I wanted to make my own way," Azel replied.

Jeriah's eyes narrowed as he looked at his brother, but he didn't push it any further.

"I think you and the children should move to Gibeath," Jeriah announced to Shelomith later that day.

She was surprised, but overjoyed. Jeriah had been returning to Mizpah less and less as his responsibilities at the king's court and in the army increased.

"Azel is entering the army as well, so he will be gone much of the time," Jeriah explained. "We decided it would be best to bring our families to be near us."

"So Dani will be moving as well?"

"Yes. We will find a compound where we can live together there."

Shelomith was happy as she thought about the prospect of once again seeing her husband every day. She knew there would still be times he was away with the army, but when he was not in the field, he would be home at night with her, Misha'el and Zaina.

The only problem she saw was that this would take her further away from her family in Beth-Horon, but she was unable to visit them very often as it was. Her parents were aging, but she did have brothers and her father's second wife there to take care of them.

About a month later, Jeriah and Azel had found a suitable house, which they purchased and added onto it. They had to make repairs because it had been empty for a while, but when they finally brought their wives and children to Gibeath, it was finished and ready for the feminine touch, which Shelomith and Dani wasted no time adding.

Jeriah had been at first concerned about moving their families from Mizpah, partly because it meant his father's heritage was gone from their ancestral home. Eldad's brother Jacob and his family were all that remained, but Jacob's sons were able to continue the metalsmith work. Even Jacob was slowing down as his age crept upward.

Jeriah's heart hurt with the memory of his father's last moments. He only hoped he could bring honor to the family, of which he was now the head.

Misha'el and Zaina were both older than their cousin, Erel, but the children played together well. They were very young to have moved, but they seemed to have adjusted quickly. Shelomith was glad.

While moving and setting up a new household in an unfamiliar place was challenging, she was glad that she could now see her husband every day and the children could know their father.

She had grown close to Dani, Azel's wife, during the time before they moved with Jeriah away so much. It was good to have someone to talk to and she and Dani got along well. Jeriah and Azel were helpful in finding the things they needed to set up their new households, which were next door to one another.

Shelomith knew that Dani was concerned about Azel joining the army, but men would do what they would do.

❧ 85 ❧

"Do not trouble the king with this, I beg you."

"But he should know!"

"Make your report to Abner," Jeriah insisted, holding back one of Saul's distant relatives, Shimei.

After moving his family, Jeriah once again stood before the king, where one of his duties was to screen those who came before him with their petitions.

Shimei was short, only about 25 and lacked any skills to serve the king, but because he had a tenuous familial connection, he was always at court, dressed as if he was an important advisor. Jeriah knew the way Shimei presented himself bore no relation to the truth. He was tolerated, but had no real influence.

"I tell you, I have a reliable report that, after Samuel rejected the king in Gilgal, he went to Bethlehem to anoint a new king! He needs to know!" Shimei insisted.

"I have heard it too, but do not trouble the king," Jeriah pleaded. "Abner is dealing with this. Speak to him."

Shimei gave a Jeriah a contemptuous look, but finally turned away. Jeriah sighed with relief, glad to have protected the king. It was an important part of his job now.

The courtiers were already walking on eggshells as their king brooded and mumbled as he went about the business of the kingdom. The defeat of the Amalekites should have been cause for glory, but Samuel's rant and public dismemberment of Agag had left Saul demoralized. Jeriah did not want to add rumors to his burdened soul.

Concerning the rumors, Jeriah had already heard that Samuel had gone to Bethlehem "to sacrifice," but Bethlehem was deep in Judah and he had never gone far from his regular circuit in the hill country of Ephraim and Benjamin. He remembered that Eliab, who had fought beside him at Havilah, was from a shepherd family in Bethlehem, but he had mustered out for the lambing season, so Jeriah could not ask him about it.

"Why doesn't he shake this off?" Abner groused to Jeriah while pacing under the portico. "He is the Lord's anointed!"

Jeriah didn't answer, but let Abner vent.

There were times when Saul seemed his old self; happy and gregarious; the humble, yet dashing, leader who had so enamored the people when he was first revealed as Yahweh's choice for king.

But then there were the other times, like today, when it seemed a dark shadow would come over the king and he would be sullen. An uneasy silence fell over the court.

"He has an evil spirit," someone whispered.

"God has forsaken him," said another, echoing Samuel.

The king was distant from everyone except his cousin, Abner, but Abner was manipulative and scheming. In spite of Jeriah's doubts about Abner's motives and activities, his proximity to the court made him one of Abner's confidants.

"His moods swing unpredictably," Jeriah said diplomatically. "Today is not one of his good days."

"Yes, he can be unreasonable, but I might have a solution," Abner answered, leaving Jeriah to puzzle over his cryptic statement.

"Lord king, I have found a young man who excels at weaving beautiful melodies accompanied by the lyre. This might soothe the king's spirit."

As Jeriah held his breath, Saul looked up at Abner with darkness in his eyes, but he replied, "Do as you wish."

Abner brought forward a young man, barely more than a boy, clad in the robes of a shepherd and carrying a crude lyre. Abner directed him to sit on a stool before the throne.

Jeriah was surprised that the young man exhibited no fear or nervousness before the king of Israel, but was at ease and poised. He immediately dipped his head in a quick bow which was unacknowledged by the king, then began to pluck the lyre in a way Jeriah had not heard before. Shortly he began to sing a psalm that Jeriah could only suppose the young man had composed, for it spoke of God as a shepherd.

"He makes me lie down by still waters; He restores my soul..." the boy sang in a high, clear voice.

Jeriah was deeply impressed by the young man, not only by his poise and skill with music, but his appearance. The young man was not terribly tall, but he was blessed with perfect skin and hair that was full and dashing. His compact body was muscular, owing to hard work, Jeriah guessed.

He looked at King Saul and saw that he was staring at the young man. His eyes had gone from dark and brooding to clear and shiny; he seemed on the verge of tears, yet the corners of his mouth were turned up in a smile.

Saul was indeed responding to the young man's music.

Soon the young man finished the psalm and sang another, after which, Saul thanked him, then called out for the first of the supplicants of the day to stand before him. Abner ushered a man from the tribe of Zebulun before the throne, who bowed, then began a monologue concerning some injustice that had been done to him. Meanwhile, Abner motioned to the young man to follow him.

"Wonderful!" Abner told him within Jeriah's hearing. "You must remain close by so I can call on you again."

"Lord, I will be happy to do as you ask," the young man answered, "but first I must return to Bethlehem to make arrangements for the flock in my charge."

"All right, but please stay one week, so the king may hear you again and the evil spirit be kept at bay." asked Abner.

"Then go to your father, but hurry back; your playing greatly benefits the king."

"As you wish," the young man said with a slight bow, then left the court and passed out the gate, as Jeriah watched.

❦ 86 ❦

Each day of that week, the young man came before the king to play his lyre and sing his psalms. Gradually the king's mood improved and, instead of being in a morose, near catatonic state, or worse, raving about imagined plotting against him, he was lucid and following the songs. Then he would talk to the young man as Jeriah looked on.

Again, Jeriah was impressed by the young man's poise and he could see a real bond forming between them. Saul began to display an almost fatherly feeling to the young shepherd. Abner's plan had worked even better than he must have hoped.

At the end of the week, the young man departed to go home, promising to return soon.

But the young man would not soon return to Saul's court, for after he had gone home to Bethlehem, the Philistines once again invaded Israel, this time in the territory closest to their own, to the southwest, in Judah.

"They appear to be moving on Gibeath-Saul from the south," Abner reported to the king after debriefing his spies. "They could be upon us in three days. We should move to meet them."

The king nodded, but his eyes were dull once again. Abner bowed and quickly turned away and spoke to Jeriah.

"Find Jonathan," Abner said. "He will need to assemble the troops. The king is not well."

Jeriah did not need to be told what ailed the king. He left immediately, believing he could find Jonathan in the camp of the professional soldiers. After asking a couple of the men if they had seen him, he did indeed find Jonathan in the camp, conferring with a couple of other officers.

"Lord Prince, General Abner sends word that the Philistines are invading Judah," Jeriah began. "He asks that you prepare a force to meet them."

"What of my father?"

"He is not well."

"Can he lead the attack?" Jonathan asked, but his raised eyebrow showed that he had already assumed his father's mental state.

"Perhaps, but Abner feels you will need to issue the orders and lead the advance."

"Yes, I imagine so. Thank you." And with that, Jonathan turned to speak to the two officers standing by.

Jeriah saluted, then left to return to the king's court.

The army of Israel had marched all day and all night to move deep into Judah west toward the Philistine border. Jeriah could sense that they had passed the safety of the last truly Israelite village when they passed Socoh. Each and every soldier was exhausted as the sun rose across a sweeping valley.

At the foot of the valley to the West was a very old, large Terebinth Oak tree from which the valley received its name: "The Vale of Elah." Elah was the word for Terebinth Oak in a Canaanite dialect.

Like so many wadis in western Israel, a small brook wound its way west at the lowest point of the valley, making its way to the Great Sea. Tall grasses grew along the banks of the brook and the clear water flowed over small stones that had been smoothed by many, many centuries of flowing water. On either side of the brook a gently sloping plain extended for many acres and then rose to high ridges facing one another across a half mile.

Jeriah once again rode at the head of his company of men of Judah who had responded to the sounding of the shofar as they topped the northern ridge. Eliab of Bethlehem rode at his side on his own donkey.

Jeriah's brother Azel marched among the Benjamites in the battle line of Saul and his son Malchishua in his first action as a professional soldier.

When they came to the northern ridge overlooking the valley, the order to halt came through the ranks and Jeriah repeated it for his troops. They stopped and looked across the plain toward the other ridge to the South and, sure enough, they could see dust rising from beyond the ridge, which could only mean one thing: a large number of horses and men were approaching.

Another order came from the king's staff: each company should deploy troops as a forward guard, while the rest of the soldiers made camp.

"I hope they don't attack until we get our camp established," Eliab commented.

"They are arriving at the high ground after us," Jeriah answered. "It isn't likely they will attack. We are more ready to attack than they."

As the camp took shape, Jeriah rotated his men so the first forward guard could set up its tents with others taking their places. It was nearing noon and Jeriah allowed some of his men to prepare food and enter their tents to rest, while others maintained a forward perimeter a little way down the slope toward the floor of the valley. Jeriah still doubted that the Philistines would attack so soon. They were also setting up camp on the facing ridge. He fully believed there would be no fighting until tomorrow morning.

Gary L. Ivey

❧ 87 ❧

About mid-afternoon, something happened which would change everything: Two men left the top of the ridge where the Philistines were setting up camp and descended into the valley. As they approached, the men of Israel watched, not sure what to expect. By the time they got to the bank of the brook, a murmur wafted through the ranks of Israel.

"It's a giant!" men exclaimed.

"He towers above his armor bearer!"

Jeriah's eyes were riveted to the scene, as were those of all the men in Saul's army. He shivered as his mind went back to the stories his father had told of the Battle of Eben-ezer and The Giant that had killed so many of his fellow soldiers in that battle.

"Men of Israel!" the giant spoke loudly with a deep, powerful voice. "I am Goliath, the champion of Gath. There is no need for all of you to die. Send out your champion to fight me. If he defeats me, we Philistines will submit to you and become your slaves. If, on the other hand, I defeat your champion, you will submit to us and become our slaves. I await your answer!"

Goliath OF GATH, the giant had said. Jeriah recalled that his father had said The Giant at Eben-ezer had fought under the banner of Gath.

Is this perhaps a son of that Giant?

No one in the army of Israel moved. But rumors were filtering through the ranks.

"He has brothers!" some said.

"He is from a race of giants," said others.

"He must be six cubits tall!"

268

"I think seven!"

"Who can fight him?" many asked. None volunteered.

Jeriah couldn't conceive of a man seven cubits tall. That would be almost twice the average height of the men he knew.

Soon Jeriah was summoned by a messenger to meet with his commanding officer, Saul's son, Jonathan. He left his men to go to the center of the camp where the king's tent was pitched. There he found his fellow captains.

"Who do you have who could defeat this giant?" Jonathan asked.

The captains looked at each other, but said nothing. Finally, one spoke.

"I have a man who is four-and-a-half cubits. He has bested all others in my company in our contests."

"Bring him to me," Jonathan said.

Jeriah sat down with the others in a circle to wait. In the distance, he saw Abner exit King Saul's tent. A clay jar flew out of the tent door and Abner dodged it. Then Saul came out. He was not wearing his crown and his hair was disheveled. He stood when he got free of the tent flap and it struck Jeriah that he was still taller by far than the men around him. The thought came into his mind fully formed, though he would have stopped it if he could have:

Saul himself may be the object of the Giant's taunt.

Presently, Jeriah's fellow captain returned to the circle with the champion he had mentioned. The man was indeed large and broad-shouldered, with sun-browned skin stretched tight over hard muscles, but he was bent over and hanging back as his captain led him to the circle.

"This is Elon, the man I spoke of," the captain said.

"Will you fight the Philistine?" Jonathan asked him.

Elon hesitated, then spoke timidly: "Lord, if you order it, I will fight, but I fear I would not be successful and my lord and all my comrades would become slaves."

Exasperated, Jonathan looked at the other captains. "Is there none other I can offer the king?"

Jeriah shook his head with the others. His father's horror of The Giant's swinging ax at Eben-ezer came to his mind once again.

❧ 88 ❧

Generals Malchishua and Abinidab had no better luck finding a champion to match the giant among their troops. Each day, morning and evening, Goliath returned to the bank of the brook and hurled insults at the army of Israel, but no one went out to answer him any day for the next week. Eventually Saul even offered a reward and the hand of his daughter in marriage to the man who would meet the giant, but there were no takers.

On the eighth day, the Israelites stood ready for battle, but once again the giant came out with only his armor bearer and stood on the rise above the brook.

"You Hebrew dogs!" Goliath growled. "Is no one of you man enough to fight? I still say, choose a man to fight me and you do not all have to die. If he prevails, we will become your slaves and if I prevail you shall be our slaves. Is there no one who will take my challenge?"

"This is unbearable!" Eliab said to Jeriah in a whisper so their troops would not hear. "Let us simply attack and fight! I want to get this over with."

"I guess the king prefers humiliation day after day to sure servitude," Jeriah answered bitterly.

"Where is the king, anyway?" Eliab said.

"He has not left his tent in three days."

Eliab turned to look again at the giant as he taunted them. Finally, Goliath grew tired and returned with his comparatively small armor bearer to the Philistine camp.

Jeriah began to seriously worry about the morale of his troops. They seemed at an impasse. Almost forty excruciating days had passed. Twice each day, the giant came out and made the same offer and the same threat of slavery and each day the soldiers of Israel cowered in fear. One morning the giant came out again as he had so many times before, issuing the same challenge and threat, but something would be different this day.

"What are you doing here?" Eliab said. Jeriah turned to see who he spoke to. "Does father know you are here? Did you abandon the sheep? I know how mischievous you are. You just came to see the battle!"

Jeriah was surprised to see the young lyre player who had soothed the king's mood.

"What have I done now?" the young man said. Then turning to Jeriah asked, "What will be done for the man who defeats this uncircumcised Philistine?"

"Uh, well," Jeriah began as the giant continued his harangue in the background. "He will receive treasure, the king's daughter in marriage and freedom from taxes for him and his family."

The young man cocked his head and walked away.

"Where are you going?" Eliab shouted after him.

"To find the king," he answered.

"Fool boy!" Eliab kicked a stone from the earth and watched it roll away.

"He is your brother?" Jeriah asked him.

"The eighth of eight of my father's sons," Eliab sneered. "He fears not man nor beast!"

❧ 89 ❧

Azel stood with the men of Benjamin not too far from where Jeriah's company of Judah faced the valley. It was after the noon meal and the men were growing agitated, knowing that the giant would again make his appearance as he did each morning and afternoon. Azel heard something going on near the king's tent but it was impossible to hear or see exactly what was happening and he could not leave the ranks to learn any more.

Shortly, two officers came through the ranks shouting: "Make way, make way!" and the men parted to see a short, but muscular and very young man, dressed in shepherd's garb, following the officers through the opening in the ranks. Soon, the officers stopped and the young man stepped between them and continued down the hill into the valley.

Azel and the other men were in shock, gradually realizing that this smallish, young man intended to meet the giant. He didn't cower or hesitate. He strode strongly and surely down the hill, his curly hair blowing in the breeze. He wore no armor, but only carried a shepherd's staff and leather shoulder bag.

Suddenly he turned and faced the men of Israel.

"Who is this uncircumcised Philistine that he should defy the armies of the living God?" he shouted and raised his staff into the air. But the men of Israel were too demoralized to cheer him on.

As he turned and continued to walk toward Goliath, Azel watched, certain they would soon witness his death.

❧

Gary L. Ivey

"David! What are you doing?" Eliab shouted. "Dear God, little brother! No!"

Jeriah went and put his hand on the shoulder of his second-in-command, who watched desperately as his youngest brother walked to certain death. He had come to comfort Eliab, but soon realized he needed to restrain him to prevent him from following his brother into the valley.

"I must find my brothers," Eliab said to Jeriah wide-eyed.

"Yes, go!"

Jeriah knew that Eliab had two brothers in another company of the army and he understood they would want to be together at a time like this.

From the opposite ridge, Achish, the newly minted king of Gath watched his champion and his armor bearer once again leave the camp and descend into the valley as he had so many times before. But something was different this time. The king squinted at the small figure that was making his way across the gently sloping ground from the ridge where the Israelites were massed toward the brook.

Surely this cannot be the Hebrew champion!

His father, Maoch, had been dead but a few months and this was the first time Achish would lead the army as its commander. Though only twenty years old, he had a great deal of training and experience in war and stood confidently beside the driver of the royal chariot, wearing the green of Gath and his father's crown of gold.

The Giant's challenge was his idea. He gladly watched the growing demoralization of Israel's army, day after day.

But now, what was he seeing from his elevated position in his chariot? The man coming forward from Israel's ranks appeared to be little more than a boy. He was not a large man, wasn't wearing armor and appeared to be carrying nothing but a shepherd's staff.

Is this a joke?

⁂

From his vantage point near the center of the battle line, Azel could see very clearly everything that was happening. He marveled at the courage of the man, younger than himself, who believed that he could alone best the giant because Yahweh would be with him.

Azel could see that Goliath was watching the young man as well. As the young man drew near the brook which divided the valley, Goliath roared, "Do I look like a dog that you come to me with sticks?"

"You come to me with sword and spear," the young man answered. "But I come to you in the name of the Lord of Armies, God of the armies of Israel, whom you defy."

The young man wasn't through.

"This very day Yahweh will deliver you into my hand and I will strike you down and remove your head from your shoulders! Then I will give all the Philistines to the birds of the air and the beast of the field. All the world will know there is a God in Israel. The battle belongs to the Lord and He will give you into my hand!"

Azel marveled at the confidence – and faith – the young man displayed, but he could also see that the giant was growing more enraged by the moment.

The young man didn't hurry, but went to the brook, where he bent down and appeared to be picking up something. Then he rose and took something from his bag.

"It's a sling!" someone near Azel shouted. "He intends to meet the giant's sword and spear with a sling!"

The army of Israel stood in rapt attention as the young man splashed through the shallow brook and climbed the bank to high, flat ground several cubits to the east of where the giant stood. Azel and his fellow soldiers could clearly see both of them in profile now.

The young man appeared like a small child compared to the giant. Goliath roared with laughter, pushing his massive helmet back and relaxing somewhat. Then he stopped laughing and spoke in a booming voice.

"Now I will give your carcass to the birds!"

He leaned forward to begin running toward the young man, pausing only long enough to lob his heavy spear. The young man nimbly stepped aside and the spear clattered harmlessly to the ground.

The giant then drew his huge sword as he continued taking long strides toward the young man, breathing heavily.

Calmly, the young man dropped a smooth, round stone into his sling and began swinging it by his side, faster and faster, gradually moving its arc over his head. The rapidly swinging sling began to make an ominous hum as it spun faster and faster.

Will he release the stone too late? Azel worried. He would only have one chance.

The giant was only about 10 cubits away when the young man released the stone, which flew fast and hard and straight, striking the giant's forehead perfectly in the center, bouncing away with a spatter of blood.

A gasp went up from both armies as Goliath's head jerked back and his legs slowed, but forward momentum caused him to fall forward until he slammed down on the ground, rolling halfway over before becoming still.

Azel saw the young man run over and pick up the giant's massive sword, lift it over his head and bring it down on his neck. The head rolled away from the huge body, guaranteeing the giant would rise no more.

The young man then lifted the head high in the air, with blood dripping from under the chin and turned to face the Philistine lines.

He didn't need to say a word. The Philistines on the facing hill panicked and broke ranks, the first line colliding with the men behind them.

Azel and every other Israelite soldier erupted in a spontaneous cheer that reverberated through the valley. They continued to cheer as they ran down the hill, relief and joy causing them to move without orders.

❦ 90 ❦

"Charge!" Jeriah shouted and his company charged down the hill, cheering and shouting, the spell that had lasted 40 days boisterously broken.

In no time his troops had splashed and leaped across the narrow brook, crossed the other side of the valley floor and climbed the opposite hill.

They crashed through Philistine stragglers. Thoroughly panicked, the Sea People were tripping over each other and even slashing and stabbing one another, trying to escape, the rear ranks impeding the forward in their chaotic retreat.

For many miles that day, the army of Israel pursued the shattered army of the Philistines, cutting down those they caught and demolishing any troops that turned to stand and fight. It was not until they reached the borders of the Philistine lands at Ekron that an order came from Saul's staff to halt and return to the Vale of Elah.

When Jeriah arrived back at the place where they had camped for 40 days, The headless body of Goliath still lay on the field and the vultures were indeed making a feast as Eliab's brother had said they would.

Jeriah and his men were exhausted and made good use of the water in the brook to drink their fill and then to bathe, washing off the dust and dried Philistine blood from their clothes and bodies. They finally collapsed and slept for a long night of satisfied sleep.

❦

The next morning, the work of plundering the Philistine camp began. In their haste and panic at seeing their champion killed, they had left everything. The well-equipped professional Philistine soldiers had weapons, armor and supplies the men of Israel only dreamed of. There were even teams of oxen and wagons in which to transport the supplies. It was several more days before the army of Israel was ready to travel once again.

Finally, the order was given to begin the march back to Gibeath-Saul.

❧ 91 ❧

The triumphant army of Israel took several days to march back to Gibeah. Most of the trip was through cities and villages of Judah, David's tribe. News of the great victory preceded the troops and people turned out on either side of the road to hail them.

The king rode his donkey at the head of the column and beside him was the young shepherd, riding on a donkey that was the first reward of his brave feat. As they passed through the towns on the road back to Gibeath-Saul to the north, people lined the sides of the road to see the hero whose name everyone now knew. King Saul waved to the cheering crowds and he prompted the young man who slew the giant to do the same.

"Wave to them, my son," the king said. "This is your day."

David waved timidly at first, but eventually caught the mood of the crowd; a look of clever confidence appearing on his youthful face and he began waving at everyone.

Sometime during the jubilant parade, a chant arose. No one knew who started it, but it quickly spread:

> *"Saul has slain his thousands*
> *and David his ten thousands!*
>
> *Saul has slain his thousands*
> *and David his ten thousands!"*

The first time Saul heard it, he paused and looked over at David, who was still waving and smiling, not aware of the king at all, it seemed.

Over and over the crowds repeated the cheer in each of the towns and villages they passed through. Saul looked at David who continued smiling broadly and waving. A shadow passed over Saul's mind, but it didn't linger, because the jubilation surrounding them was infectious.

Behind the king, David and the royal guard, marched the men of Benjamin, including Azel. The soldiers were fairly skipping and cheering with the citizens lining the road. They were extremely giddy after the long forty days of strain during which the giant taunted them.

As he rode along with the jubilant army, David thought back to when Samuel had come to visit Bethlehem. He had not been invited to the sacrificial service. He was alone, watching the sheep outside of the village. He had not expected to be called to leave the flock.

His brother just older than him, Ozem, had come to relieve him in the field and he had gone into Bethlehem, where he had been surprised to find Samuel alone with his family after the service.

He had seen a variety of emotions in the faces of his family, ranging from embarrassment, to frustration, to anger. They all had looked at him when he arrived. At first he had feared he was about to be punished for something he had done, but he couldn't imagine what that would have been.

Then Samuel, with eyes closed, had slowly released a long breath. When he opened his eyes he had said, "This is the one the Lord has selected."

David had had no idea what he meant, but his family had reacted; the emotions that David had seen on their faces now evident in their body language.

After that, Samuel had wasted no time bidding David to kneel before him, and when David had done so, Samuel informed him that Yahweh had selected him to be the next king of all Israel and he proceeded to anoint him with the sweet-smelling olive oil from his horn.

David had been confused as the oil ran through his hair and down his face and neck, but he then had felt something go through him like a fiery shock.

He hadn't felt the same since. When he had come to the camp and heard the giant's taunt, he had felt that fire again, knowing exactly what he should do and knowing exactly what the result would be.

So would Samuel's word now come true? Would he truly become king in place of Saul, who was riding beside him?

The king's family was among the noisy crowd lining the road when they arrived at Gibeath-Saul. The news of Israel's victory in the Vale of Elah had preceded the army's return to the capital. Saul's wives and other children were there, waving at the procession of victorious warriors. Jonathan was in the vanguard, riding his donkey.

Michal, the fifth of Saul's children and the younger of two daughters, was with her mother, older sister and baby brother, waving to the marching soldiers. She was in her teens and in recent months, her body had been changing, developing womanly curves. She was feeling emotions she hadn't felt before, too. She had begun to be concerned about her hair and clothes, trying to look as grown up as possible.

When her father went by, Michal saw David for the first time, riding beside him. She stopped waving and calling out. He was smiling and waving, his eyes bright. Michal felt a flush of heat on her cheeks, but she didn't know why.

Back in Gibeath-Saul, the mood at court was jubilant as those who had been at the battle told and retold the story of how the young shepherd slew the giant no one else dared face. In each telling, the victory grew in glory. Jeriah was one of the few who noticed that all was not well with the king. As he stood guard once again to the left of the throne, he could see that the "evil spirit" some spoke of had returned.

❧

Gradually, those who had volunteered for the campaign just past melted away, going back to their homes, their flocks and their shops, leaving just the professional soldiers like Jeriah and Azel.

By all outward appearances, over the next few weeks, everything was happening as one would expect: David was awarded treasure fit for a prince and was given his own command. A thousand soldiers of Judah now marched under David's banner. However, the promise of the hand of the king's daughter in marriage remained unfulfilled.

Jeriah sat on a stone before his company's quarters, repairing the thong of one of his sandals, when he saw someone approaching. It was his brother Azel.

"Azel! Hello, brother."

"I wanted to let you know, I've requested a transfer."

"That's wonderful!" Jeriah cried. "I will put you in charge of a squad."

"No, I'm sorry, you don't understand," Azel replied, suddenly looking down. "I have requested a transfer to David's command."

"What? But his cohort is of Judah!"

"And that means I may not be admitted, but I had to try."

"Well," began Jeriah, disguising his disappointment. "I wish you good fortune, however it turns out."

"Thank you, brother."

Michal's older brother Jonathan was spending time with David quite often now, orienting him to the ways of the army, since he had been given a command. What he didn't know was that Michal followed him several times into the encampment, slipping between tents, so she could catch a glimpse of Israel's hero as he and her brother bonded over their discussions of military strategy.

She watched from a distance as David talked and gestured, his ready smile made her swoon.

He is so handsome!

Everyone knew he was to receive the hand of the king's daughter in marriage, and Michal would love to be that daughter, but there was a problem.

❦ 92 ❦

"You must be so excited!" Michal gushed to her big sister.

"But I love Adriel!" Merab sobbed.

"But this is your opportunity to marry the hero of Israel! He's so dashing!"

"You know nothing of love, little girl," Merab cried. Her cheeks were red and wet from sobbing.

"I would gladly marry him!"

"I would gladly give him to you," Merab cried. "But it is father who will give each of us to marry whom he wills."

Michal looked at her older sister forlornly, wishing something could happen to change the events that were already in motion, but knowing that culture and tradition were strong. The king's daughter had been promised to the hero, and while no one had been named, it was unthinkable to give away the younger daughter before the older.

"But I love David," she whispered so quietly she was surprised that Merab heard.

"You love him? And do you think that will matter at all?"

Azel's request to transfer into David's command was granted and soon, owing no doubt, Azel reasoned, to his brother's rank, he was elected a captain over 50 men, so he sat in council with David and gradually grew to know him. The Battle of Elah had left no doubt as to David's courage, but the intervening days would demonstrate his strategic ability as a commander as well.

"We have been ordered to raid the borders of Philistine land," David announced to the officers of his command. Azel and the others cheered. "At last we will take the battle to the enemy, rather than fighting defensively when invaded," said Joash, one of Azel's fellow officers.

David began outlining the plan. The thousand men would march toward Ekron to the west. They would not attack the main city but, were to raid unwalled farming villages on the periphery of the city-state.

The first time out, they planned to attack a small village at night. It was defended only by a detail of a dozen soldiers in an outpost barracks.

"We will surround the post, approaching silently as the dew," David said, outlining the plan. "Azel, Ben-Zedek, and Joash, your companies will attack, setting fire to the barracks and killing the soldiers when they exit the burning building. Then we will capture the townspeople and burn the town."

The officers gasped at the audacity of the plan. It was in stark contrast to Saul's usual defensive posture and apparent paralysis at Elah.

"We will bring the townspeople back to Israel," David continued. "We will enforce the giant's promise that the Philistines will serve us." The men nodded obediently, awed by David's decisiveness and courage.

The next night, David's troops surrounded the village and Azel's company joined two others in silently approaching the Philistine garrison with bundles of dry straw and fire hidden in clay pots to conceal the light of the fire in the darkness. When they had set the straw around the four walls of the mud-brick-and-wood barracks, they ignited a bundle of straw from the clay pots and then threw burning straw through the windows and doors of the building.

Soon soldiers began running out of the burning building and Azel's men cut each one down as they came out of the door and windows. It took only a couple of minutes to kill the entire garrison in the darkness, confusion and smoke.

The village's defenders gone, the townspeople were quickly rounded up by David's 1,000 soldiers and tied together under guard.

As Azel watched his men tie the people to a rope that would be tied to a donkey for the trip back to Israel, a shopkeeper resisted the soldier tying his hands, attempting to take his sword. As the two men briefly struggled, Azel motioned to another of his men, who quickly went and slashed at the villager's neck and he fell to the ground without a sound. The members of his family cried out, but the message was received and no one else resisted.

A surprisingly large amount of gold, silver and iron was brought out of the houses of the town along with the captured townspeople. As soon as they were ready, the soldiers designated as guards began marching the captives back toward Judah and the ultimate destination of Gibeath-Saul. Meanwhile, David gave the order to torch the town.

"Wait!" David said to those making ready to set the town ablaze. "Gather the gods of wood and stone and bring them to the square."

Azel's men carried out the order, finding several household representations of Dagon, the god of harvest, Baal, the storm god, and Ashtoreth, the goddess of fertility, some sculpted from stone, some of wood, some metalic.

"Place them in a heap," David ordered. "And shatter them to pieces."

Some of the men hesitated. Even though they worshipped Yahweh, they seemed reluctant to defile the gods of others.

"They must see that the God of Israel is greater than gods of stone," David explained.

The night sky was alight with the pyre that had been the Philistine village as David's men withdrew. The return trip was difficult because they were driving several hundred prisoners, as wells as hundreds of sheep, goats, donkeys and cattle taken in the raid on the village. In addition, no small amount of valuables was captured. Much of the heaviest burdens, the gold, silver and iron, were being carried by the prisoners, but donkeys and oxen were also utilized to carry the booty.

Azel's company was delegated as the rear guard. While they would have been surprised if a pursuit had been mounted so soon, they would be ready for any hastily mounted attack. Azel wished David's army, with the prisoners and booty could move faster, but he knew there was a limit to how fast they could go.

It was late in the afternoon of the second day before they reached the hills of Benjamin and ascended to Gibeath.

The sun was setting when Azel's company arrived in the town and he was able to dismiss them to go to their lodging. Before turning in, he walked toward the king's court and joined his fellow officers in David's army.

"Did you see the shock on their faces as we cut them down?" said one. "The Philistines never expected that."

"I've never seen such a plan," said another. "Flawless in design and execution."

"Astounding is what it was," a third officer added. "With David's leadership, there's no telling what we can do. Maybe we can be rid of the Philistines once and for all."

The others nodded, then stopped talking and looked to the side. Azel, followed their gaze and saw that David himself approached.

Amazing, Azel thought, *he has such boyish looks, with a quick, winning smile, but he displays such confidence and strength. Always sure of himself; always knowing what to do. Amazing. Surely God is with him.*

The men watched as their commander walked up to another man. It was Prince Jonathan.

"David!" Jonathan spoke first. "A great victory."

"It was a small village, but we have brought back much spoil, for the glory of Yahweh and the house of Saul."

"May this be repeated over and over," Jonathan replied. "You are certainly welcome to the family."

"Yes, begging your pardon, I am but a humble shepherd. I am not worthy to be the king's son-in-law."

"You are more than worthy and this is what was promised. It will be done. Then you will be my brother-in-law!" Jonathan slapped David's shoulder.

"I am wondering if your father, the king, truly intends to give me his daughter's hand as he promised?" David ventured. "Has he said anything?"

"That's a delicate matter," Jonathan answered. "You should know my sisters are perhaps not as pliable as the women in Judah."

David smiled. "I would not expect a king's daughter to be easily commanded to marry anyone."

"Oh, don't worry, my brother," Jonathan said, clapping his hands on David's shoulders exactly like David's older brothers might have done. "She will want to marry you, I'm certain. How could she help it? Come, let us make your report to the king."

❦ 93 ❦

But an audience with the king would have to wait, for he had already retired to his chambers. Only Jeriah remained in the court finishing some clerical duties when Jonathan and David entered.

"Jeriah, my father is not here?" Jonathan asked.

"He ended the business of the day about an hour ago," Jeriah replied, saluting the general.

"Ah, well," Jonathan turned to David. "Tomorrow then."

"Commander," Jeriah said, looking at David. "Is my brother performing his duty satisfactorily?"

"Who is your brother?"

"Azel of Mizpah, son of Eldad. You made him a captain over fifty."

"Oh, yes. Most certainly he is. In our campaign just concluded, his company led in the attack and then served as our rearguard. He serves well indeed."

"Good. Thank you."

"And what is your name again?"

"Jeriah, of Mizpah."

"Jeriah? It means 'taught of God,' does it not?"

"Yes."

"And you stand before the king?"

"Yes, when we are not at war."

"And then?"

"And then I command a company from Judah, including, it happens, YOUR brother, Eliab."

David laughed loudly at the coincidence.

"I trust he treats you with more respect than he does me!" David said.

"He is my second in command and a good officer."

"I'm not surprised. Well, I'll let you get back to your duties. Until tomorrow then," David said as he shook Jeriah's hand warmly.

Jeriah watched the two of them leave the court, still chuckling over the exchange. He marveled at the self-confidence David displayed for such a young man.

The next day, Jonathan stood nearby as David gave his report of the raid to the king. Azel and other officers of David's 1,000 men stood behind him, each holding a sack. As always, Jeriah stood to the left of the throne.

"And king, we have brought gold, silver and bronze for your kingdom," David said motioning to the officers, who took their cue and withdrew shiny bowls and goblets and chargers from their sacks.

"All this from a fairly small village," David said. "All for the glory of Yahweh."

King Saul sat hunched over looking at David as if his mind was somewhere else. Then he sighed and leaned back.

"And was this victory complete?" he asked.

"Total. We had the advantage of surprise and overwhelming numbers."

"Hmph." Saul shifted on his throne and sneered, "I have no more rewards to give my champion."

Jeriah saw a question on David's face, but he recovered.

"No additional reward is required, my king."

"Lord King," Jonathan spoke from the portico.

"What is it, my son?"

"I'm sure his majesty has not forgotten the promise to give his daughter to the man who slew the giant?"

"No, of course not," he said, looking at David through narrowed eyes. "I will inform my daughter right away. I guess you will be my son-in-law."

"My king," David said as he bowed, "I am unworthy to be the king's son-in-law." He then turned without waiting to be dismissed, motioning to his officers to leave with him.

David and his cohort continued to raid the edges of Philistine lands, sacking villages and harassing far-flung Philistine garrisons. His reputation, which had been celebrated since he killed the giant, only grew with each passing success.

One day, Jonathan summoned David to his quarters in the permanent camp of the army.

"Lord, you called?" David said as he entered the tent.

"Yes, I have something for you. Here, take these."

Jonathan handed David a fine tunic and coat with colorful fringe on the sleeves.

"General, this is too much!" David exclaimed.

"You need a good suit of clothes. You are going to be part of the royal family after all."

"But the gift is too generous."

"It's nothing. I have many more like it."

"It is yours?"

"Yes, and I insist you take it. I also have this for you." Jonathan went to a corner and took a fine sword and leather scabbard in the Philistine style and held it out to David.

"I won't take 'no' for an answer. Please take it."

David took the weapon and slipped it a little way out of the scabbard to admire the workmanship.

"David, my brother, you have come to mean a great deal to me. Your natural ability as a leader and a warrior is unmatched in anyone I've ever known. You deserve this."

"Thank you, lord."

"Come now, call me by my name. We are to be brothers, are we not?"

"When the king sees fit to honor his promise, Jonathan."

❧ 94 ❧

The winter wet and cold was reflected in the king's attitude. Courtiers spoke in nervous whispers and those who were required to stand before the monarch were sweating in spite of the chill. Saul's face was as dark as the sky and he spoke rarely and only in monosyllables. Today, he had come to court dressed as if going to battle, with a sword at his side and a javelin, which he thrust into the ground so it stood beside him as he sat on his throne.

Midway through the afternoon, Abner came to Jeriah.

"Go and find David," he began. "Have him bring his lyre. Perhaps that will help."

Jeriah nodded and slipped out the door, making his way to the barracks for the professional soldiers. He knew where David's quarters were, in one of the best spaces in a stone building near the center of the camp.

The hero of Elah was seated by his front door repairing a wood-and-leather shield.

"Commander," Jeriah began. "Abner requests your presence before the king, with your lyre."

David looked at Jeriah and nodded, knowing the full implication of Jeriah's words. He rose and went inside his quarters, while Jeriah waited outside.

Shortly the tanned, muscular young man emerged with his instrument, looking not much different from the way he looked some months before, the first time Jeriah saw him play. Yet he had grown, not just in stature, but in poise and power. Jeriah couldn't help feeling he was in the presence of a kind of greatness he hadn't encountered before.

They made their way to the king's court and were quickly inside. Jeriah returned to his post to the left of the throne and David stood in the shadows until Abner motioned for him to come forward and sit on a stool near Jeriah.

"Play well, David," Abner said. "The king needs soothing."

There was a man standing before the king just finishing his business. As he bowed and turned away, David began playing. After a few notes, he began to sing.

> *Give ear to my words, O Lord;*
> *Consider my meditation.*
> *Hearken unto the voice of my cry,*
> *My King and my god:*
> *For unto Thee will I pray.*
> *My voice shalt thou hear*
> *In the morning, O Lord;*
> *In the morning will I*
> *Direct my prayer unto Thee,*
> *And will look up.*
> *For Thou art not a God*
> *That hath pleasure in wickedness:*
> *Neither shall evil dwell with Thee.*
> *The foolish shall not stand in thy sight:*
> *Thou hatest all workers of iniquity.*

Saul for a time stared straight ahead, but gradually he became aware of the music and he turned his head to look in David's direction.

Jeriah waited for the music to have its desired, customary effect, but instead, Saul suddenly looked up, then grabbed the javelin at his side and, with great violence, threw it at David.

The agile young man leapt backwards, nearly tripping over the stool. Jeriah flinched as the javelin flew by in front of him, missing David only by inches, skidding to a stop on the packed earth as others waiting for an audience leaped aside.

Saul glared at David, who glared back, then stalked out of the room with his lyre. Neither man had spoken a word.

Jeriah still stood, eyes front as if nothing had happened.

❧

"Why am I betrayed by all who are near me!"

It was late and Jeriah wanted to go home, but the king became belligerent and was talking nonsense, accusing anyone and everyone of treachery.

Finally Abner got him calmed down enough so that he and Jeriah could help him out of court and to his house, where his wife and concubine would have to deal with him.

Jeriah put his papers in order for tomorrow and left to go home for the night.

⤜ 95 ⤛

It was dark when Jeriah arrived home after a long day in court. It was so late in fact, Shelomith and the children were already in bed.

He lit an oil lamp which threw long, flickering shadows on the walls of their new home. Then he wearily sat on a chair and began to lay aside his arms, armor and uniform tunic to prepare for bed.

It had been difficult to deal with the king after his violent attack on David. Jeriah wondered why David's playing hadn't soothed the king like it had so many times before? Could it be that the king was jealous of David's notoriety after his success at the battle of Elah?

That was a better option than what others said of Saul, that he had an evil spirit. Jeriah didn't want to believe that, but there were times he wondered.

"Jeriah!" came a whisper from outside the open window.

"Azel?"

Jeriah went and opened the front door. His brother slipped inside, looking ashen.

"What is it, at this hour?" Jeriah demanded, returning wearily to his chair.

"Is it true?"

"Is what true?"

"That the king tried to kill Commander David today."

"Where did you hear that?"

"Is it true?"

"Yes, I'm afraid so, but the king missed."

"Where is David now?"

"I guess he's gone. He was pretty angry when he left."

"Gone? Has he left Gibeah?"

"I don't know. It wouldn't surprise me."

"What about us?" Azel asked.

"What do you mean?"

"Those in David's command; what will become of us?"

"I'm sure another commander will be found for you."

"I mean," Azel said in a whisper. "What will become of those of us who are loyal to David?"

"I should think a pledge of allegiance to the king would be sufficient."

Azel looked down at his sandals.

"Is that a problem?" Jeriah demanded loudly.

"If forced to choose between the king and my loyalty to David, I'm not sure I could choose the king."

"Are you a fool?" Jeriah shouted, leaping to his feet. "The king can order you executed with a wave of his hand. In fact, he can order our entire family executed and I would probably be ordered to carry out the execution! Except I am part of our family, so I might be included in the execution!"

Azel petulantly turned his head to look at the lamp.

Jeriah seized his brother by the arm. "And more than that, Saul is the Lord's Anointed, so, if a pledge is laid before you, you WILL sign it, because this isn't just about you. Do you think any of us will be spared? A Benjamite family disloyal to a Benjamite king?"

"But how can I, when I believe the Spirit of God is upon David?" Azel jerked his arm and freed himself from Jeriah's grasp. "Besides, our mother was of Judah."

Before he thought, Jeriah swung his fist, hitting Azel in the jaw. Azel staggered back, then ran at Jeriah, his own fist swinging forward. Jeriah dodged so the blow didn't hit him full force, but Azel's momentum caused them to crash together to the ground. Azel was on top, but only briefly, as Jeriah pushed him up and over, then climbed over him and pinned him to the packed-earth floor.

"Stop it!" Jeriah shouted.

"You hit me first!"

"Yes, I'm sorry. I'll let you up if you promise not to try to hit me again."

"I promise."

Jeriah cautiously released his hold on Azel and partly stood, before sitting on the chair. Azel sat up, then stood, steadying himself by holding a table.

"It is inevitable," Azel said softly.

"What's inevitable, our execution?"

"No. That David will replace Saul."

Jeriah's mouth fell open. "You believe David is the one anointed by Samuel; the one of whom the rumors are told?"

"I don't just think he is," Azel's whispered. "I know he is."

When Azel was gone, Jeriah pondered what he had said. Had Samuel truly anointed another and was it David?

How can two be anointed king at once?

Jeriah put the thought from his mind. Yahweh wouldn't do that. It would mean civil war. At present, he knew of only one who had been anointed king: Saul, whom he served every day and had for more than 20 years.

And he determined to continue serving him, come what may...

...To the death.

THE END...until

Gary L. Ivey

Coming... *Exile of the King*

The second novel in the "Age of the Kingdom" series begins where *Quest for a King* left off.

When David, whom many believe will be the next king, is forced into exile, will Azel desert his post and follow? Will Jeriah continue to loyally serve Saul? How can the young nation survive the forces of jealousy and violence that threaten to rip it apart?

God's curse still hangs over the house of Eli. After one of the priests, a son of Ahitub, helps David, Saul orders a massacre of the whole town of Nob, which once again leaves the Tent of Meeting without priests to serve there. History repeats itself when again a single young priest survives.

Saul is intent on killing David, the primary threat to his dynasty. In desperation, David and his band of 600 men and their families flee from one hiding place to another, then finally to the haven of Philistine Gath, of all places. Achish, king of Gath, is just as taken with David as anyone and so is blind to David's divided loyalties. How will David and his men avoid fighting shoulder-to-shoulder with the Philistines against the army of Israel?

Faced with another Philistine war, Saul is desperate to hear from the Lord, but Samuel is dead, so he seeks out a witch he once tried to kill. Jeriah is with him when a voice from the grave predicts death on the mountain for Saul and his sons. Can Jeriah avoid being caught up in the king's self-destructive obsessions?

For release date, go to www.ageofthekingdomseries.com

Gary L. Ivey

About the Author:

Gary L. Ivey wrote *Quest for a King*, the first book of the "Age of the Kingdom" series, from his home in Hawaii. He is a husband, father and grandfather.

He has written two other novels in the "Backlash" series: *Backlash* and *Backlash 2: Justice Denied*. He has also written a number of screenplays which have been honored at a variety of film festivals.

He has been a music minister, a pastor, a Christian magazine editor, media producer and a TV ministry director.

He is Vice President of a marketing and web development firm in Georgia, which he co-owns with his wife of 50 years.

www.garyivey.com
www.backlashbook.com
www.studioiv.productions

Want more?

Check out **www.garyivey.com** for blog posts about what he's working on, freedom and the free market, and other random thoughts.

Follow Gary L. Ivey on Facebook at
www.facebook.com/GaryIveyAuthor/,
on Instagram **@garyivey**, and on Twitter **@gary_ivey**.